VALLEY OF THE DAMNED

Sonja Williams

Cover by Wayne Beauchamp

Editing, typesetting and publishing by UK Book Publishing

www.ukbookpublishing.com

ISBN: 978-1-917329-84-2

VALLEY OF THE DAMNED

(A horror story. Be afraid, be very afraid. Even the cat is petrified.)

PROLOGUE

'Looking back it really was an evil place,' said Jane, in answer to her friend's question.

Sitting back in her chair, she glanced across the room at her daughter Emma, lying sprawled on the floor, engrossed in a large colourful picture book. Instantaneously the child looked up, hatred burning in her eyes, and Jane, feeling a damp patch forming on the nape of her neck, turned away quickly.

'You're lucky to be alive,' Dee rambled on, unaware of the mounting tension she was causing. Jane nervously brushed a few stray wisps of hair away from her face and remained silent.

'I've never been so frightened in my whole life. I'll always remember the expression on Paul's face when he came home early the evening you went over to Hanslope. I suppose you've not heard from him?'

'No,' Jane replied. 'I don't know why he left, where he went, or even if he is still alive. To be frank, I try not to think about him, or any of the things that happened in that dreadful place. It's all in the past, Emma and I are safe now and looking forward to a happy future, aren't we?' she said to the robust little four-year-old.

The child looked up at her mother and smiled.

CHAPTER I

P aul slowed down the car and looked across at his wife Jane, intently studying a large map spread over her knees.

'I should think we must be nearly there now. We've driven about ten miles along this road.'

'Yes,' she answered, glancing up to look out of the window.

'Look, there's a signpost about a hundred yards up on the left. Can you see it?'

The car came to a halt. Paul sat back stretching his limbs and yawned. Jane folded the map, stuffed it into the glove compartment and got out.

The grass verge, wet and soggy underfoot, squelched as she clambered on to the footpath. She shivered, hastily buttoning up her coat as the wind buffeted against her legs and swirled her hair about, making it difficult to see. Gripping the pole with one hand to keep her balance, Jane swept the hair away from her eyes and read the directions.

'Phew, it's wild out there,' she exclaimed, sliding back into the passenger seat.

'Turn left here and it's a mile further on.'

They turned the corner into Boundary Road and drove past several ugly Victorian cottages on their left, all with tiny front gardens, privet hedges and steep steps leading up to the front doors. At the end of the row stood an empty derelict building, Ashingham Post Office barely visible on the weather-beaten board hanging over the door. On the right, fields, broken up here and there by small clumps of trees, undulated away gently into the distance.

After approximately half a mile the road disappeared from sight, dropping sharply down a steep hill and Paul and Jane saw the valley for the first time. The view from the brow of the hill was breathtaking, and steering the car into a passing place at the roadside they got out to have a closer look. They crossed the road and leaning against a dry-stone wall, gazed down into the valley, their eyes greedily devouring the panoramic scenery stretched out before them.

The hills encircling them fell sheer, downwards into the valley basin where a small river had cut its way through the rock on one side, creating a deep gorge, and meandered across the floor vanishing into the trees at the other end. From where they were standing they could see no sign of habitation, but thin tendrils of smoke, rising up from the treetops at the bottom of the hill, suggested the village lay hidden close by. Returning to the car, they continued their journey down the hill, bearing round a sharp left bend under the canopy of trees and finally entered Ashingham village.

Ivy Cottage proved easy to find as it was the only one displaying an estate agent's board in the front garden. Jane reached over to the back seat to retrieve the details sent to them through the post, and Paul confirmed that the key was in his pocket.

'It's lovely,' said Jane, peering out of her window. 'Come on, let's go and look at it.'

'They stood together on the path, their arms entwined around each other, mentally absorbing the property and its surroundings. Set beneath a grey slate roof it was a large, square stone-built cottage with raised strap pointing. Above the porch on a level with the upstairs windows was a date stone denoting it was built in 1660. To the left of the front door were four leaded casement windows, two down and two up. Ivy Cottage had been aptly named, the porch covered by this climbing evergreen shrub whose tentacles stretched out menacingly in all directions, threatening the entire facade.

Approaching the gate Jane peered over the wall into the front garden. There wasn't anything in it apart from the agent's board, but she did notice a tiny brook running across it parallel with the front wall which disappeared under the front path and into the adjoining property.

'This will be my herb garden,' she said to herself, following Paul up to the solid black oak front door with its enormous wrought-iron hinges.

It opened directly into the living room. Paul and Jane stood on the threshold, captivated by its charm and character. Light filtered into the room through the leaded panes, casting soft diamond shaped patterns on the floor, and was reflected back by the brilliance of white rough plastered walls, broken up at intervals by vertical oak supports. The ceiling was only about six feet high and Paul found it was better to walk down-beam in order to avoid banging his head. The pièce de résistance was a magnificent inglenook fireplace complete with dog-grate which filled an entire wall.

The door from this room led into a large airy kitchen with a raised dining area at one end. It looked out on to the back garden and a paddock beyond. The original stone walls had been left exposed in here and the old roofing slabs had been used as the floor covering which made it rather uneven.

'It's very cold in here, don't you think?' enquired Jane, pulling her coat more tightly around her.

'Well, what do you expect, it is January you know.'

'No, I don't mean that sort of cold,' said Jane. 'It's very odd, but the coldness in this cottage is sending shivers down my spine.'

'Oh, come on, don't be silly, you've been watching too many horror films,' said Paul, laughing.

Returning to the living room they mounted the stairs to the first floor, which consisted of two bedrooms and a bathroom.

'Well, what do you think?' said Paul.

'It's absolutely delightful,' replied Jane, opening the front bedroom window and leaning out.

There was a faint stirring in her pelvis as she felt the baby she was carrying, moving about inside her. Patting her stomach she turned towards Paul. 'I think we could all be very happy here.'

He put his arms around her protectively.

'I think you're right,' he said, his lips brushing the crown of her head.

'Let's lock up now and have a walk through the village. We'd better see it all before we decide whether to buy this or not.'

'Alright,' Jane said, 'but I don't think I'll change my mind.'

CHAPTER 2

Paul and Jane stood in the porch together while Paul carefully locked the heavy front door behind them. They turned to walk back down the path, simultaneously glancing upwards as they felt the warm rays from a watery sun filtering through the clouds. They both saw it at the same time.

'Bloody Hell!' said Jane, startled. 'I never noticed it before, even when we got out of the car at the top of the hill. Did you?'

'No, it must have been hidden by the trees,' replied Paul.

Ashingham Castle, set high up on the top of an escarpment of sheer rock cliffs, skirted on three sides by thick forest, bore down upon them like a vulture guarding its prey, completely dominating the entire valley.

'If we walk back to the village shop on that sharp bend at the bottom of the hill we'll get a closer view of it,' suggested Paul.

They stood opposite the shop by the telephone box looking upwards in awe at the magnificent grey stone fortress towering above them, its crenellated turrets piercing each cloud that passed overhead. Crossing back over the road they went into the village shop to buy some sweets. A little bell jangled as they opened and closed the door.

The interior was very cluttered and seemed to sell just about everything imaginable, it even housed a Sub Post Office, fighting a losing battle for space in one corner. A plump, rosy-faced woman in a pink and white check overall stood behind the counter unpacking a case of tinned food. Jane picked out a selection of sweets and walked over to pay her.

'Do you know when the castle on the hill was built?' Jane enquired.

'Sightseeing, are you?' the woman said, smiling at her.

'No, not exactly,' replied Jane. 'We've been to see Ivy Cottage.'

'Brenda, stop gossiping and get on with your work, time's money.'

The unpleasant voice was followed by the lumbering frame of Len Potter, the shopkeeper, appearing through the doorway separating the shop from a small back store-room. He eyed Paul and Jane up and down suspiciously, his wife scuttling away like a frightened mouse, leaving the three of them together.

'We don't care much for strangers in these parts,' said Len Potter. 'What can I do for you?'

'We were just enquiring about the castle,' replied Paul, 'but it's not important.'

'Thinking of buying Ivy Cottage, are you?'

'Could be,' said Paul, ushering Jane hurriedly out of the door. 'Might see you again soon.'

'Objectionable man,' said Jane, as they strolled back into the village. 'I didn't like him at all.'

'Don't worry about it, these country yokels are always suspicious of outsiders. If we buy the cottage they'll get to know us soon enough.'

As they passed Half Acre Farm, two collies came bounding out of the gate towards them. Paul bent down to stroke them.

'Well, at least the dogs are friendly,' he said, looking up at Jane grinning.

She laughed and they continued walking, the dogs trotting after them.

The 'Castle Arms' pub was directly opposite Ivy Cottage. It couldn't have been better situated, Paul thought to himself, making a mental note to drop in for a quick one if they had time before leaving. Next to the pub was the eyesore of the village - namely a derelict mill, so tall it cast a deep shadow over the row of tiny cottages.

'That needs pulling down,' remarked Jane. 'It's cutting out all the light and blocking the lovely view across the valley.'

'The Estate Agent told me on the phone that there are plans to have the mill restored, but if it's found to not be possible the site will be cleared,' said Paul, reassuring her.

They were approaching the river now and the road widened, creating a large turning circle for vehicles. A narrow footbridge provided the only access to the farm on the opposite bank, and all farm traffic had to cross via a ford a little way further on. Jane rested on the bridge for a while, idling away the time dropping stones into the water. The river was fast flowing under the bridge, cascading haphazardly over a mound of stone slabs which looked as if they had originally been part of the mill. Paul had crossed to the other side and was sitting on a bench studying the map they had brought with them.

'According to this, there's a footpath straight through the farmyard and across the hills to the next village,' he said.

'In that case, I wonder why there's a large notice saying 'Heronsford Farm, Keep Out' on the gate,' she replied drily. 'By the way, don't look now, but we're being watched from an upstairs window.'

Although they would have liked to continue their stroll by the river, they turned back as the track was too muddy to go on.

'What do you think that deep gully running alongside the mill and down to the river bank is for?' asked Jane, pointing towards an overgrown ditch.

'It looks like the old mill race,' said Paul. 'Further along the river there'll probably be a man-made weir and small waterfall with a channel leading directly from it. The water then flows downhill gathering speed to turn the mill wheel, and the overflow collects in the mill pond over there behind the mill,' he said. 'At least that's what I remember from my engineering lectures at college. When the better weather comes we'll have a wander across the valley and see.'

Paul looked at his watch and saw it was already two o'clock.

'Shall we pop into the 'Castle Arms' for a drink before we leave?'

'You go ahead,' she said, 'I'd rather have another browse round the cottage, if you don't mind.'

Paul handed her the key.

'When you've finished, ·come into the pub and get me.'

'OK,' she said, 'I won't be long.'

The 'Castle Arms' was exactly as Paul imagined it would be. The bar with its brightly coloured hand pumps displayed a comprehensive range of local brews, while the usual hard spirits sat on the shelves behind. He couldn't see any of the drinks that women asked for, such as sherry or Martini, and he wondered what on earth he could get for Jane when she came into the pub. He'd have to mention this to his friend Ian Sharp, head of the Martini Drive Team next time he saw him.

It's ridiculous to have a pub that doesn't cater for women, he thought to himself, feeling rather annoyed as his wife didn't drink beer as a rule.

There were about a dozen men in the bar as Paul walked in, the general buzz of conversation dying away as they stared at him.

'Pint of bitter in a straight and twenty John Player 'Black' please,' he said to the barman.

Looking at his pint ruefully, he wondered if they had a tie to go with the collar – a London pub wouldn't dare serve beer with such a large head.

Drink in hand, he scanned the room for a seat, but all the tables seemed to be occupied. The furnishings and decor were not going to impress Jane, it was definitely a man's pub. Simple wooden tables and chairs, harsh strip lighting and red linoleum were hardly suitable accoutrements for idling away a couple of hours in the evenings together, not to mention the lack of anything she liked to drink being available.

Propping up the bar he unwrapped the cigarettes and lit one up.

'Saw you looking at the cottage opposite,' said the man behind the bar, making polite conversation. 'I'm Terry Smith, the Landlord.'

'Pleased to meet you,' said Paul, grateful that someone was prepared to talk to him.

'Thinking of buying it, are you?'

'I'm not sure yet, we haven't finally decided.' 'Quite a surprise, it was, when the builder turned up to renovate it. We didn't realise it was for sale,' continued the landlord, pulling a pint for one of the men playing darts.

'I can't tell you anything of the background to the cottage,' said Paul. 'The Estate Agent sent us details of everything available in this area as I've just taken a job in Prestbury which means my wife and I will have to move up here from London.' Paul endeavoured to sound casual with the intention of gently pumping the landlord for information.

'Why are you surprised it's for sale?' he prompted, offering Terry a cigarette.

The landlord took one, produced a box of matches to light it, and exhaling slowly, continued.

'A couple of years ago the last mill-owner died leaving no heir to inherit the estate. As a result the Trustees closed the mill and put the whole valley on the market. Luckily for us all Bert Grimshaw and Arthur Briggs, who own the two farms, were able to raise the cash and buy the valley in order to expand. Ivy Cottage was not included in the sale and Bert and Arthur assumed the omission was due to its derelict condition. But unknown to any of us the Trustees had already sold it to this builder who spent the whole of last summer modernising it to resell for a fat profit. Naturally enough Bert and Arthur were furious, but there was nothing anyone could do about it.'

'I suppose they could have bought it from the builder,' said Paul, pushing the conversation further.

'What, and pay the fancy price being asked for it. You've got to be joking.'

'What would you say if I bought it?'

11

The landlord shrugged his shoulders and moved off to serve another customer.

The pub had become quite busy and trade being brisk, the possibility of continuing his chat with Terry looked doubtful. Paul concentrated on his pint, detaching himself from the general hurly-burly surrounding him. Suddenly a deathly hush descended on the room, jolting him from his reverie. Looking round to see what had happened, he noticed Jane standing in the doorway. She saw him and waved. As she walked purposefully towards him at the bar, the men stood back, leaving her a wide berth to pass through.

'Hello,' he said, putting his arm round her. 'Let's find you somewhere to sit.'

Realising that the couple intended staying on, the customers began silently filing out of the door until Paul and Jane found themselves alone in the bar apart from the landlord. Jane sat at a table by the window watching the men dispersing in various directions while Paul returned to the bar.

'I'm sorry, sir,' said Terry curtly, 'but the bar is closed.'

'Not to worry,' replied Paul cheerfully, 'I didn't see how late it was.'

He had turned to collect Jane and leave when Terry called him back.

'In case you do decide to buy Ivy Cottage,' he said quietly, so as not to be overheard, 'I have to tell you that women are not served in this pub.'

'I don't drink them either,' replied Paul, utterly fed up now with all the hassle.

Leaving the bar he moved over to Jane, who was still sitting at the table waiting for her drink.

'The idiot behind the bar won't serve me now as he says the bar's closed.'

Looking at his watch he didn't let on to Jane that the real problem was that women were not welcome and that the bar shouldn't have closed for at least another ten minutes.

'Come on, Jane, I'll buy you a coffee at the 'Little Chef' we passed on the way up here.'

Jane suddenly felt very cold and wanted to get out of that pub as quickly as possible. Something felt wrong, something very strange and evil was present in this place. There was a cold atmosphere which chilled her to the marrow. She knew she had to go right now. There was no logical reason to feel like this but leave she must. Pulling at Paul's sleeve she whispered nervously, 'Paul, let's go, I want to go now.'

Terry followed them across the room and, stepping outside into the cold January afternoon they heard the door thud to a close behind them and the iron bolts being drawn into place. A heavy, overcast sky hung down over the valley and it had started to snow. 'What's the matter with you?' said Paul, as they made their way to the car.

'I don't know,' she replied, 'I just had to get out of that pub. I'm fine now. If only we could find somewhere where everyone and everything seemed friendly, but that's the story the whole world over I suppose.'

'Never mind, Jane,' said Paul. 'We don't have to buy Ivy Cottage you know.'

'Oh, yes we do,' she replied vehemently. 'It's a lovely cottage and I'm not going to be put off it by this damned place and the people living in it. Anyhow, they can't all be bad, can they? We shall see.'

CHAPTER 3

P aul carried the last suitcase outside to the car and heaved it into the boot.

'Is there anything else to go in before I close it?' he called to Jane, as she placed the last empty milk bottles on the front step.

'No, that's the lot, apart from the cat. His travelling basket can go on the back seat,' she said, disappearing back inside.

He slammed the boot closed and trundled back in after her to check round for the last time.

Jane stood in the centre of the living room, stripped of its furnishings and fittings, her eyes attracted by the bright patches of wallpaper where pictures had hung in contrast with the rest which had become dingy with age. Paul came up behind her and kissed the nape of her neck.

'Come on, love, let's go. The flat looks depressing now that all our possessions have gone. Remember, our new home is that beautiful old stone cottage we saw up in the north, and it's waiting patiently for the three of us,' he chuckled, patting her stomach.

Glancing at his watch, he saw it was already 7 a.m. 'We must hurry because we have to collect the keys from the agent in Prestbury, and I would like to arrive at the cottage before the removal men just in case any problems crop up.'

In spite of the fact it was Easter Saturday, the M1 motorway remained fairly quiet and they made good steady progress. The sun broke through the cloud, its warm rays penetrating the windscreen. Paul lowered his visor to cut out the glare from the road.

'The weathermen are right for once,' he said, looking across at Jane. 'It's going to be a hot day.'

'I agree,' she replied dozily, fighting off the sleepiness engulfing her from the heat and the steady purr of the engine.

'How are we doing?' she asked, pulling herself upright in the passenger seat.

'We're in Northamptonshire now and the M6 is coming up shortly.' Paul rolled up his sleeves.

'Go to sleep if you can, we've a busy day ahead of us.'

Arriving in Prestbury at half past ten, they stopped only the length of time it took for Paul to pick up the keys, after which they headed out of town towards Ashingham. Jane, refreshed after her long sleep, attentively looked out of the window at the lush rolling countryside as the car sped onwards to their destination. Her pulse began to beat faster with excitement as they approached familiar landmarks on the road, indicating their close proximity to the village. Passing the signpost they had stopped at on the previous visit, Paul turned into Boundary Road.

They drove swiftly towards the crest of the hill which led down into the valley.

The arrival of Spring had softened the austerity of the scenery. Tiny pale green leaves were sprouting on the blossom covered chestnuts and the first clumps of wild bluebells nestled in the grass at the roadside. Animals grazed in the fields. There were sheep with their tiny newborn lambs, cattle and horses. It seemed the valley had burst into life as if to welcome them to their new home. Jane turned to Paul and smiled.

'We're going to be so happy here,' she said, squeezing his hand.

Bearing left into Hunters Lane, under the leafy canopy of trees they saw the row of cottages in front of them, brightly lit up in the morning sunshine.

Paul got out of the car. Walking up to the front door he filled his lungs with the fresh country air. Jane retrieved the cat basket from the back seat and followed him into the cottage.

Although the temperature outside had reached the mid 70s and the sun beat down relentlessly upon the cottage, the interior felt cold.

'I don't understand why it's so chilly in here. The sun is streaming through the windows, yet the warmth doesn't penetrate through the glass,' remarked Jane. She unfastened the two casement windows, letting the heat from outside rush against her face as if she had opened the door of a hot oven.

'That's better,' she said.

'While we're waiting for the removal men to arrive, I'll fire up the boiler to give us hot water later on, and I'll check the radiators while I'm at it,' said Paul.

Jane bent down to undo the basket.

'Come on, Oedipus, out you get.'

The enormous long-haired black cat poked his head over the rim, surveying his surroundings cautiously before jumping out. He remained motionless beside the basket for some time before padding stealthily around the room.

'Your new home, Oedipus,' said Jane triumphantly. 'I hope you like it.'

She noticed the cat's back twitch, and the hair on his backbone rise up in defence as Oedipus explored the new territory. On reaching the corner where the stairs rose out of the living room to the first floor he stopped, ears flat against the side of his head, He backed away mewing.

'Stupid animal,' thought Jane, walking through into the kitchen.

The control panel for the oven and hob lit up when she switched it on. Turning on the taps she found the water supply working as well.

'Would you like a cup of tea?' she called to Paul as he filled the coal hod from the bunker in the back garden.

'Admirable suggestion,' he replied. 'I'll fetch the kettle and things for you from the car,' he said, staggering into the kitchen under the weight of the hod which he dumped next to the boiler.

'OK, I'll walk up to the farm and get some milk,' she said, walking out to the car with him.

Half-Acre Farm appeared to be deserted. Jane rang the doorbell but no-one answered. Picking her way carefully across the filthy farmyard, balancing from stone to stone to avoid the mud and cow turds, she approached the dairy, from where the sound of a generator droned monotonously over the farmstead. She opened the door and stepped inside. A short, middle-aged woman was bending over a sterilising machine sorting milk bottles. The atmosphere, thick with steam from the boiling water, formed heavy condensation which poured down the tiled walls, creating large pools of water on the concrete floor. The woman stood upright, smiling.

'Hello, I'm Maureen Briggs, the farmer's wife.'

'I'm Jane Richardson from Ivy Cottage. My husband Paul and I are moving in today and I wondered if we could have some milk?'

'Take what you want from the crates over in the corner,' she said, wiping her hands on a towel. 'I deliver the milk every day,' she added. 'Would you like me to leave you a couple of pints?'

'Yes please.'

Maureen Briggs brushed the beads of perspiration from her forehead with her arm.

'I hope you settle in comfortably. It's lovely to see some fresh faces in the village.'

'I'm sure we'll be very happy here.'

A sudden stab of pain shot down Jane's right leg. She winced and lifted her foot off the ground to relieve the pressure.

'When is the baby due?' asked Maureen, noticing Jane's discomfort.

'About the 14th of June,' replied Jane, rubbing her thigh. 'The doctor at the clinic told me that sciatica is quite common in pregnancy.'

'Yes, it's nothing to worry about. It'll disappear when he arrives.'

'Have you any children?' asked Jane.

'Yes, I've four, and they've all given me trouble,' laughed Maureen.

'Boys or girls?'

'Boys, of course,' she replied stiffening, her laughter halting abruptly. 'There's not been a girl born in this village for over three hundred years.'

'Perhaps I'll break the tradition,' said Jane light-heartedly. 'It would be nice to have…'

She didn't finish her sentence. The expression on Maureen's face had changed dramatically from a friendly smile to a rigid icy stare. Her eyes pierced into Jane's abdomen as if to ascertain the sex of the unborn child. Bewildered, Jane held the bottles of milk in front of her stomach and stepped back.

'It will be unfortunate if you have a girl,' said Maureen gravely.

'I must get back to help Paul. He'll be wondering where I am.'

Jane stumbled out of the dairy and limped back across the farmyard to the gate as quickly as she could manage, desperate to run, but unable to, since the pain in her leg jabbed every time her foot touched the ground. In her hurry to get away she carelessly trod several times in the disgusting mire underfoot as she lost her balance on the slippery stones. On reaching the gate she saw that the removal van had arrived at the cottage and the men were already unloading the furniture. Leaning against the farm wall to catch her breath and recover, Jane decided not to mention to Paul the conversation with the farmer's wife. He had enough on his mind to worry about with the move and a new job without her whimpering at him as well. She cleaned her shoes as best she could on the grass verge and walked back to the cottage.

'Tea for four coming up in a jif,' she announced cheerfully, marching into the kitchen to reboil the kettle.

The incident at Half-Acre Farm faded from Jane's mind as she became preoccupied with supervising the location of furniture, sorting out her new kitchen, unpacking tea-chests, making up beds and hanging curtains. By five o'clock the removal men had finished and left.

Jane flopped exhausted into one of the armchairs, while Paul sat cross-legged on the carpet connecting up his hi-fi equipment.

'I hope we don't have to move too often,' she said, 'I'm completely shattered.'

'Don't let me hear the word 'move' for at least another five years,' laughed Paul. 'Are the radiators hot yet?'

'Yes,' she replied, leaning across to the window to touch the one which ran the width of the room beneath the two sills.

'My next job is to load up the dog-grate. Tonight you and I will celebrate by eating supper and toasting our feet in front of a roaring fire.'

'There's a casserole in the oven for dinner. In the meantime I'm off to soak in a hot bath,' she said, easing herself out of the chair.

'Fine. As far as I'm concerned, once the fire's going I've finished for the day myself,' said Paul.

Several minutes later Jane immersed herself shoulder high in a steaming, bubble-filled bath. She closed her eyes, the heat and steam relaxing her tired, aching muscles. The day's events wafted through her thoughts. The valley and Ivy Cottage were as delightful, if not even more so now that Spring had arrived, as she could recollect from her first visit after Christmas. However, the inhabitants were definitely a problem. There had to be a way of being acceptable in this tiny rural community. It might take time and considerable effort, but Jane was determined to break through this hostile barrier between the villagers and themselves.

There was a knock at the front door. Paul bent over to tip the final pieces of coal into the dog-grate. He stood up, arched his back in doing so, and made his way over to answer it. Raising the latch and easing the door ajar with one elbow to prevent the coal dust on his hands spreading everywhere, he was confronted by a gigantic figure, so vast it blocked out the daylight, standing in the porch.

'Bert Grimshaw from Heronsford Farm,' bellowed the voice of the man towering above him on the threshold. The farmer thrust out an arm, grabbed Paul's hand which he shook vigorously before barging past into the living room. Inside the cottage, Bert Grimshaw stooped almost double to avoid the beams. Bringing his head down on to an equal level, the man's cold slate-grey eyes scrutinised Paul closely, his full flowing beard reaching to within an inch of Paul's face. He flinched and drew back cautiously.

'I can't stop,' growled Bert. 'I've called to tell you you're expected at the 'Castle Arms' across the road tomorrow evening at 8 p.m. sharp. Alone.' Turning abruptly, before Paul could reply, he marched out, slamming the door behind him.

'Who was that?' said Jane, peering over the bannisters.

'Bert Grimshaw from the farm across the river.'

'Didn't you offer him a cup of tea or anything?'

'No chance. He just stomped in, issued an instruction and stomped out.'

'How incredible!' She paused reflectively. 'What's he like?'

'Built like a brick shit-house, he sounded like a regimental sergeant-major and dressed like Worzel Gummidge.'

Jane dissolved into laughter.

'Well, what did he want?'

'Apparently I've been ordered to present myself at eight o'clock on the dot tomorrow night at the pub.'

'A welcoming party perhaps?' she said, wryly.

'I don't know, I'm keeping an open mind on this one.'

'Dinner should be ready now,' said Jane, reaching the foot of the stairs. She walked into the kitchen. Paul drew the living-room curtains and switched on the lamps. The fire had caught easily, red flames darted up the chimney and Oedipus had finally emerged from his hiding place in the corner by the front door to sit in front of it and bask in the heat. A few minutes later Jane appeared with dinner. Paul uncorked a bottle of wine and they sat down to eat in front of the hearth, trays balanced on their knees. The food and wine, combined with the warmth from the fire, lulled them both into contented drowsiness and then sleep.

Outside, night had spread its black cloak tranquilly over the village. The lamps from the cottages provided the only source of light along the deserted street. Paul and Jane slept peacefully, the intermittent crackly from the fire, the one sound breaking the silence surrounding them. Sinking deeper into sleep, they were unable to hear the tapping from the corner by the stairs.

Oedipus stirred, raising his head to look in the direction from whence the noise came. It stopped. The cat settled down uneasily, resting his head on his paws, eyes fixed on the wall, as if on guard.

Only he was sensitive to the mounting evil in this place and the inevitable horror to come. Tap, tap tap. The sound started up again, more urgently this time. The ears of the cat pricked up, keen and alert. Silently he rose, padded stealthily across the floor, stomach close to the ground in a stalking position. He reached the stairs. The tapping ceased. Nose to the floor he sniffed, gently clawing at the wall with one paw. The noise began yet again, but this time it was a scratching sound accompanied by a whining hiss. Oedipus retreated, arching his spine. He mewed piteously.

Jane woke with a start to see him backing away from the corner, eyes as large as saucers. The volume of sound had increased dramatically, and the draught she had felt from that direction earlier in the evening swirled around her legs and feet.

'Wake up, Paul,' she said, shaking him urgently. 'Something odd's happening.'

Adrenalin pumped through her veins, triggered by anxiety. As he awoke, silence descended upon the room once more.

'There are strange noises coming from under the stairs. The cat appears to have seen a ghost by the look in his eyes.' She shivered. 'I'm frightened, Paul.'

'I can't hear anything,' said Paul, wearily standing up. He crossed the room and knelt down by the stairs to listen. Nothing. What he did observe, however, were several large cracks in the new plaster. They were definitely new. Twisting round he said, 'Did you notice any cracks down this wall today?'

'No, and those would have been clearly visible in the daylight,' she replied, acknowledging his discovery.

He traced the path of the largest crack with his index finger and sighed.

'It's probably all due to the new plaster drying out and the stairs contracting now the central heating has been turned on. I'm not doing anything about it now, it's far too late. I'm off to bed. Are you coming?'

Paul flaked out the moment his head touched the pillow. Jane, however, lay next to him staring up at the ceiling, thinking to herself. She knew that no matter what excuses Paul put forward in explanation for the weird occurrences, something evil was happening, and judging by what she had already experienced in this village, it was only the beginning.

CHAPTER 4

The village slumbered peacefully, protected by the encircling hills. Man and beast alike were at rest. Jane, however, slept fitfully, waking up on the hour every hour. Turning to look at the clock on the bedside table she saw it was only three o'clock. She lay completely motionless for a minute or two listening - but there was nothing, only the overpowering silence of night. Flipping back the covers, she sat on the edge of the bed, her feet searching for her slippers. She wriggled her toes into them and tiptoed quietly towards the window. No moon, no stars, just blackness. Blackness and silence. Would morning never come? She lay down again, flat on her back, arms resting on each side, palms upwards and slightly clenched. She thought back to her yoga classes and began to concentrate on her breathing to relax her mind. In, out, in, out.

Meanwhile, downstairs, Oedipus lay curled up, his head resting on the rim of his basket. Oedipus, like Jane, was not asleep. Only, in his case he had elected to keep watch through the dark hours. Although one eye was closed, the other remained wide open, rigidly fixed on the corner.

Chink. Chink. Jane woke immediately to the sound of the milk bottles being placed on the stone floor in the porch. The clock said seven a.m. She remembered the hands pointing to five a.m. Two hours uninterrupted sleep. Not enough. Pregnant mothers needed at least eight hours a night according to Dr Browne at the clinic. He had advised her to rest as much as possible and pointed out the dangers of moving house during pregnancy.

Registering with a new GP headed her list of tasks for the week, together with securing a hospital bed at the local hospital, wherever that might be. Only two months' pregnancy remained, the baby was due to arrive in the middle of June.

The cottage felt cosy and warm until she reached the foot of the stairs, where an icy draught swirled around her ankles. Oedipus rubbed himself against her legs and followed her into the kitchen. The overcast sky had cleared and strong rays of sun filtered into the kitchen. In the paddock beyond the back garden a small jet black horse trotted up and down, while a herd of cows sauntered out of the cowshed, one at a time, slowly making their way to a field further on. Two collie dogs accompanied the herd, running and weaving around them to keep the cows on a straight course. Oedipus pricked up his ears at the sound of them barking, the noise prompting all the other dogs in the village to join in.

Jane poured out two cups of coffee and headed back upstairs. The noise had woken Paul.

'What's the time?' he asked, rubbing sleep from his eyes.

He pulled himself up into a sitting position.

'Half-past seven,' replied Jane, handing him a large cup of coffee.

'It's a bit early, isn't it?'

'I couldn't sleep.'

'What's all the noise outside?'

'The farm dogs are herding the cows back to a field behind the paddock. Milking's just finished I think.'

Jane curled up on the bed next to Paul and sipped her coffee.

'What shall we do today?'

'The timetable looks pretty full already to me. I'd better repair the cracked plaster downstairs, and, of course, I've been summoned across the road to the pub this evening.'

'If the wall doesn't take too long to patch up, perhaps we could go for a walk along the river this afternoon after lunch?'

'Yes, sounds fine to me.'

After a leisurely breakfast, Paul strolled out into the back garden, while Jane cleared away and washed up. The back door led directly out onto a small patio constructed from the old roofing slabs left over after the kitchen floor had been laid. The garden itself remained untouched although the builder had cleared the site of weeds and rubble. He lit a cigarette and slowly walked towards the back fence where the black horse stood looking over at him. The sun beat down into the garden and Paul raised his head upwards to feel the heat touch his face. The black horse whinnied, pawing at the ground impatiently. Patting the animal's nose with one hand, he placed the other on the fence and gazed across the paddock to the hills in the distance. Time to get on, he thought.

Turning, he saw Jane standing at the door wiping her hands on a tea-towel.

'I'm coming,' he said, retracing his steps over the rough turned soil.

The interior of the cottage felt distinctly cold compared to outside and he rubbed his arms vigorously to disperse the goose pimples that had appeared.

In the living room he pulled the carpet away from the skirting board by the stairs and knelt down to examine the cracks more closely. A shaft of cold air rushed around his knees. The thought that this wall under the stairs might be hollow suddenly occurred to him. He pulled a small hammer out of the toolbox on the floor beside him and gently tapped at the wall. He had previously assumed that the recently constructed staircase rested on a concrete base, but the dull thuds produced by the hammer confirmed his new theory of a hollow cavity behind the plaster.

Jane wandered in with two cups of coffee.

'It's hollow behind here, you know,' said Paul, standing up. He took one of the cups from her and stepped backwards to survey the wall.

'I'll fill in the cracks for now, but sometime in the near future I'll take the boarding down and have a look behind it.'

'Yes, we ought to find the source of the draught before next winter or we'll freeze to death,' replied Jane, returning to the kitchen to prepare lunch.

Selecting a chisel from the toolbox, Paul chipped away at the cracks to remove all the loose pieces. Gradually, what appeared to be green paint came into view from behind the plaster, and as Paul bent over to look more closely, the chisel slipped, his full body weight behind it as he struggled to regain his balance. As a result several large lumps of plaster fell to the floor around him, but Paul's attention was on the green wooden door in front of him.

'Jane, come and see what I've found,' he said, brushing the plaster from his clothes.

'My God,' said Jane, staring at the door in amazement. 'No wonder there is a draught. The builder must have just plastered over it. I wonder why?'

'I've made a dreadful mess,' said Paul. 'The damned chisel slipped.'

'Never mind. We would have discovered the door sooner or later and there's no point in re-plastering over it. The more storage space we have, the better. A cupboard under the stairs will be very useful.'

Paul slid his fingers across the green painted surface. Four old rusty nails down the opening edge secured the door firmly to its frame. The handle had been removed.

'This door has been closed up for a very long time, judging by the state of these nails,' said Paul.

With the aid of a pair of iron pincers, he prised each one gently away from the wood, finally pulling them clear of the door with a hammer claw Despite the pressure inflicted on the wood by the removal of the nails, the door remained firmly in place.

'Christ, it's still stuck,' said Paul, sitting back on his heels. 'Pass me the crowbar please.'

Slipping it into the gap between the door and the floor he carefully eased it upwards into position. Paul stood up and pressed downwards on the jemmy to attain enough leverage, then pulled sharply until the door separated from the frame with a shuddering groan. He stumbled back a few paces as it broke free. Jane moved towards the opening and peered in. She began to choke and withdrew before her eyes could focus in the blackness. A nauseating smell of damp and decay filled her lungs and nostrils. Retching, she stumbled back into the living room, clasping her throat.

'My God,' she spluttered.

Paul helped her into a chair.

'Stay there, I'll go and fetch the torch from the car.'

On his return, he switched it on and shone the beam directly into the opening. A flight of stone steps descended into the blackness, but the foul air barred him from further investigation and he withdrew also.

Jane had opened the front door and was standing outside in the fresh air. Paul came out to join her.

'It's not a cupboard. I saw some steps – there must be a cellar down there.'

'Full of dead bodies, I shouldn't wonder. I've never experienced such a bloody awful smell in my whole life.'

'Well, we can't just leave it, hoping it will go away, I'll have to go down and see what's causing it. Have we anything better than a torch?'

'Yes, you'll find a storm ·lantern in the broom cupboard.'

The stench from below had permeated into the living room, devouring any oxygen in its path. Jane opened the windows as wide as possible to dispel the rank odour.

Armed with the paraffin lamp and the crowbar, Paul negotiated the stone steps, Jane bringing up the rear with the torch. The treads had become uneven with the passage of time and they made their descent with care. Standing side by side at the bottom, Paul held the lamp in the air while Jane shone the torch slowly in a circle around the chamber. The cellar appeared to be roughly the same size as the ground floor of the cottage. It comprised a vaulted stone ceiling, supported by walls constructed of rectangular slabs and a solid flag floor. The source of the overpowering smell became obvious as their eyes grew acclimatised to the poor light. Filthy black slime oozed through tiny gaps between the slabs, searching out random crevices in which to hide, the remainder clawing its way downwards to hang, suspended by its own viscosity. The dank atmosphere penetrated through their clothing to chill them to the marrow. They both shivered uncontrollably, not only from the cold but also from mounting apprehension within themselves. Three large slabs lay piled up to one side of a narrow opening to reveal a passageway leading off from this subterranean chamber.

'I'm scared,' said Jane, stepping behind Paul to put his body between her and the unknown stretching away in front of them.

'Why don't you go back upstairs, it's far too cold for you down here. I'll be up shortly.'

'Why, what are you going to do?'

'I thought I'd see where the passage leads to. I won't be long-.'

'I'd rather come with you. What on earth would I do if you didn't come back?'

'Don't be silly, nothing's going to happen,' he laughed.

'Well I'm still coming, whatever you say,' she retorted.

'OK, let's go, but be careful you don't slip in the dark, the floor is wet and slimy in places.'

The constricting space inside the tunnel forced them into single file with Paul leading. The floor progressively sloped downhill. Jane was able to walk normally, but the low ceiling subjected Paul into an uncomfortable stoop, making his shoulder blades ache. After what seemed an eternity, but, in fact, was roughly only about fifty yards or so, they reached what looked like a T junction. The passage forked sharply backwards at an angle of approximately forty-five degrees in one direction whilst bearing off at a more gentle angle to the left. Paul stopped, contemplating the situation for a few moments.

'I wouldn't be at all surprised if the tunnel leading back doesn't go to The Hermitage next door or even to the farm. Come on, let's go on a little further.'

They continued slowly, taking the left fork. This passage was wider than the one leading from their cellar; the floor kept to a constant level from this point onwards. Paul finding that he could stand straight, gratefully stretched his aching muscles. Although they had become accustomed to the appalling smell, Paul's head began to thump, sending spasmodic shafts of pain across the top of his skull. His stomach churned and he felt bile rising in his throat. His vision blurred as the pain and nausea swept through his body. At that moment they stumbled into an intersecting chamber from where several tunnels led off in different directions.

Paul clutched his head in both hands, the pain reaching its climax. The walls spun round and round. Unable to see any more, he dropped to his knees and passed out.

When he came to, Jane was cradling his head in her lap, her face contorted with fear and anxiety. The pain had disappeared.

'What happened?' she asked, trembling.

'I don't know, but I'm OK now, just a bit shaken up.' He sat up and looked around the walls.

'Christ Almighty, it's incredible, totally unbelievable.'

'Paul,' Jane whispered, tugging at his sleeve to attract his attention. 'Paul, I don't think we're alone down here.'

'Have you seen anything?' he replied, lowering his voice.

'No, but I can hear something breathing, and I'm convinced we're being watched.'

'From where?'

'I don't know, and it's too dark to see clearly in here. Please can we go back, I'm petrified.'

'Alright,' he said, placing a protective arm around her shoulders.

'Which way do we go?'

Jane pointed to one of the exits. Paul retrieved the lamp and struggled to his feet, leaning on Jane for support. They walked at a brisker pace on the way home, both anxious to return to the more familiar surrounds of their cottage. The feeling that someone or something followed them on their journey back through the tunnels caused Jane to turn round on several occasions and shine her torch into the murky labyrinth behind. She saw nothing, but the breathing continued, at a constant pace to the rear, causing her flesh to crawl at the thought that whatever it was could attack at any time. What have we done? she wondered to herself. We could have bought a pleasant three bedroomed semi-detached house on a friendly estate like most other normal people. But no, we had to be different and buy a cottage, full of charm and character, in a picturesque village, miles from anywhere, full of unfriendly people, underground tunnels and strange inexplicable noises.

The cellar came into view up ahead. Paul and Jane sighed with relief as they saw the staircase leading back up into the cottage.

'I'll push these slabs into place to block the passageway,' said Paul. 'You go on upstairs.'

Jane stepped back into the living room. She shielded her face from the light, blinded momentarily by the sun streaming through the windows. In the kitchen she filled the kettle and switched it on, before opening the oven door to check on the lunch. It was nearly ready. The clock on the control panel said nearly three o'clock, which meant they had spent nearly two hours down in the cellar and tunnels. Hearing a thud as Paul, returning upstairs, pushed the cellar door closed, Jane poured out cups of tea and carried them through to the living room.

'What are we going to do about the cellar?' she asked, handing him a cup and sitting down.

'What do you want me to do about it? he replied wearily.

'It's evil down there, it frightens me. I don't think I'll be able to settle here unless we can block it up.'

'Yes, I feel the same way as you, but apart from nailing up the door, there's not a lot more I can do at present.'

She nodded.

'I've pushed the loose slabs against the entrance to the tunnel to close it, and I'll nail up the door presently. Sometime next week I'll get some bricks and cement, permanently seal up those slabs in the cellar and brick up this doorway under the stairs,' he added.

'How are you feeling now?' she asked.

'The pain has gone but it's left me completely shattered.'

'Well, just stay where you are and rest while I go and serve up some lunch,' she said.

They ate in silence, both deep in thought. Paul's main concern lay with Jane. His new job commenced on Tuesday which meant leaving her alone during the day. That, combined with the fact that the G.P.O. were not able to install the telephone until the end of the week would leave her totally isolated. He also knew that the problems encountered so far could adversely affect her health, which, in her present condition would be disastrous. Jane and the baby had to come first, their entire future happiness depended on his successful career at work and a stable family lifestyle at home. They had both grabbed at the opportunity to leave London and settle in the countryside within easy reach of a small town where he could work. The concept of bringing up a family in the country far outweighed the mad bustle of the London rat-race, where no-one had time to unwind from the pressures of city life. But, in retrospect, had they just made the biggest miscalculation in their lives? Who could say at this early stage. Even if it was, they had no alternative but to make the best of a bad job for the present. Perhaps things would improve, in time.

Glancing over at the clock on the mantelpiece he saw it was five o'clock.

'If you don't mind, I'd like to relax in a hot bath before I go out this evening.'

'No,' said Jane. 'You go ahead, I've plenty to keep me occupied.'

At eight o'clock sharp Paul walked into the 'Castle Arms'. Nothing had changed, not even the stony silence that greeted his entrance into that establishment. He strode purposefully towards the bar, making a point of attracting the landlord's attention.

'Hello there, I'm Paul Richardson from Ivy Cottage across the road. I called in here for a drink last January when the cottage was up for sale, if you remember.'

Terry Smith, the landlord, nodded briefly.

'Yes, I never forget a face. Bert Grimshaw's expecting you, he's waiting in the private bar through there,' he added abruptly, pointing to a door at the side of the bar counter.

'What'll it be while I'm here?'

'Pint of bitter and twenty 'black' please. You'll get to remember the order after a time, won't you?' said Paul jovially.

Terry glared at him icily, making no reply.

Not a brilliant start, thought Paul, moving over to the door. The twenty or so pairs of eyes fixed intently upon him, and the overwhelming silence in the bar frayed his already tattered nerves, causing him to spill some beer down the front of his trousers and on to the floor.

'Shit,' he muttered. 'This beer's so bloody weak it hasn't the strength to fall to the floor.'

He chuckled to himself and turned the handle of the door to enter the private bar.

The events that took place in that stuffy, claustrophobic room during the course of the next two and a half hours were to dramatically reshape the pattern of Paul's entire life.

Jane and Oedipus spent the evening curled up together on the sofa watching television. Although the film being televised starred one of her favourite actors, Robert Redford playing his famous role of Washington Post reporter together with Dustin Hoffman in 'All the President's Men', her attention became distracted on several occasions, not by the draught, because her legs were firmly tucked under the cushions, but by the resumption of incessant scratching from the corner.

Hearing Paul insert his key in the front door, she sighed with relief and jumped up to switch off the set.

'Hi there,' she said, turning to greet him with a smile. 'Did you have a pleasant...?'

She tailed off, seeing him standing woodenly in the doorway, his face set rigid like a piece of stone sculpture.

'Everything OK?' he asked mechanically, looking not at her but straight ahead.

'I'm fine, but whatever has happened to you?'

'Nothing.'

'Oh come on, you're not yourself.'

'I don't know what you're talking about.'

He crossed over to the television, turned it on and sat down in front of it.

'Paul, talk to me.'

Silence.

'Paul, will you please speak to me?'

Again he ignored her.

Fighting to control her temper, she leaned across to the wall and pulled the plug from its socket.

'Answer me, damn you. Did you have a pleasant evening?' she demanded.

'I'm going again tomorrow,' he replied.

'Over my dead body. If spending the evening over the road results in you coming home in a strange frame of mind, you are most definitely not going again.'

By this time they were both standing up facing each other.

'I'll do exactly as I please, how and when I choose,'

he said, evenly. in the village.

'I'm beginning to make friends here You should be doing the same instead of walking about as if there's a rotten smell under your nose, like the stuck-up bitch that you are.'

'Don't you dare speak to me in that way,' she retorted, her hackles rising. 'Who the hell do you think you are?'

'The lord and master of this household from now on. Step out of line and you'll regret it.'

Paul bent over to stoke the cat, who had remained seated on the sofa, gazing wide eyed from one to the other as they parried insults to and fro. In a flash Oedipus leapt to his feet, hissing and spitting, his back arched high in defence, his tail swishing from side to side. On reaching to within a hair's breadth of the animal, Oedipus pounced upon the outstretched hand, sinking his sharp claws and razor-edged teeth deep into flesh and muscle, gouging and tearing, again and again until Paul's blood dripped freely from the wounds opened by this savage attack. To rid himself from this onslaught, he raised his arm shoulder high, his hand still caught in a vice-like grip and with all the force he could muster he violently threw the cat across the room with a whip-like action. Oedipus crashed against the opposite wall and dropped heavily on to the floor, stunned.

Clutching his injured hand to staunch the flow of blood, Paul staggered to the front door, wrenched it open and disappeared into the night.

CHAPTER 5

A strained atmosphere hovered over Ivy Cottage during the course of the following day, namely Bank Holiday Monday. Jane had woken to find the other half of the bed unslept in, and, on coming downstairs discovered Paul huddled up asleep on the sofa. In the kitchen she busied herself making coffee, dumping one of the cups on the small table next to Paul before returning upstairs with her own.

Outside, the sun, already high in the sky, beat down over the village rooftops. Jane decided to take advantage of the good weather today and make a start on her front garden, which she intended to lay out as a formal herb garden in the traditional cross pattern. She dressed quickly, selecting trousers and maternity top as suitable gardening attire, and hurried downstairs, picking up her handbag and keys on the way out to the car. Paul, still asleep, grunted as she walked past him, the keys jangling in her hand disturbing his slumber.

The village street was deserted. She started up the engine, aware of the considerable noise it created in the surrounding silence. The road surface shimmered in front of her as the car slowly glided past the farm, under the canopy of trees beyond and up the hill towards the main road. She made a right turn at the T-junction and headed in the direction of Prestbury. Ten minutes later Jane pulled into the Garden Centre she remembered passing on their drive out from the market town two days previously. During the course of the next hour, she chatted to one of the nurserymen on duty, who not only helped her pick out an assortment of plants, but also enlightened her as to their various culinary and medicinal properties.

She drove back to Ashingham, pleased with her morning's progress and relieved that she had finally spoken to a friendly person, who had gone out of his way to be helpful. On arriving home she found that Paul had gone out, obviously in a hurry by the state of chaos he had left behind him. Normally such untidiness would have irritated her, but today she mentally rose above it, not caring a damn.

The herb garden in the forefront of her mind, she set to work. The rubble heaped up in one corner by the builder contained a considerable number of small stone slabs which Jane utilised to form walkways, in the shape of a crucifix. These paths ·performed two functions. On the one hand they gave access to all corners of the garden without having to tread on the soil, and, on the other they permanently displayed the sign of the cross, the historical and religious aspects of this ancient horticulture.

Engrossed in her work, Jane failed to notice Eve Simpkins emerge into the garden of Crabtree Cottage, two doors along the row. Jane lay the Sorrel in position by the wall, gently pressing the earth around the base of the plant. The top right hand bed now complete, Jane stood up to admire her handiwork.

'Hello there,' shouted Eve across the next garden.

CHAPTER 5

Jane turned in the direction of the voice, not believing her ears.

'Oh hello, I'm Jane Richardson, we've just moved in.'

'Yes, I know,' said Eve, opening her front gate and advancing along the road towards her. 'I knocked yesterday morning, but as there was no reply I presumed you were out.'

Jane thought for a moment.

'No, that must have been around the time we were in the cellar,' she replied cautiously, studying Eve's face to see if there was any reaction to her statement.

No flicker of surprise, however, crossed Eve's smiling face, thus confirming that every cottage possessed a cellar, and the fact that the builder had concealed the one in Ivy Cottage had been his own decision. Not able to leave the subject through curiosity Jane asked, 'Do you use your cellar at all?'

'My husband does, but I never venture down there. Besides the fact that cellars frighten me, ours is very damp and smelly. It's the water level from the river, you see,' she added as an afterthought. 'During the autumn when the sea tides are at their highest, the Colne River which flows into the sea at Prestbury Dock backs up into the Lune here in the village flooding the cellars. It happens every year.

'Is that a fact?' said Jane. 'I must remember to tell my husband Paul.'

In the course of conversation Eve had hoisted her petite frame onto the front wall and sat, dangling her legs into Jane's garden.

'What are you doing?' she asked with genuine interest.

'I'm laying out a herb garden. I thought it might add to the general character of the cottage.'

41

'What a good idea. I like the tiny paths intersecting the beds.'

'Do you enjoy gardening?' asked Jane.

'Yes, but I don't have a lot of time to spare, so my efforts mainly consist of keeping down the weeds and mowing the back lawn. You'll find your own hands full soon enough,' she added with a twinkling laugh, looking directly at Jane's stomach.

Jane stared down at her ever-widening girth and nodded in agreement.

The sun had moved behind the derelict mill, enveloping the entire street in dark shadow.

'What a pity the old mill blocks out so much light. Have you heard whether it's to be restored or not?'

Eve turned her head to gaze up at the gaunt stone building across the street. Towering three storeys high, its roof open to the elements, the unglazed windows of the mill stared vacantly over the cottages to the hills beyond, like empty sockets in a skeleton.

'The local Preservation Society are sending a team of architects and surveyors into the village this week. I think they start work tomorrow,' said Eve. 'Personally, I'd like it pulled down, it's an eyesore from our cottage situated directly opposite.'

'I agree entirely,' said Jane. 'The view from here would extend right across the valley if it were demolished.'

At this point Jane glanced down the street to see Paul crossing the footbridge. She turned back to Eve.

'I suppose at one time nearly everybody in the village worked at the mill?'

'Yes. It came as a terrible blow to the village when it closed down two years ago. But luckily, Bert Grimshaw and Arthur

Briggs managed to raise enough capital to buy the village from the estate and take on the existing workforce. Otherwise I don't know what would have happened, the cottages are tied to the mill, you see.'

Paul approached the gate and stopped dead in his tracks.

'This is Eve Simpkins from Crabtree Cottage, next door but one,' Jane said in introduction.

He nodded curtly in Eve's direction but said nothing, opened the gate and headed up the front path.

Damn him to hell, thought Jane, glancing at Eve with a strained smile.

'Don't take any notice of Paul, he's been a little odd since yesterday. I don't think he's feeling very well,' she added, prickling with embarrassment.

'Oh. Forget it,' said Eve, dismissing it lightly.

'All the men down here act strangely on occasions. The women are used to it.'

Eve pulled up her sleeve to look at the time.

'Good Lord, I had no idea it was as late as this. It's three fifteen. I must go back, my family will be wondering where I am.'

She lifted her legs, swung them gracefully over the wall, and dropped nimbly to the ground.

'Why don't you pop in for a brew sometime tomorrow?' she said, smoothing her skirt into place.

'I'd love to,' responded Jane cheerfully.

'See you soon then.'

Eve disappeared indoors, the heavy oak door closing firmly behind her.

Jane bent down to gather her tools together. The gardening had proved quite a strain for her, and she could feel the baby moving restlessly around inside. She longed for a cup of tea. Tomorrow, weather permitting, she would plant out the remaining beds.

Indoors she found Paul lounging in a chair watching the television.

'I'm making some tea,' she said. 'Would you like some?'

He grunted his assent, his eyes firmly fixed on the screen.

On her way to the kitchen she noticed Paul's hand and lower arm had been professionally bandaged. She made the tea and carried a cup through to Paul.

'Have you been to the hospital?' she asked, addressing the question more to the bandage than to her husband. 'Does it matter?' replied Paul, still engrossed in the programme he was watching.

Jane refused to rise to the bait. Instead, she collected her cup from the kitchen, climbed the stairs to the bedroom where she lay down to rest.

She awoke some hours later to find it was already dark. She was sure she could sense a presence other than her own in the room. She moved her hand slowly across the bedspread. Fingers and fur touched. Oedipus lay curled up asleep beside her. Sighing with relief she stretched across to the bedside table and switched on the lamp. Opening the bedroom door she stepped out on to the landing and peered through the bannisters.

The living room curtains still open, allowed the full moon to cast a silvery pool of light on the carpet, transforming the furniture into indefinable murky shapes, which, enlarged in shadow, reflected back from the walls. Although the radiator at her side felt hot to the touch, she shivered, realising her isolation inside the dark, deserted cottage. Paul had gone out, presumably to the pub again. She retrieved a cardigan from the bedroom and made her way carefully downstairs, Oedipus finally tucked under her arm for support.

Jane moved around at speed, switching on lights and drawing the curtains to shut out the night. She picked up a box of matches, lit the fire and turned on the TV, increasing the volume control to a level she could hear in the kitchen while she rummaged through the cupboards to prepare herself a meal. The prospect of another solitary evening ahead of her, she sat in front of the roaring fire, Oedipus beside her, watchful as ever. Disturbances from the corner distracted her occasionally, as they had on the previous evening. She made a mental note to ask Eve if she heard similar noises.

Paul rolled in from the 'Castle Arms' after closing time. Tonight, however, his face broke into a watery smile as she stood up to greet him.

'I'm sorry, love,' he said, extending his arms towards her. Jane accepted his invitation and buried her head in his shoulder.

'I've not been feeling myself.'

'Are you OK now?' she enquired with concern.

'No, not really. I don't know what's wrong. Everything is hazy and my head feels like a ton weight.'

'Go on up to bed. You'll feel a lot better in the morning. It's nerves, that's all, the house and the new job worrying you.'

'I hope to God you're right,' he said. 'I've never felt like this before, it's weird.'

The next morning Paul left the cottage at eight-thirty sharp to drive into Prestbury. Jane waved him off from the porch.

Today he commenced his new job, today she remained alone in the cottage for the first time during the day in her new role as housewife.

Overnight stormy weather had pounded the valley as driving rain and gale-force winds circled the hills continuously, felling trees, smashing chimney pots and sending roof slates crashing into the street. Even now the icy rain pricked at her face like shards of broken glass as she stood, shielded by the porch. Jane drew back into the living room, pressing her full weight behind the door to close it, the swirling wind on the outside defying her in her efforts. She went through to the kitchen to clear the breakfast dishes, gazing out of window as she washed up. The trees beyond the paddock bowed almost double as the wind thrashed down upon them, worrying and fretful, pushing them to the limits of their elasticity. Jane, unused to being left alone with the prospect of a long dreary day ahead of her, listened acutely for unusual sounds, turning round occasionally as if she expected to see someone or something behind her. If I go on like this, people will begin to think I've gone crackers, she thought to herself. I must make a concerted effort to pull myself together. After an hour or two she became calmer, moving about the cottage in a more relaxed frame of mind.

Suddenly, somebody knocked on the door. She froze on the spot, her heartbeat rising, everything achieved over the last hour or so wiped out. She opened the door, to find the postman with a bundle of letters in his hand. He said he had a parcel for her on the van. She followed him outside as far as the gate and took it from him.

Further down the street a dark-green transit van had pulled up outside the old mill. Three men got out. One of them

46

opened the rear doors of the vehicle and began unloading its contents. The blond-haired man, standing nearest to Jane, donned the yellow tin helmet he had carried, tucked under one arm, then leaned into the van to retrieve a large clipboard. The van unloaded, the three men divided the equipment equally between them, locked up and disappeared inside the mill. Jane did likewise into her cottage, clutching the parcel.

Sometime later, the housework completed to her satisfaction, she changed into a clean dress, brushed her hair and set off to Crabtree Cottage, carefully locking the front door behind her. Eve looked delighted to see her. Jane was reverently ushered into the cosy living room, where a glowing log fire crackled cheerfully in the g-rate. A small wire-haired terrier bounded into her lap as she sat down in one of the comfortable chintz armchairs and proceeded to lick her face in frenzied delight.

'Get down, Cookie,' shouted Eve from the depths of the kitchen where she was making a pot of tea. 'How is your husband feeling today?'

'He's still not well, but I think it's nerves,' replied Jane. She changed the subject, not wanting to talk about Paul.

'I think I saw the surveyors arriving earlier.'

'Yes,' said Eve, 'but I wonder how much they will get done in this atrocious weather.'

While she waited, Jane cast a look around at her surroundings. The living room of Crabtree Cottage differed from her own in that it was rectangular in shape rather than square, but the olde worlde features, the low-beamed ceiling, latched wooden doors and inglenook were of similar design. Her visual tour stopped abruptly at the cellar door. Unable to wrench her eyes away, she remained staring at it until Eve broke the spell by handing her a cup of tea.

'Do you ever hear strange noises coming up from the cellar?' Jane asked.

'No,' laughed Eve. 'What sort of noises do you mean?'

'Tapping and scratching sounds, oh, and whining noises as well.'

'No,' repeated Eve. 'I can't say I've ever heard anything like that. The draught from under the cellar door is the only thing that bothers me, and that's something I can't seem to cure. But that's all.'

Jane decided to drop this particular conversation. She certainly had no intention of frightening her new friend.

'It's probably my imagination. I've never lived in an old cottage before.' She changed the subject.

'I'm looking forward to bringing up my new baby in the country.'

'When is he due?' asked Eve.

'It could well be a girl you know,' suggested Jane, waiting to see Eve's reaction.

'Never. It will be a boy, without doubt. There's not been a baby girl born in this village since the Civil War, over three hundred years ago.'

'I wonder why?' asked Jane, pumping for information.

'I've no idea,' replied Eve.

Jane valued this new friendship. She desperately needed someone close to her that she could confide in.

In these early days, however, certain subjects would be better avoided, especially cellars and the sex of yet unborn children. Later as their relationship developed, perhaps these areas could be touched upon, but not now, definitely not now. She rose to leave, thanking Eve for her hospitality and also returning the invitation.

Outside, the stormy weather had died away completely, leaving in its wake a muggy atmosphere of wet mist, as the first rays of sun filtered through the broken cloud to merge into the warm vapour rising up from the ground. Jane inserted her key in the front door and stepped inside the cottage. She progressed no further than the threshold. Paralysed with fear, she remained rooted to the spot, wide-eyed in disbelief. The cellar door stood open against the wall, the large nails which Paul had used to secure it, protruding from its inner side like a formidable row of shark's teeth. The immense power invoked by this unknown intruder to gain entry had resulted in the door itself crashing against the adjacent wall, gouging out great chunks of plaster, which now lay scattered across the carpet.

A hideous moan rose up from the bowels of the cellar, gathering momentum as it climbed the stairs, finally escaping into the room, howling, shrieking, swirling, lifting up and hurling any objects obstructing its path. Jane looked on, mesmerized, watching the devastation. A paperweight spun through the air and hit her on the left temple, jolting her brain into action. A wind tunnel. She slammed the front door closed. The last of the flying objects dropped to the floor. Silence descended upon the room.

Her heart pounding, Jane remained by the door, holding her breath hard, listening. Intuitively, she knew she was not alone. She was sure she could sense a presence other than her own in the cottage. In the front bedroom, immediately above where she stood, something fell on to the carpet with a dull thud. Christ, she thought. There is somebody moving around upstairs. Jane scanned the living room for a suitable weapon with which to defend herself. The solid brass poker in the hearth glinted in the sunlight as if to attract her attention. Four steps and she held it in her grasp. To test its clout capability she flexed her wrist and wielded it in the air several times. Yes, it would suffice. A considerable volume of adrenalin pumped through her body, bolstering up the courage and physical strength necessary for the task in hand.

Never had a flight of stairs looked so daunting. Would she reach the top, or be attacked and sent crashing back down. After what seemed an eternity her feet gained the landing, from where the whole of that bedroom could be seen. It remained exactly as she had left it, with the exception of a tiny porcelain figurine, which had fallen off the bedside table onto the floor, its head parted from its body in a clean break. As she stooped down to pick up the pieces, a shadow flashed in front of her, blocking out the light from the window. At the same time, a smell of decaying flesh wafted up her nostrils. In a second the shadow had disappeared, but the stench remained. She jumped, her senses prickling with fear. An evil coldness filled the room, the temperature dropped sharply and a smell of death flooded the atmosphere causing Jane to retch. Gripping the poker, she struggled to a standing position, contaminated air coursing into her lungs, sending acute pain shafting through her ribcage. Jane lunged towards the doorway, but one foot became entangled in a corner of the bedspread, sending her sprawling across the floor.

A message from her brain repeated itself continuously like a scratched gramophone record - get out, get out. My God, she thought. If I can't escape, I shall die. She dug her nails into the carpet and heaved her body in the direction of the door and out onto the landing. Unable to apply any pressure to the injured ankle, Jane hobbled down the staircase, one at a time. Something followed only a pace behind, she could feel its cold, clammy breath on the back of her neck. She swung around, flailing the poker frantically in wide circular sweeps of emptiness. Overreaching herself, she lost her balance and tumbled awkwardly down the remaining stairs.

The brain message purged onwards – Get out, get out. 'Shut up,' she screamed aloud, losing the last threads of self-control, as she lay sobbing in a crumpled heap at the foot of the staircase. This outburst echoed round the walls of the deserted cottage and died away. She needed one last effort to reach safety. Jane crawled painfully towards the front door, the last obstacle blocking her route to freedom. Nearer and nearer it came. At last it stood within reach.

Exhausted, she stretched upwards, fumbling for the wrought iron latch. Droplets of sticky liquid spattered onto her hand. Warm, sticky red liquid. Jane glanced up uncertainly, then looked away quickly, her vision clouded by pain. No, it wasn't possible. She stared up again in total disbelief at the horrific spectacle displayed in front of her. Oedipus the cat, her beloved companion and friend, gazed down at her, his amber-green eyes a vision of bewilderment as he hung, spreadeagled across the front door, impaled upon a large butcher's hook, his four limbs stretched taut and secured to the wood by rusty iron nails. Although dead, the cat's life-blood continued to drip steadily from the gaping wounds, saturating the long jet-black fur of his body and once beautiful brush-like tail, on to Jane's hand, finding its final resting place in a red pool on the floor.

The shock forced her hand downwards, the latch sprang open and the door opened. Jane collapsed into unconsciousness in the porch.

CHAPTER 6

J ane opened her eyes to find herself staring up at an unfamiliar ceiling. She blinked hard several times to clear her vision, but although the haziness disappeared, the ceiling remained exactly the same. Unlike the exposed oak beams in Ivy Cottage, this ceiling had been close-boarded and painted glossy white. Without moving her head, Jane's eyes apprehensively scanned the room in a semi-circular sweep to ascertain her whereabouts.

The room, decorated in modern style, had no rough-plastered walls, but instead, delicate floral print wallpaper with matching curtains and loose-covers in a soft pastel pink, delightfully feminine, and totally out-of-character with what she had seen so far in this down-to-earth farming community. Completing their survey, her eyes came to rest on a young fair-haired girl sitting in front of the fire upon a creamy-grey goatskin rug. Turning her head slightly to see better, Jane noticed a tiny baby cradled in her arms. The girl, sensing movement, looked up to see Jane regarding her steadily from where she lay on the sofa. Handing the baby gently to a young man standing on the opposite side of the fireplace, the girl approached Jane and knelt down beside her.

'Hello,' she said quietly. 'I'm Susan Entwistle.'

Aware of Jane's bewilderment in these strange surroundings, she continued.

'Please don't worry. You're in Hermitage Cottage next door. My husband Graham found you lying unconscious in your porch and carried you in here.'

Susan paused, momentarily, her face showing genuine concern.

'How do you feel now? Are you in any pain?'

'I'm OK, but my ankle is throbbing.'

'Would you like me to call a doctor?'

'No, it's not necessary.'

'Are you sure? It might be a good idea to be examined and make sure the baby is alright.'

'No, honestly,' repeated Jane, struggling to sit up.

'Stay lying down a bit longer,' said Susan, coaxing Jane's head back onto the cushions. 'I'll make some tea.'

Graham Entwistle, who had disappeared upstairs with the baby while the two women were talking, had returned and now sat in the corner, silently observing Jane.

'Thank you for helping me,' said Jane. 'I'm most grateful.'

'No problem. I was passing by at the time.'

Tears welled up in Jane's eyes as she thought of Oedipus. She fought them back, searching in her pocket for a handkerchief.

'Will you do something for me when I go home?'

'If I can.'

'Someone has killed my cat and nailed him up on the inside of my front door. You wouldn't take him down for me, would you?'

Graham's whole countenance changed at this request. His face adopted a fixed, taut expression transforming his once friendly eyes into dark narrow slits.

He said, guardedly, 'Cat, what cat? I didn't see a cat.'

At this point Susan bustled in from the kitchen with the tea and the conversation ended, much to Jane's relief.

'Now, are you quite sure I can't ring your husband,' asked Susan, showing genuine concern for Jane's condition.

'No, please don't worry him. It's his first day in a new job and I don't want to fetch him home.'

'Fair enough, but let me bandage your ankle.'

'Please don't go to any trouble on my account.'

'Don't be silly, it's the least I can do.'

Jane looked across at Graham. He hadn't moved a muscle. She could feel sinister vibrations emanating from his direction and resolved to leave as soon as politeness would allow.

Susan appeared not to notice the strained atmosphere as she fussed about tending to Jane. Jane drank her tea quickly while Susan tightly strapped up her ankle, then stood up to test it.

'That's lovely,' she said. 'I'll go home now, I don't want to take up any more of your time.'

'Hey, not so fast,' said Susan. 'Graham told me it's quite a mess next door. I'm coming with you to help clear up.'

Realising that nothing she could say would deter Susan, Jane smiled gratefully to acknowledge and accept the offer. She turned to thank Graham and say goodbye, but instantly changed her mind in view of his threatening glare.

'Come on,' said Susan, oblivious to her husband's mood. 'Lean on my shoulder for support and mind the step as you go out.'

Arriving back at Ivy Cottage, Jane cautiously raised the latch on the front door and pushed it open. The living room resembled a battlefield with occasional tables, lamps, in fact everything portable overturned and strewn haphazardly across the floor. The pictures, without exception, hung skew-whiff from the walls. Most of Jane's precious lead crystal vases and porcelain figures, collected lovingly over the years, lay on the carpet, smashed into myriads of tiny fragments, the glass shards twinkling as they picked up the odd ray of sun through the windows.

Both girls stood on the threshold, unable to move. The state of chaos had completely overawed Susan, rendering her speechless, her mind trying to co-ordinate some semblance of order to the task that confronted them.

Jane, on the other hand, knew, unlike Susan, that her cat hung impaled on the reverse side of the door, and she could not bring herself to look upon his pitiful, lifeless body for a second time. A lump formed in her throat and the tears, bravely contained until now, began to course freely down her cheeks. Jane sank to her knees and sobbed as if her heart would break. Susan bent down and helped Jane to her feet, gently guiding her to the nearest chair.

'Please don't cry,' she said. 'It's a terrible mess, but we'll soon clear it up between us.'

'It's not the mess,' said Jane, continuing to weep.

'It's my cat. Someone has killed Oedipus and impaled him to the back of the front door.'

Susan got up, visibly shocked and stared over at it. Slowly, but with deliberation, she walked across the room, stretched out a shaky hand and pushed the door to close it. She gritted her teeth for the shock to come. With a clunk the door secured itself on the latch. Susan looked, blinked, then looked again to make sure. The pounding in her heart abated as she saw that nothing hung there. Christ, she thought to herself. The poor girl's so wound up she's hallucinating. I knew I should have called the doctor.

She crept back to where Jane sat and gently clasped the other woman's hands between her own.

'Jane,' she whispered. 'Jane, there's nothing there, nothing at all.'

Jane turned to look for herself in disbelief. But Susan had spoken the truth. Oedipus had vanished. He was no longer there.

'What about the pool of blood on the carpet?' said Jane, pointing to the doorway. Susan went back to look.

'I can see a wet patch here, but that's all. It doesn't look like blood to me, just a water mark.'

Jane struggled to recall the events leading up to the time she passed out. Had the things she remembered happening actually taken place or, more to the point, were they a figment of her imagination? Had the complete change in her lifestyle, the move from London, her job and her friends, to a country cottage with the new role of housewife and mother-to-be been too much to handle at one stroke? Jane's nervous system, wound up to maximum tension, teetered on the brink of collapse. Yet she clung desperately to her past reputation of being rational, clear headed and reliable. She needed proof of the cat's death to maintain her sanity. If Oedipus had been impaled on the door, the marks from the butcher's hook and the nails would still be there as evidence.

Jane rose and slowly walked to the door. The proof she sought openly presented itself, four holes at right angles forming an almost perfect square with a somewhat larger rent between the top two where the hook had scored the wood before securing itself into place. Jane turned to Susan, thinking she was behind her, but Susan had vanished into the kitchen to look for a dustpan and brush. On reflection, she decided to say nothing further. Past experience had shown that the villagers turned hostile for no apparent reason and there seemed little point in pushing her luck with the two women she had made friends with so far.

Susan and Jane spent the next hour restoring the room to its former state as best they could, miraculously retrieving a few ornaments intact from the debris which they swept up and deposited in the dustbin outside. Jane limped painfully as far as the gate with Susan to say goodbye and after she had departed, remained standing, turning over the day's events. Above all else, she pondered the fate of her cat. Where was he now? Who had removed his body and cleared up the blood?

'Hello there.'

Jane looked up, startled to see the blond-haired surveyor she had noticed earlier in the day unloading the van outside the mill.

'Oh, hello. How are you getting on?'

'Could be worse, I suppose,' he said, laughing.

'Does the restoration look favourable?' she asked.

'Well, the structural condition of the building above ground level is shaky, to say the least, but not impossible to rebuild and make safe. The foundations are the important factor.'

Jane's face dropped on hearing the surveyor's comments.

'You don't look too pleased at the suggestion to rebuild,' he said, grinning.

'No, not really. The mill blocks out a lot of light and obstructs the beautiful view across the valley. Personally, I'd like to see the building demolished.'

'You're probably in luck, as it happens,' he replied, amicably.

'Down at the river bank, just by the bridge, we opened up a bricked-up tunnel this morning. It led directly into a cave immediately beneath the foundations of the mill, which made our survey relatively easy, as we were able to see the whole of the sub-structure.'

'And,' prompted Jane.

'Well, the fact that the mill has been left empty and derelict for some years, combined with the common subsidence problem in this area due to the geological sand strata, have caused the foundations to tilt roughly thirty degrees, leaving the structure in an extremely dangerous condition.'

'Can it be rectified?' she asked.

'Yes, but in my view the whole project would be uneconomic,' he said.

'I've just completed my written report and posted it to the Preservation Society. I get the feeling you've not a lot to worry about,' he added. He glanced at his watch. 'I'd better get back and help my colleagues to clear up.'

'Is there a lot?'

'Well, we'll do most of it now, but I'll probably come back tomorrow to re-seal the tunnel.'

The surveyor had begun to saunter slowly down the road when Jane called him back.

'Were there any tunnels leading off that cave under the mill?' she enquired.

'Yes, about half a dozen I should guess. I didn't venture any further than the cave though. To be honest, I experienced the most weird sensations down there and hurried to complete the survey as quickly as possible. The whole time I was working in the cave, I had the distinct feeling that someone was looking over my shoulder, even though I knew I was alone. Then my head started throbbing, and by the time I emerged into the daylight again, the pounding had become so acute I thought I would collapse.'

'Are you OK now?' Jane enquired, thinking back to the previous weekend and the exploration of the tunnels with her husband Paul. She noted the comparison by which both men had suffered severe headaches and nausea while underground.

'Yes, I'll be fine. I just feel a little washed out, that's all.'

Jane watched the surveyor make his way back to the mill, then disappeared indoors herself to prepare the evening meal.

Driving home from Prestbury at the end of a hectic first day in his new job, Paul decided to call in at the 'Castle Arms' for a drink before going home for dinner. He left his car by the village shop and walked the rest of the way to the pub to avoid being spotted by Jane. Although most people experience numerous difficulties on day one in a new job, fumbling around unable to find anything they require, or anyone to ask if a problem crops up, in addition to these common obstacles Paul became acutely aware, as the day progressed, that his new colleagues disliked him. In fact, intensely disliked him. By the time five o'clock arrived, Paul's only thought was to get away as quickly as possible. However, having left the building another problem loomed up. He didn't want to go home either.

Sitting in the car, he visualised walking through the door to be greeted by Jane, to his mind, gross and ungainly as her pregnancy advanced. His feeling towards her had definitely soured since the move from London and the thought of facing her after a bad day was too much to contemplate. No, he needed to unwind and have a few drinks with the lads before going home to Jane.

Paul found the bar surprisingly crowded, considering the early hour. The local clientele stood in small groups, some at the bar chatting, while another was busily engaged in a game of darts in the far corner. As he strode across the room to the bar, he was delighted that several villagers acknowledged his presence by raising their hands in greeting, and to crown it all, Terry, the landlord, offered to buy him a drink. Wonders would never cease. For the first time that day, things were looking up. At the far end of the bar stood a man Paul had not seen in the village before. He stuck out like a sore thumb, being blond and head and shoulders taller than everyone else.

'Who's the man Bert and Arthur are talking to?' he asked Terry as he took his first mouthful of beer.

'One of the surveyors working at the mill. There've been three of them messing about down there all day.'

'Doing the survey for the Preservation Society?'

'Reckon so.'

'What's the outcome?'

'No idea, you'd best ask him yourself.'

Paul remained at the bar chatting to Terry for several more minutes, not wanting to interrupt Bert and Arthur, who appeared to be deep in conversation with the stranger.

However, at the first suitable opportunity, Paul sidled along the bar and approached the group, to find himself warmly invited to join in the discussion. Paul already knew the views held by the two farmers regarding the mill restoration, the whole matter having been discussed at length at a meeting held at the pub the previous evening. The main cause for concern in the village lay not with the restoration, but what it would inevitably lead to. The Preservation Society's desire to convert the restored building into a craft museum would, without doubt, result in a popular tourist attraction, with hordes of visitors pouring into the valley, bringing their cars, families and litter with them, poking about and generally making themselves a nuisance to everyone.

The villagers hated strangers, they remained apart, a separate breed. Paul could vouch for that. He had witnessed their initial hospitality at first hand, although now, of course, he had started to integrate and become one of them. Paul regarded every man in the valley as a friend and, eager to please his new comrades, committed himself wholeheartedly to endorsing any decisions made by Bert and Arthur, the leaders of the community. It had been agreed at the meeting that a museum in Ashingham was totally unacceptable to its inhabitants, and in the event of a favourable survey, the entire village down to the last man would stand united in its struggle to prevent any development of the site.

Paul, impressed by the skilful handling of the conversation by the two men, stood passively on the sidelines, nodding in agreement at the appropriate moments, reverently hanging on every word uttered by the two leaders. Nick, as Bert had addressed him, chatted away amicably, recounting the day's progress on the site, totally unaware that Bert and Arthur were methodically extracting every scrap of information from him. During the period of time Paul looked on, five empty glasses were removed from Nick's hand, only to be replaced by another pint of ale.

Suddenly Nick broke off in mid-sentence and asked Arthur about the tunnels. Paul's eyes darted from Arthur to Bert. Neither man batted an eyelid. Unperturbed by a nil response, Nick continued, announcing that he had decided to carry out his own survey of the passages the following morning before re-sealing them. He scanned the group for their approval. Bert, the first man to recover his composure, laughed heartily.

'How do your colleagues feel about it?'

'They aren't scheduled to return tomorrow, I'm the only one coming back to clear up.'

'Well, I can't see any reason to object to it, can you, Arthur?' Bert said, looking directly at him.

'No, I've no objection at all. Go ahead, it's fine by me.'

Paul glanced at his watch, and seeing the time, excused himself to go home. As he approached his front gate, he felt a heavy hand clamp down on his shoulder. He spun round to be confronted by Arthur Briggs.

'Not so fast, laddie,' he said. 'You're needed back at the pub later. Ten o'clock sharp. Make sure you're on time.'

Paul nodded his assent, and waited by the gate until the farmer disappeared back into the pub. Paul had not intended to stay in the bar so long. It was late and he knew Jane would be annoyed. The last thing he wanted was the inevitable argument. He stood in the porch and composed himself. Drooping shoulders, rumpled suit and weary smile should do the trick. Satisfied with his appearance, Paul inserted his key into the lock and went in.

Jane limped into the living room to greet him. Her angry expression dissolved as she met his tired, but cheerful face.

'Bad day?' she enquired.

'Yes,' he replied, flopping into a chair. 'You don't look so good yourself. What have you done to your leg?'

'I'll tell you about it when I've served dinner,' she replied. 'I won't be a moment.'

So far, so good, thought Paul, inwardly grimacing at his wife's swollen stomach. Keep the peace and life flows smoothly. Bert and Arthur had demonstrated the theory perfectly in their subtle handling of the surveyor. From now on he would utilize this method, both at home and at work. No more rows or upsets. Eventually, subtlety would lead to a position of dominance.

During the meal, Jane recounted, at length, the events of the day, and Paul played a distinguished role any actor would have been proud of. He made all the appropriate noises Jane expected, and the look of concern on his face made her feel closer to him than at any time since the move to Ashingham. He promised to find and deal with the person responsible for the cat's death, and even suggested she should buy another one when she felt up to it. He had to admit to himself, Jane positively glowed with health and happiness, and he regretted his inability to cope mentally with her advanced pregnant condition. In his mind, his wife had been transformed from a beautiful girl into a grotesque ugly woman, and there was nothing he could do but wait for the outcome.

Jane continued to glance lovingly in his direction, making him feel uncomfortable.

'You look very tired,' she said. 'Why don't you sit by the fire with your feet up?'

Paul glanced at the clock on the mantelpiece.

'I wouldn't mind popping over the road for a drink. I could put out a few feelers regarding the cat at the same time.'

Jane didn't turn a hair at his suggestion, in fact, she agreed it might do him good. Paul, unable to believe his luck, got up and made his way upstairs to freshen up before she changed her mind. She was still smiling, however, when he said goodbye and closed the door behind him.

Jane woke early the next morning completely refreshed following all the trials and tribulations of the previous days. She looked fondly across at Paul, still fast asleep, his face relaxed in the familiar half smile she had become accustomed to over the years. Although the hands of the clock only pointed to six thirty, the sun streamed through the bedroom window, openly inviting her to make the most of the day ahead. Jane slipped quietly out of bed and gathering an armful of clothes, tiptoed to the bathroom. Ten minutes later she emerged into the front garden, savouring the early morning country air, a cup of coffee in her hand. Bending down to check on the progress of her newly planted herbs, she decided to continue working in the garden if the weather stayed fine.

Suddenly she heard a mew. Standing up, Jane looked around her, but saw nothing. Then she heard it again. This time she walked to the gate and looked down the road. Another mew attracted her gaze across the street to where a large black cat crouched, his eyes fixed firmly on her face. Oedipus. No, it wasn't possible. Oedipus was dead. A lump formed in her throat as she thought back to yesterday.

Opening the gate, she walked towards it. The cat resembled Oedipus exactly. The nearer she came, the more she was convinced it was him. Then, reaching to within arm's length, the cat scampered off down the road, stopping to turn around and mew plaintively at her as if to ask her to follow. Jane's curiosity forced her to obey, and she limped behind him down the road towards the river. The cat constantly checked that she was following, then ran a little further on, until he reached the middle of the bridge where he resumed his crouching position. Jane arrived at the bridge and hung on to the rail to catch her breath. What did the cat want? Why had he brought her down to the river? She looked at him questioningly. He returned Jane's gaze and, acknowledging her unspoken questions, slunk across to the handrail, halfway along the bridge where he lowered his head over the edge. From where she stood on the bridge, Jane could see nothing. The cat looked at her, then lowered his head once more, mewing in frustration. Then she understood. He was asking her to look underneath the bridge.

Jane stepped back onto the bank. In front of her a little further along the path she clearly saw the unblocked tunnel the surveyor had mentioned during their conversation the day before. She took half a dozen paces towards the gaping hole, then turned abruptly to look back at the bridge. Jane stopped dead, rigid in her tracks, unable to believe her eyes. A body hung from the central bridge support. She raised her head to where the cat crouched a little higher up. His work done, he withdrew his head and scampered away into the undergrowth on the opposite bank. In her heart, Jane knew the cat was Oedipus. He had returned from the so-called twilight zone, in order to lead her to the river. She wondered if she would ever see him again. Of one thing she was certain. Oedipus would never be replaced.

The corpse twisted gently in the light breeze, making it difficult for Jane to identify. She stepped closer to the water's edge to see more clearly. Then it turned towards her to reveal the most horrendous injuries she had ever seen. Jane's eyes stared directly into those of the blond-haired surveyor. Unable to wrench her gaze from the hideous spectacle, she clutched her throat as her stomach churned in preparation to vomit. The once blond hair lay flat on the man's head, matted with congealed blood, so that it looked a dark reddish brown. His eyes bulged from their sockets, horribly contorted by the pressure from the knotted rope which had also forced his tongue from his mouth. Deep, livid score marks ran vertically down the heavily bruised face, the blood from these wounds forming a thick crust on the beard line. What remained of the man's clothes, hung open and loose, torn to shreds, exposing large areas of torso, also gouged by what appeared to be claw-like talons.

'Christ Almighty!' muttered Jane under her breath, almost as if she was frightened at being overheard. Her knees wobbled as they turned to jelly, forcing her to the ground. Unable to hold back any longer, she emptied the contents of her stomach into the river, her body heaving and retching uncontrollably.

Jane pulled a handkerchief from her pocket to wipe her mouth and looked around her. Nothing stirred, apart from the body, swinging in the breeze. The village street remained deserted, there was nobody about. She struggled to her feet and walked back along the street, past the row of cottages, past the farm and on towards the phone box to call the Police.

CHAPTER 7

B y the time Jane arrived back at Ivy Cottage she was completely exhausted. Paul had already left for the office, passing her in the car as she emerged from the telephone box. He pipped his horn and waved to attract her attention before accelerating up the hill. A dull ache in her lumbar region which Jane had first noticed about half an hour previously, now throbbed relentlessly, making her feel giddy and sick. She struggled into the kitchen to make a drink and carried it upstairs to the bedroom where she collapsed on the bed.

Outside, the sleepy village stirred itself at the beginning of another day. Jane heard milk bottles being placed in the porch followed by the clinking sound of the empties being gathered up and taken away. The farm dogs barked as a tractor engine burst into life. Children's voices rang out as the youngsters trudged past the cottage on their way to the village school at the top of the hill.

Jane drifted off to sleep, only to be woken up minutes later by the sound of police cars, sirens blaring, sweeping down the street towards the river. Unable to move from the bed, Jane lay motionless, straining to listen to what was happening outside. The sirens stopped abruptly, car doors slammed shut and she heard footsteps from all directions running down the street towards the river. Then silence again.

The ache in Jane's back edged its way round to her stomach and changed to spasmodic bouts of sharp pain which coursed through her body, building up slowly to a powerful climax and then ebbing away to leave her sweating and breathless. Several tiny spots of blood appeared on the sheet beneath her, clearly indicating that she was in the first stage of labour. Another contraction slowly gathered momentum. This time Jane lay back to ride the pain and concentrated hard on her breathing. Gradually the second contraction died away. She sat up, wiping away the beads of perspiration from her forehead, her brain racing. She needed to get help, and quickly. The telephone was not due to be installed for another two days and Paul had taken the car to work.

Jane swung her legs off the bed and stood up. At that moment she felt a warm rush of fluid gush down her legs and onto the carpet as her waters broke.

'Oh. Christ. What a bloody mess,' she said to herself, staggering towards the stairs.

A third contraction prevented any further progress, forcing her to the floor like a crumpled piece of waste paper. Jane wondered if she would be able to find help in time. The short intervals between contractions signalled a rapid birth, and the fact that she was only in her thirty-second week of pregnancy frightened her. The pain eased again. She scrambled down the stairs and across the living room.

Somebody hammered on the front door before Jane reached it. Thank God.

'I'm coming,' she shouted.

A policeman stood on the threshold. She looked at him, about to speak, when his outline dimmed and swayed in front of her as the fourth contraction took its course.

Jane remembered little of what happened during the course of the next few hours. Vague recollections of blue flashing lights and people giving orders, followed by an extremely uncomfortable car journey at high speed wafted through her mind, only to be released again, as if of no importance. She felt drowsily content, at peace with the world she looked down upon from her elevated plane. Drifting in and out of consciousness, she had no desire to be hauled back to real life. No, she never wanted to return. Hours and hours floated past, as well as people in white, who approached, lowered their faces close to her own, then disappeared.

At last, her batteries recharged, Jane opened her eyes furtively and peered around the room. She chuckled to herself, as, in her case, waking up in strange surroundings seemed to be habit forming. This time, however, she was in no doubt as to where she found herself. Dreary green and cream gloss painted walls, white ball-shaped lights and highly polished linoleum added up to a typical hospital interior. No other beds though, obviously a private room or a side-ward. Jane glanced sideways at the tall bedside locker. The absence of flowers, fruit and get-well cards indicated her recent occupation of the room. Then she remembered the pain and the mind-bending contractions of childbirth. The baby. What had happened? Jane frantically ran her fingers across her stomach. No baby, only flabby excess skin. Oh my God, she thought, raising herself higher on to the pillows, her eyes searching in vain for a clear perspex fish tank, the modern hospital equivalent of a cot.

CHAPTER 7

No cot, but instead, the last thing she expected to see in her hospital room, a policeman sitting quietly in the corner by the door, reading a newspaper.

The constable, hearing movement, lowered the paper and smiled at her.

'Stay where you are,' he said kindly. 'I'll just let the staff know you're awake.'

Seconds later, a nurse popped her head round the door to announce that Sister Anderson was on her way. Jane looked questioningly at the policeman.

'Sister will fill you in with all the details. I'm here on a completely different matter.'

The swing door flew open as the Sister breezed in.

'Hello, my dear,' she said, unclipping a chart from the end of the bed. She studied it meticulously, then pulled up a chair and sat down.

'It's Mrs Richardson, isn't it?' she asked.

Without waiting for a reply, she continued.

'Congratulations. You've just presented your husband with a beautiful baby girl.'

'My husband?' said Jane, bewildered. 'Is Paul here?'

'Your husband was present at the delivery, but as the experience became too painful for him at the end, we sent him home to recover.'

'Has he seen the baby?'

'Oh yes, he knows he has a daughter.' Sister smiled benevolently at Jane.

'He'll be back to visit you this evening.'

'Please tell me about the baby,' said Jane.

Sister Anderson flicked through a file of notes in her lap.

71

'Right, here we are. Baby Richardson. Date and time of delivery 30th April, 1980 at 11.35 a.m. Birth weight – four pounds one ounce, length – forty-five centimetres.' She paused, looking up from the notes to smile again.

'As you can see from these statistics, baby is very small and we have placed her in an incubator in the Special Care Unit. Physically speaking, however, baby is quite perfect and medically sound, apart from a minor infection, which we are treating with antibiotics. The infection is nothing to worry about, in fact it's fairly common in such tiny babies.'

Her monologue completed, Sister Anderson sat back in the chair, beaming triumphantly.

'Now, my dear. Is there anything else you would like to ask me?' she enquired.

'Only one thing,' replied Jane. 'When can I see her?'

'We normally request patients to remain in bed for about six hours after delivery to give the drugs time to wear off. We don't want our mothers fainting in the corridors.'

Sister Anderson paused briefly to re-open her file. 'In your case, the delivery had complications. By the time you arrived here, it was too late to manipulate baby into the correct position for birth, which resulted in a breech delivery with forceps and more stitches than normal.'

A worried expression crossed Jane's face. The Sister patted her hand, reassuringly.

'As I said before, there's no cause for alarm. Everything is fine. If I were you, I'd ring for a wheelchair and pop along to Special Care about five o'clock.'

She stood up and leant over to straighten Jane's pillows. 'Oh yes, before I forget, Constable Deacon, the policeman who brought you in, would like to ask you a few questions. I'll pop in later to see how you're feeling. Right, Constable, you may talk to Mrs Richardson now, but please don't be too long,' she said, before disappearing through the door.

The policeman hauled his burly frame out of the chair he had been sitting in and ambled towards the vacant seat by Jane's bed.

'Congratulations,' he said, reaching into his breast pocket for a notebook and pencil. Sorry I couldn't say anything before, Sister's instructions you see.' Jane smiled.

'It doesn't matter. What can I do to help you?'

'I won't keep you long. If I could just ask one or two routine questions now, perhaps you wouldn't mind if I came back again tomorrow when you're feeling stronger?'

'OK, that's fine by me.'

He wrote down Jane's name and address, and confirmed the fact that she had been responsible for the telephone call to the Police regarding the death of the surveyor in Ashingham village. He closed his notebook, returning it to his pocket and stood up.

'That'll do nicely for today,' he said, glancing at his watch. 'It's five o'clock already. If you like, I'll fetch a wheelchair and escort you to the baby unit on my way out?'

'Thank you, I'd like that very much,' replied Jane.

Constable Deacon arrived back a couple of minutes later, but any hopes of visiting the baby, even in a chair, were dashed for the present by Jane's inability to get out of bed. She lay back on the pillows, too weak to move and resigned herself to wait until Paul came. Perhaps they could go together during the visiting hour. Jane drifted off to sleep.

Some time later a petite nurse popped her head round the door.

'Hello, Mrs Richardson, I'm glad to see you're awake now.'

The nurse walked across to the bed and plumped up Jane's pillows again.

'It's visiting time and your husband is waiting outside. Shall I let him in?'

'Yes please,' said Jane, rummaging through her handbag for a mirror and comb. 'Do I look OK?'

'You look fine to me,' she laughed, heading for the door.

Jane heard the little nurse talking to Paul in the corridor. She sat up in bed excitedly, waiting for him. Mr and Mrs Richardson, proud parents of baby --- . They hadn't chosen any names as yet, not expecting such an early confinement. Perhaps Paul might have one or two suggestions. Jane wished he'd hurry up, she wanted to be close to him, to thank him for being with her at the birth. From now on they were not just a couple, but a family, a self-contained unit and she desperately wanted to go and see their baby.

The expression on Paul's face as he marched into the room drained every ounce of happiness from her. Sister had said he had become overwrought at the delivery and the staff had sent him home. Obviously, Paul had not recovered. His eyes blazed angrily in Jane's direction, seemingly not at her, but through her. His mouth, contorted by rage, spat obscenities so foul, she raised the sheets to her shoulders for protection. Frightened for her life, Jane reached behind the pillow and rang the bell for assistance. The nurse answered her call almost immediately.

Paul's expression changed instantaneously. He smiled charmingly at both women.

'I wonder if I could have a wheelchair?' said Jane, stuttering nervously. 'I'd like to go and see the baby.'

'Yes, of course. I'll fetch one straight away.' The nurse disappeared.

Jane turned to Paul.

'Just keep away from me. Take one step nearer and I'll have you thrown out.'

On arriving at Special Care, the sister-in-charge of the unit conducted Paul and Jane to a locker room, where they donned specially provided protective overalls, before entering the closed ward. The unit comprised half a dozen brightly lit glass cubicles, each one containing its own incubator, open cot, washing facilities and specialised medical equipment. The temperature remained at a steady eighty degrees Fahrenheit, which Jane found somewhat stifling- after the average heat level in the maternity section.

Ignoring Paul totally, Jane chatted to the sister-in-charge as they walked to the end cubicle to look at the baby. Jane voiced her relief at seeing her free from the drips and feeding tubes being used in the intensive care room next to the unit office.

'Oh no,' said Sister cheerfully. 'If your baby continues to progress at her present rate and the infection clears up, quickly, I can see no reason why she cannot be discharged as soon as she reaches five pounds in weight.'

'How long... will that take?' asked Jane.

'About fourteen days, allowing for an initial weight drop.' Sister fished out the folder she had been carrying, tucked under her arm.

'Have you thought of a name yet?'

'Yes,' answered Jane, to Paul's astonishment. 'Emma Louise.'

'Fine. 'I'll just make a note of that in the file.'

Inside the incubator, baby Emma lay on her back, wearing nothing apart from a nappy. She stared up intently at Jane and their eyes locked together to form an inseparable bond between mother and child, a bond, so unshakeable, that Jane would only become aware of its significance as time went on. Her tiny arms reached out frustratedly towards her mother as if pleading to be released from the perspex prison. Reading Emma's mind, Jane turned to the Sister.

'Would it be possible to hold her for a short while?'

'Just for a moment. We don't want her to get cold. Babies as small as Emma find it difficult to maintain their body heat.'

Lifting Emma gently out of the incubator, the Sister offered her to Paul. Horrified, he stepped backwards and stuffed his hands into his pockets.

'Give her to Jane, I'm frightened I'll drop her,' he said, trying to sound convincing.

Jane, her face a picture of adoration, relieved the Sister of her tiny burden, clasping Emma protectively in her arms and savouring this special moment for all time.

'What's the tiny mark in the centre of her chest?' she asked.

'Nothing to worry a bout,' replied Sister. 'We call it a third nipple. It's rather unusual but something that can be easily removed at a later stage by minor surgery.'

Paul's mind reeled. Christ, it was bad enough the baby being a girl, to add a witches' mark to the catastrophe was way over the top. He stepped forward to see for himself. Yes, a witches' mark, without a shadow of a doubt. To the amazement of the two women, Paul began to ruffle Emma's hair, meticulously examining every inch of her tiny head. They had no idea that he was searching for three sixes, denoting the Sign of the Beast. Thank God, he could find nothing. He stepped back again. outwardly smiling, inwardly badly shaken.

'I think we'd better put her back now,' said Sister, making a mental note to instruct her staff never to leave Mr Richardson alone with Emma, while the child remained in Special Care.

Back in her room, Jane turned sharply on Paul.

'What the hell are you playing at? Last night you were the Paul I know and love. Today I don't recognise you.'

'I'm sorry, love. I've been worried about you and the baby, that's all. The delivery this morning was rough and I felt the baby was hurting you, which I resented. It's silly, I know, but there it is.'

Yesterday's mask sat firmly on Paul's face again, and Jane, unable to see through it, believed him. She smiled.

'Don't worry, Paul, everything is fine.'

In the distance a bell sounded to signal the end of visiting. Paul got up and kissed Jane on the cheek.

'Look after yourself, I'll see you tomorrow.'

He turned at the door.

'Is there anything you want?' he enquired.

'Just you,' she replied, laughing.

On his drive home to the cottage, Paul pondered the problems which lay ahead. The village already knew Jane had given birth to a little girl, Bert Grimshaw having made a point of calling at Ivy Cottage to enquire, on Paul's arrival earlier in the day. Paul had asked him why a baby girl presented such a problem and had learnt that way back during the Civil War a woman born in the village had betrayed the valley to the opposing forces, resulting in the deaths of the entire male population of Ashingham. Since that time no female child had been born in the valley, and any pregnant woman that miscarried was found to have conceived a female foetus.

Paul's second problem centred around the fact that no matter what the hospital might say to the contrary, baby Emma was a witch. Whether she possessed any power was something that would remain to be seen, but Paul had no intention of disclosing this important information. Things were bad enough as it was.

Within five minutes of arriving home, a knock on the door announced a visit from Arthur Briggs. As yet, Paul had not even had time to remove his coat. Clearly irritated by the intrusion, he off handedly pointed Arthur to a chair, while he set about lighting the fire, before switching on the lamps and drawing the curtains. At last Paul sat himself down to face the other man.

'What can I do for you, Arthur?' he asked, brightly.

'I'll not beat about the bush, Paul,' he replied. 'Bert asked me to call on you to clear up one or two things.'

'Fire away. I'm all ears,' said Paul, although openly smiling, in fact, inwardly dreading the following chat.

'The first matter concerns the Police visit to the valley this morning. According to Len Potter, your wife was responsible for the telephone call to the Police Station. He saw her leaving the kiosk as he was about to open the shop at around seven thirty. The entire village regards this action as an act of betrayal on the part of your wife, a crime that carries stiff penalties in our community. No-one in this valley would ever call out the Police for any reason whatsoever. We handle everything of this nature ourselves. However, bearing in mind your wife's condition, it has been agreed that you, as her husband, make it your business to severely reprimand her and take any action you feel necessary to keep her in check, which leads me to the second matter.'

Arthur got up and paced the room to stretch his legs. Paul, meantime, shifted uneasily in his chair while he waited for the other man to resume his seat and continue.

'You were saying,' prompted Paul.

'The second matter is somewhat delicate,' said Arthur, rubbing his eyes wearily. 'It concerns the baby. As Bert told you earlier, there have been no females born in this valley since the betrayal of the men during the Civil War. The present male population see the new female child as a threat to their existence, even now, over three hundred years after the incident involving one of our women. We held an extraordinary meeting, in your absence, a couple of hours ago, and I have to tell you that the valley refuses to accept the child to live within its boundaries. The ball being firmly in your court, therefore, leaves you with two choices. Either the child goes up for adoption, or you leave the valley.'

Paul sat, his head cupped between his hands, staring down at his feet, engrossed in his own thoughts.

'Have I made myself quite clear, Paul?' asked Arthur.

'As crystal,' mumbled Paul.

'Right, I'll be off then. Don't get up. I'll let myself out.'

Christ Almighty, what a bloody mess, thought Paul. Although tired, he remained where he sat, until the fire finally died, turning- over in his mind what he would have to say to Jane on his next visit to the hospital. Perhaps God would be merciful and he wouldn't wake up tomorrow. Some hopes, he thought, making his way up to bed.

Seven o'clock the following evening found Paul confidently ascending the hospital steps, complete with bouquet of flowers. His day at the office had passed uneventfully, his present amenable attitude standing him in good stead with his new colleagues. Checking through a draft report he had compiled the day before, Paul had plenty of time to mull over his personal problems and prepare himself for the evening. His speech, memorised to the last full stop, was word perfect. His affairs in order and under control, Paul had the appearance of a happy man.

Jane was sitting up in bed, flicking through a magazine as she waited for her husband. He breezed through the door and approached the bed, presenting the bouquet with a flourish.

'Hello, darling,' he said, throwing his arms around her. 'How are you both?'

'We're fine. How about you?'

'The same as you,' he replied.

They strolled together down the corridor to Special Care and saw baby Emma, under the watchful eye of the staff, who had been told about Paul's odd behaviour the previous day. Emma was progressing steadily and, indeed, she certainly looked happy enough, kicking and gurgling in her incubator. One thing Paul noticed, however, was that Emma clearly idolised her mother, but never once looked at him.

On their return, Jane clambered back into bed and gazed lovingly at Paul.

'The baby's absolutely gorgeous, isn't she?' she said ecstatically. 'I feel so grateful to the Policeman who rushed me here before it was too late.

Emma would not have survived without his help. This was the opportunity Paul had been waiting for. 'Jane, did you call the Police from the telephone box yesterday morning?'

'Yes,' she replied. 'As it happens, that call helped me out of quite a dilemma, didn't it?'

'Absolutely,' agreed Paul. 'However, in future, if you need to call one of the Emergency Services, would you refer the problem to either Bert or Arthur first. Apparently, that happens to be the way things are done in Ashingham.'

Paul waited for her reaction. Would Jane explode in temper, or accept his request?

'I don't see why not, she said.

'Unless, of course, it's a matter of life or death.' Paul smiled. His subtlety had worked. One down, one to go.

'Jane, there's something else I would like to discuss.'

She looked at him attentively.

'Go on,' she said.

'Baby Emma will be the first little girl to live in Ashingham For over three hundred years. Life could become very difficult for her being surrounded by boys. Obviously she will find it hard, if not impossible to mix with the other youngsters, and her isolation could lead to great unhappiness for her. Neither of us want to see that happen, do we?'

Jane shook her head. Paul continued.

'I've given the matter considerable thought and quite honestly, I think it would be better if she were adopted. We could go on and try for a little boy, if you like?'

Jane stared at Paul, wide-eyed in disbelief. She had imagined it. He hadn't really suggested that Emma should go to strangers. She laughed.

'You're joking, of course.'

'No, I'm perfectly serious. It would be in her best interests.'

She had heard correctly.

'It's ridiculous. I'll never agree to it,' she said.

'It's a shock at first, I know,' he replied. 'But in a day or two I think you'll agree with me.'

'Rubbish, you're jealous. You're afraid Emma will form a wedge between us.'

'No, that is untrue. I'm thinking about her future.'

'Her future. My arse. How dare you take it upon yourself to suggest what happens to her. Emma is my daughter as well as yours and any decision regarding her future will be decided upon jointly. However, any thoughts on adoption can be forgotten, permanently. I won't have it. Do you hear me?'

'I hear you, Jane, but on a matter as crucial as this, I must be the one to decide, and my mind is quite made up.'

'The hell it is,' Jane snarled.

Her fingers searched behind the pillow for the buzzer. A nurse appeared in seconds.

'Ask Sister to come in please,' said Jane.

'What can I do for you, Mrs Richardson?' asked the Sister on her arrival.

'Please ask my husband to leave,' replied Jane. 'So far I Have found his visits distressing and I would be grateful if you could prevent him harassing me any further.'

'I think you had better leave, Mr Richardson. Your wife is obviously upset. We'll discuss this matter further in my office, if you'll follow me.'

CHAPTER 7

Jane saw nothing more of Paul during her stay in hospital. Two days later she travelled home to Ashingham by taxi. Baby Emma remained behind in Special Care.

Ten days later, Jane called another taxi. This time she travelled back to the hospital to collect baby Emma and take her home to Ivy Cottage.

CHAPTER 8

Eve Simpkins and Sarah Watts broke off the conversation they were holding across the dividing hedge between their houses to stare at the taxi which had cruised to a halt outside Ivy Cottage. Taxis were rarely to be seen in Ashingham village. The driver leapt out and opened the rear passenger door to allow Jane to alight with care, cradling a tiny infant, tightly wrapped in a woollen shawl. Relieving her of a bunch of keys, he unlatched the gate and proceeded up the path to open the front door for her. Jane stood on the pavement, fumbling in her handbag to find her purse.

'Here, let me hold the baby for you while you see to that,' said Eve, relieving Jane of her precious bundle.

'Come on, Sarah, let's put the kettle on and give Jane a chance to sort herself out.'

The two women disappeared into the cottage with baby Emma, leaving Jane to pay for the taxi and follow them inside.

Eve sat on the sofa, from where she set about organising everyone.

'Go and take your coat off. Sarah's making some tea.'

'Are you ok with Emma?' asked Jane.

'Oh, I think I'll manage,' Eve chuckled.

The rest of the afternoon passed swiftly, the three women completely absorbed in the new arrival. Eve and Sarah reminisced about their own children as babies, dishing out endless hints on how to do this and that, making Jane feel that now, at last, she had a common link with the majority of the women in the community. She was sorry when the two women left to go home to their own families.

Jane had made no visible preparations for bringing Emma home, in view of Paul's determination to proceed with the adoption plans. She had decided that the only course of action open to her was to present him with a fait accompli, Once Emma came home he would have to change his mind. While she waited for him to return from work, Jane occupied herself clearing out Emma's new bedroom, which had become the dumping ground for all manner of odds and ends, the room now being surplus to requirement in Paul's mind. Occasionally she popped downstairs to the living-room to check on the baby, sleeping soundly in her carrycot on the sofa. The bedroom neat and tidy, she then set about unwrapping the new bed linen to make up the cot. Engrossed in her work, Jane didn't hear Paul come home.

Wearily her husband walked in, setting his briefcase down by the door. The past two weeks had certainly taken their toll, the strain showing plainly on his face and in the way he moved. Yet, despite the arguments and long periods of icy silence, he was still resolved to carry through his plan for adoption. The papers had arrived in the post this morning and during the course of the day he had perused them carefully, it being his intention to complete them this evening and return them tomorrow. He was well aware that time was running out,

Emma could not remain in the hospital indefinitely, but neither could she come home, Bert making this fact quite ·plain every time he saw Paul.

He shook himself free of his overcoat and stretched across towards the chair to drape it over the arm. Then he saw the baby. Silently he stood looking down at her, sleeping peacefully, a tiny picture of innocence, cocooned and protected from the world around her. Waves of paternity surged through him.

Here lay his flesh and blood, his baby daughter, so small and vulnerable. At that moment Emma woke and stared up at him. He returned her gaze, feeling a strange power being transmitted between them as their eyes locked together in a mental struggle, each intent on dominating the other. Emma's eyes, now fully dilated, blazed with hatred and bore into Paul's like lasers, the burning sensation sending tears flowing down his cheeks.

He tried to look away, but the power held him in a vice-like grip, not yet satisfied in its victory. At last the spell broke and Paul stumbled backwards, wiping his face with the back of one hand. Emma's eyes appeared to act as the transmitter for the power she possessed, but Paul knew that if she really was a witch, her mystical influence would not be confined to this one outlet, it would be limitless. Although dreading the consequences, this theory had to be put to the test, otherwise he would never know for sure exactly what he was up against.

He crouched behind the sofa, the back of which hid him effectively from Emma's sight.

On all fours, Paul furtively crawled towards the arm rest nearest to the baby's head. Emma, however, using her powers of extra sensory perception, was acutely aware of her father's plan. She waited patiently for his approach, her tiny fists tightly clenched in preparation. Steady, steady, she told herself. Wait until he reaches the point of no return and catch him off guard. She inhaled deeply, still waiting. Then, in a flash Emma opened her tiny lungs and screamed for all she was worth, her body writhing and her arms thrashing in all directions.

The uproar brought Jane rushing downstairs to see Paul on the verge of grabbing the child around the throat.

'What the hell is going on?' she screamed at him.

He stood up to face his wife.

'What on earth are you playing at?' she demanded, scooping Emma swiftly from the carrycot to comfort her.

'I'm the one who should be asking that question,' he snapped. 'Who gave you permission to bring the child home? The hospital staff are fully aware that Emma is to be adopted and I have forbidden them to let you visit her.'

Jane threw back her head and laughed.

'Your ignorance never ceases to astound me. The adoption-machinery may well be in full motion, but firstly, I am Emma's mother and no-one will prevent me from seeing my daughter and secondly, I refuse to give my permission for this adoption to take place. As for the matter of bringing her home, according to the Paediatrician Emma's infection has cleared up, she weighs five pounds and the hospital was only too willing to discharge her into my care.'

Emma had stopped crying, and Jane placed her back into the cot, where she lay, looking up at her mother, her little face a picture of adoration.

'This happens to be my home. It is also Emma's home. We both intend to live here and if I have to choose between you and Emma, you lose hands down, Paul,' Jane added. 'Either become part of the family unit, or get out. It's up to you.'

In a surge of anger, Paul lashed out at his wife. He rained blows down upon Jane with all his strength, yet not one touched her. Unable to believe it, he flew at her, punching and kicking, but an invisible force field of protection surrounded her. In frustration he turned to Emma, directing his blows at her, only to find that she also remained beyond his grasp. Defeated, he swung round and stormed out of the cottage.

Across the road in the 'Castle Arms' Paul sat quietly in a corner by the fire nursing a pint of beer. Luckily, neither Arthur nor Bert had come in yet. He hoped he could remain undisturbed for a little while longer to think through his problem. If either man called in, they would have seen a worried man, a man ashamed to admit his inability to be master in his own house. He shivered. They would make mincemeat out of him, and no mistake.

The next morning Paul got up, washed, dressed and left for work in silence, not even bothering to go into the kitchen for breakfast. Jane, too busy preparing Emma's bottle to care, watched him drive away, before casually tipping his untouched meal into the waste bin. Tiptoeing into Emma's room, Jane saw the baby was still fast asleep. She drew back the curtains and stood by the cot for a few moments looking down at the angelic little girl snuggled under the blankets.

She cast her mind back to the argument of the previous evening. Something had happened to Paul since the move from London. At this point in time, however, Jane could not determine whether the cause of his change lay with the valley itself or a specific incident since their arrival in Ashingham. But, whatever the cause, his mental state, and their relationship, was deteriorating rapidly. She reflected on her ultimatum to him – be a husband and father or leave. Although she knew her statement was justified, Jane wondered if she had the willpower to stay the course and remain here in Ashingham with Emma. Several times during the previous evening she had glanced at the newly installed telephone, her fingers itching to dial her parents' number in London and ask for help. But no, she held back. Things were bad, but not desperate enough for her to worry her mother and father just yet.

The tapping in the corner had also resumed again last night, following an interlude of silence for over two weeks. Paul had used cement to seal up the tunnel during her confinement in hospital, but on venturing into the cellar yesterday afternoon ·with a pile of junk from Emma's bedroom, Jane saw the gaping black hole once more, the loose slabs strewn across the floor with the new mortar still attached to them. Panic stricken, she had fled back upstairs, forcing home the bolt Paul had fitted on the door to secure it.

Movement brought her back to the present. Jane looked down to see the baby awake, staring up at her. One tiny hand had emerged from the blankets and was trying to reach the cot bars. She bent down and gently picked her up, wrapping her in a warm shawl. As Jane cuddled the baby in a protective motherly embrace, the warm, sleepy, baby smell rose up and floated under her nostrils.

Downstairs in the kitchen Jane settled Emma into her feed while mapping out the day's routine in her mind, in retrospect a complete waste of time as a knock on the door heralded the first of a stream of women from the village to see the new baby. Hang the routine, Jane thought to herself, never having felt more popular. I should have expected the first few days at home with Emma to be chaotic.

Her first caller was Joan Bennett from Elderberry Cottage further down the row. Clutching a pair of knitted bootees, the tiny mouse-featured woman stood nervously on the doorstep as if afraid to cross the threshold. Not wishing to force her, against her wishes, Jane took the proffered gift and chatted to her at the door. Unfortunately for Joan, however, Dorothy Haresnape from The Barn at the end of the row arrived on the scene and pushed her forcibly from behind into the living room.

'Come on, Joan, stop cluttering up the doorway and get inside, will you,' she thundered.

Dorothy slapped a couple of towelling bibs into Jane's hand as she brushed past her and headed straight for the carrycot, sweeping the baby into the air with a dramatic flourish.

'Well now, just look at you. And how does it feel to be the first little girl in Ashingham for three centuries?' she enquired of the startled little bundle who stared back at this large woman with a look somewhere between shock and bewilderment.

Jane retrieved her baby from Dorothy's clutches and placed her back in the cot. Joan sat rigidly on the sofa, looking most uncomfortable, like an animal cornered and ready to bolt to safety at the first available opportunity. Seeing Joan's consternation, Jane gave her the loophole she sought.

'Would you like a cup of tea?'

'Oh, no thank you. I must be going. One of my boys is unwell today.'

'Nothing serious, I hope?' said Jane, ushering her out.

'No, just a bad cold, but I'd best get back to him.'

'I'll join you in a cup of tea,' said Dorothy after Joan had gone.

I had a funny feeling you'd say that, Jane said to herself, smiling at the overpowering woman on her way to the kitchen.

To begin with Jane chatted amicably to her overbearing guest, despite the fact that Dorothy's loud voice was exhausting. But after a while she realised that her neighbour was interrogating her, the line of conversation gently probing to extract information on several things, ranging from the fact that Jane had produced a female child to the statement she had given to the police on the village murder enquiry.

A ring- on the doorbell announced the arrival of Susan Entwistle and saved Jane from the embarrassment of asking the insufferable Haresnape woman to leave, as Dorothy got up immediately and went.

'Thank God you've arrived,' said Jane.

'If I'd realised Dorothy was here, I'd have come earlier.'

'I thought she had come to see the baby like everyone else, but I was wrong. She seemed intent on prying into my personal affairs and I was just on the point of throwing her out when you came.'

'I'm not surprised. All the women in Ashingham steer clear of her. Arthur Briggs is her brother-in-law you know. He uses her to spy on people. She is a very dangerous woman and should be avoided.'

'Thanks for the warning. I'll keep her at arm's length in future.'

Jane handed Susan a cup of tea and sat down opposite her.

'By the way. Sarah and Eve called in yesterday. Are they to be trusted?'

Susan laughed. 'Oh yes, everyone else is OK.' She went on. 'Actually the reason I called is that as it's such a lovely day I wondered if you would like ·to take Emma out for an airing. I'm just about to take little Robert for a walk.'

'Sounds lovely. I haven't had a chance to try out the pram yet.'

'OK. Come and give me a knock when you're ready.'

The two women and their respective children spent the next few days in each other's company. Jane enjoyed herself immensely. The fine, dry weather enabled them to go for long walks across the valley. Only a couple of· things marred the happiness she felt. If any of the men happened to be walking through the village at the same time as herself and the baby, they automatically crossed the road and passed by on the other side. And, in the evenings, the same treatment applied at home, Paul totally ignoring her as his mind grappled with the problem of Emma.

He had filled in the adoption papers and returned them. Now it was just a question of waiting. This interim period, however, was proving to be more unsettling than he had anticipated. On the one hand, the villagers continued to pressurize him, while on the other, having already experienced Emma's mystical power of which the villagers knew nothing, he refused to remain in the same room as the baby. Emma knew what he planned for her, of that he was certain, and he feared her, afraid of what she might be capable of doing to him. Unable to cope with this situation at home, he thought out of sight, out of mind, the best policy to adopt until he could gather together some information on the subject of witchcraft and how to deal with it. Secretly, Paul wished that Jane would pack up and leave him, taking the baby with her. In that way he would be rid of them both and could start afresh. However, the village would take a dim view of this action and he would be made a laughing stock, regarded as a weak man unable to maintain his role as head of his household. No, his present course of action seemed the only way.

Jane still firmly believed that Paul would get used to the idea of Emma at home and that his present incomprehensible attitude towards them would change. Mothers frequently suffer from post-natal depression and Jane wondered if perhaps fathers experienced similar problems as well. She decided to ask the doctor on her next visit to the hospital.

In the meantime she set about organising a routine for herself and the baby and enjoying the company of her newly acquired friends, without whose support she would have given up, packed her things and left for London to seek sanctuary among her family.

At about four o'clock on the Thursday afternoon, Susan said goodbye to Jane and took her baby son Robert home for his tea.

By five-thirty, fed and bathed, Susan tucked him into his cot for the night. She made her way downstairs and into the kitchen to prepare dinner. Glancing at the clock she knew Graham would be home shortly. A few minutes later there was a knock on the front door. Graham must have forgotten his key Susan thought as she went to answer it. She looked surprised to see Arthur Briggs on the step.

'Graham's not home yet,' she said.

'It's you I've come to see,' he replied, smiling.

Susan stepped aside to let him in. With dismay she watched him tramp across her light beige carpet in his muddy shoes and sit himself down heavily in one of the dainty upholstered chairs. He refused her polite offer of tea and came straight to the point.

'You seem to have become very friendly with the new woman next door,' he remarked-,.

'You mean Jane Richardson?' she said enquiringly.

Arthur nodded and went on.

'The Richardsons have one or two problems to sort out at the moment. We don't think you should be visiting your new friend for a little while.'

'I don't understand. What problems?' she asked.

Arthur declined to answer the question.

'Will you do as I ask?' he said.

'Not without an explanation,' she replied.

Arthur sighed. The polite approach wasn't working. He became more insistent.

'Look, young lady. You are not to associate with that woman next door until I say so. Is that clear?'

With indignation Susan rose from her chair and glared at him.

'I happen to enjoy visiting Jane and baby Emma. Until you can actually give me a good reason not to see them, I shall continue to call.'

By now Arthur had risen also. He drew himself up to his full height to emphasise the minute stature of the young woman in front of him.

'If you know what's good for you, you'll not venture next door for the foreseeable future,' he said, jabbing the index finger of his right hand into her chest several times.

Shocked, but unrelenting, Susan retaliated.

'How dare you. Just because Jane saw through your spy, Dorothy Haresnape, drying up your information, doesn't give you the right to come into this house and threaten me.'

Arthur's patience snapped. He lunged forwards, grabbed Susan by her hair and proceeded to drag her up the stairs. Struggling and screaming, she clawed at the bannisters for an anchorage to gain breathing space and a chance to defend herself. Her efforts proved futile. Arthur weighed at least sixteen stone. The excruciating pain from having her long blonde hair wrapped tightly around his wrist like a dog leash brought tears to her eyes, blurring her vision. Although no match physically against him, Susan fought on, inwardly knowing that no-one would hear her cries for help through the two foot thick stone walls, yet determined to continue the struggle in the hope that Graham would turn up and rescue her. The scuffle woke baby Robert who began to cry pitifully. Arthur shoved Susan into her bedroom and slammed the door closed behind them. Robert's cries sounded muffled now with two doors and the landing separating the rooms.

Arthur still had Susan trapped by the hair with one hand, his other hand grasping the wrist of the arm he now pinned behind her back. The clock on the small mahogany bedside table said five forty-five, the time her husband usually came in from work. Reaching into his back pocket Arthur produced a coil of rope which he deftly tied to Susan's wrist. He twisted her round to face him before flinging her backwards on to the bed, looping the rope around the right bed post and securing it firmly. Before Susan could reach across with her free hand he pinned her chest down with his knee and fastened the rope to her other wrist, pulling it taut round the other post.

Relaxing slightly he sat back on Susan's thighs, leering at her as he ran his hands roughly over her breasts.

'Changed your mind yet, Susan? It's not too late.'

He bent forwards towards her face. She could feel the stubble on his unshaven chin rasping against her cheek. A dirty unwashed smell wafted up her nose, its sweet cloying aroma making her choke for fresh air.

'You filthy ignorant pig,' she hissed. 'I despise you.'

Arthur laughed at her and bent close again. Susan raised her head and spat full in his face. The surprise made Arthur jolt upright. Brushing away the spittle running down his cheek with his jacket sleeve he bared his teeth, then replied with a searing blow across her face with the back of his hand. A strong direct blow to the cheekbone, stunning her into semi-consciousness. On recovery, Susan found herself completely immobilised, both ankles manacled to the bottom of the bed. 'Never let it be said that I didn't give you a last chance. Will you obey our instructions?'

'Go to hell,' she answered.

'Fair enough,' he retorted. 'You've made your choice, now you must pay the penalty.'

Without further hesitation Arthur took hold of Susan's dress lapels and expertly ripped the dress she wore into two pieces, the buttons on it systematically flying across the room, leaving her body exposed apart from the flimsy underwear she wore. She stared bleakly up at him, not fully comprehending his actions at this stage, her head still recovering from the earlier blow she had received. Reaching again into his back pocket he produced a sheath knife which he skilfully slid under the bra elastic between her breasts and sliced the fabric cleanly, to expose two milky white mounds of flesh, the nipples erect in terror. Easing himself down the bed slightly he flicked the knife again to lift away the front of her panties which he speared with the tip of the blade and dangled mockingly in front of her face.

'I'm beginning to enjoy this, but I'll not rush, there's plenty of time,' he said, casting admiring glances at her trembling, nakedness.

Lifting himself off her, Arthur stood by the bed and unzipped his trousers. Even with his pants on, Susan could see his male organ throbbing and erect, the excitement within him producing a premature trickle of semen which formed a damp patch on the crotch. Trousers and pants discarded, he climbed back and sat astride her once more, his penis hard against her stomach. Susan squirmed in desperation, anticipating the events to follow. Her eyes studied the tassels of the Tiffany lampshade directly above her head as she silently prayed for her husband's return.

Arthur set to work, meticulously exploring her body, caressing, probing her most intimate private places as she lay completely open to his every desire. She screamed. It was the only defence mechanism left open to her. Determined that she should submit silently and allow him to work at his own pace, Arthur punched her full in the face. They both heard the brittle crack as her nose fractured, the impact of the blow forcing her front teeth through her lower lip. Arthur stared at the blood streaming from her mouth and nose, but chose not to staunch the flow. What the hell did it matter anyway, the bits further down were what he desired.

Susan heard the front door open downstairs. Thank God. Her husband had finally arrived. Graham called her name, not finding his wife in the kitchen. To Susan's amazement Arthur replied. 'We're upstairs in the bedroom. Come on up.'

Bewildered, she wondered why Arthur was inviting her husband to witness this act of violation. Graham's footsteps pounded up the stairs and stopped dead in the doorway. Susan looked helplessly across at him, expecting some sort of instantaneous reaction from him on seeing the bloody humiliating spectacle in front of him. Instead he remained standing passively on the threshold, holding the door jamb for support. Graham looked towards Arthur, as if for guidance.

'Come in and sit down,' said Arthur impatiently, jabbing a finger in the direction of a chair near the bed. Graham sat down and opened his mouth as if to say something.

'Just shut up, damn you,' Arthur snapped at him. 'There's nothing to be said. Your wife had every opportunity to acquiesce to our demands, but chose to remain defiant, the consequences of which you can see for yourself. If you remember, you were asked at the meeting if you would prefer to deal with the matter yourself and you said it would be better for me to handle it.'

Susan glanced from one man to the other, scarcely able to believe the conversation. She had always known the male population in the valley differed significantly in makeup from their counterparts elsewhere, but she had never realised before the extent to which their warped minds functioned.

'Now pull your chair up closer and watch what I'm doing. If any other woman in the village is punished in this way in the future, you will be qualified to carry it out.'

Arthur turned his attention back to his victim. He sank his teeth firmly into Susan's left breast in several places, leaving a trail of livid impressions. He looked up at Susan's battered face and laughed at her discomfort. Then his tongue caressed her nipple turning the pain into sensual ecstasy.

Sensing her change of mood, Arthur moved across to the other breast and subjected it to the same painful treatment. Susan's mind reeled. This had to be some ghastly nightmare.

What she was experiencing could not possibly happen in reality. Surely no husband on earth would sit passively and watch the violation of his wife without making some effort to defend her.

She heard them laughing and she squirmed in a futile attempt to stop the torture, only to find Graham had approached the bed and was holding her shoulders down to stop her twisting about. Arthur worked further down her body, reaching nearer and nearer to his ultimate goal. Susan braced herself for the inevitable. The room revolved in front of her eyes as the penetration occurred followed by thrusting, slowly at first, then faster and faster until the walls disappeared completely, creating the sensation of falling at tremendous speed into a bottomless void. The heaving motion and the pain, together with the mind bending raucous laughter of her captors became swallowed up in the overwhelming sound of wind rushing in her ears as she plummeted further and further downwards into the depths of unconsciousness and oblivion.

CHAPTER 9

J ane glanced up from her newspaper as the clock on the mantelpiece chimed the half hour. Eleven-thirty already and no sign of Susan Entwistle. The two women had arranged the previous afternoon to go on a shopping expedition to Prestbury today, Susan's last words being that she would call for Jane at ten o'clock sharp. Emma, dressed and ready to go out, had fallen asleep in her carrycot on the sofa, next to which Jane's coat and handbag lay in preparation for the outing.

Jane walked across to the window to see if anything was happening outside. As usual the street was deserted and Susan's car stood outside patiently waiting for its owner of whom there was no sign as yet. Jane sighed and returned to the paper. If her neighbour hadn't turned up by lunchtime she would pop next door and check that everything was OK. The minutes dragged by and Jane became increasingly anxious. At last the tiny hour hand disappeared from view and the clock laboriously chimed twelve times.

Jane hesitated for a few moments, then stood up, determined to find out whether they were going shopping or not. The front gate to Hermitage Cottage whipped back into place with a loud clang as she approached the heavy oak door, making her feel somewhat conspicuous. For, although the road remained devoid of people, Jane was in no doubt that a dozen or so pairs of prying eyes were following her every move from behind the lacy curtains adorning most of the cottage windows. The milk on the door-step caught her eye. Nobody had bothered to take it indoors yet although it stood in the full midday sunlight. Jane thought this was most unlike Susan who always set a time for everything – including retrieving the milk from the step as soon as it was delivered.

She knocked loudly on the door and stepped back to wait for an answer. None came. Jane knocked a second time, then walked across the front lawn towards the downstairs window to look inside the cottage. The living room seemed to be deserted, as was the kitchen beyond, from what she could see through the door dividing the two rooms which stood slightly ajar. Jane could only think that Susan must be ill in bed and unable to come down to answer the door. Without further delay she returned home to give Emma her lunch, confident she would hear from Susan later in the day.

The afternoon seemed endless. Jane buckled down to household chores, but her thoughts constantly returned to her neighbour, and no-one else from the village dropped in to alleviate the boredom. Finally to kill time, Jane took Emma for a walk in her pram hoping she might bump into one of the other women. But no, apart from the cows and sheep grazing in the fields and the occasional rabbit, nothing broke the monotony of her stroll.

As she approached Ivy Cottage on her return home, she looked across at 'The Hermitage' and noticed, with dismay, the untouched milk. She hoped to God Susan was OK and that nothing had happened to her. In this valley of strange people anything was possible and nothing would surprise her. Without her new friend, Jane had to admit she felt isolated and to some degree frightened. Had a cruel trick of fate plummeted Paul and herself into Ashingham, a village caught in a sort of time warp, where nothing was as it actually seemed? An old film she had seen on television years ago sprang to mind. Now what the hell was it called. Oh yes – The Stepford Wives. The film portrayed a small community in America where the women had been carefully manipulated to be the objects of their husband's desires. Although Ashingham differed in its end result, the manipulation was definitely in a similar vein. From what she could remember, however, the women in the film made a dramatic turn about face, rebelling violently, creating havoc and mayhem throughout the entire community. Jane wondered whether something could happen here - an interesting thought, but somewhat unlikely, judging by what she had seen of the womenfolk in the village. Without organisation and leadership they would continue to function like a flock of sheep, completely dominated by their masters, and Jane doubted if she would remain in this village long enough to even set a few wheels in motion.

Paul came in from work at his normal time. They sat down together for their evening meal which passed in stony silence as was the routine these days. Any attempt at conversation inevitably led to bitter arguments despite Paul's efforts to adopt a smooth approach to the problems confronting them. Jane instinctively saw through him every time. Paul's mask of sincerity, never more than wafer thin, collapsed miserably under attack. The meal hurriedly eaten, he excused himself, went upstairs to change, after which he sought refuge in the pub for the evening, leaving Jane to clear away and spend another lonely evening in her own company.

She checked the television programmes to find nothing worth watching until much later in the evening. She left the set switched on, with the sound turned low to provide background noise. This had become a habit of late, mainly to blot out the disturbing sounds from the cellar which taunted her night after night, as well as providing a link with the outside world.

Sitting in front of the fire, watching the flames darting up the chimney, Jane reflected on her situation, endeavouring to detach herself so as to look at her problems objectively. She didn't hear the telephone for several seconds, although the bleeping tone had penetrated her thoughts enough to bring her eyes to rest on the small glass-topped mahogany table upon which it stood. She returned to the present and dashed across the room, unsure how long it had been ringing. She almost knocked over a table lamp in her attempt to grab the receiver before the caller rang off.

'Hello dear,' said her mother. 'We've been getting a little anxious down here as we haven't heard from you recently. Is everything alright?'

'Yes,' replied Jane breathlessly. 'I'm fine.'

'And little Emma and Paul?' 'They're fine too,' she said.

'You sound a little strained, dear, are you sure you're OK?'

'Just out of breath, I didn't hear the phone ring at first. The line is crackling quite a lot, don't you think?'

'It's perfectly alright this end,' her mother replied. 'I've called to find out if you're all coming down to see us soon. Everyone is dying to see the baby.'

'I hope we'll be able to visit you in the next couple of weeks. I'm just waiting for the nursing sister to give us the go-ahead and discharge Emma,' said Jane. 'It shouldn't be too long now.'

'That is good news. Oh, by the way, your friend Dee has been asking after you. Could you give her a ring? She'd love to hear from you.'

'Yes, of course I will. Thanks for ringing. Love to everyone and I'll let you know as soon as I have any news.'

Jane slowly replaced the receiver. Her train of thought had been interrupted by the phone call. Moreover she felt too tired to grapple with problems any more tonight. Making her way upstairs, Jane ran a bath and half an hour later retired to bed for an early night.

She woke the next morning to the sound of activity from downstairs. Reaching across the bed she found the other half empty. Frightened by the crashing of saucepans and the slamming of doors from the kitchen immediately below her bedroom, Emma started to cry.

'For Christ's Sake, what's he up to now,' Jane said under her breath as she struggled into her dressing gown and hurried downstairs.

The aroma of bacon wafted up the staircase to meet her.

Paul was busily emptying the contents of the frying pan onto a plate as she entered. Jane saw the table had been laid for one only – obviously her husband had not expected her to join him.

'You're up bright and early,' she remarked, watching him tuck into the heaped pile of bacon, eggs and fried bread on the plate.

'I haven't made any for you,' he said, unabashed by her expression of disappointment. 'Didn't reckon you'd be up yet.'

'I wouldn't have been, had it not been for the dreadful noise you've been making down here.'

Jane sat down opposite him.

'Can't you hear Emma crying?'

'That is your problem. It's nothing to do with me,' he retorted angrily. 'As far as I'm concerned that child has no place in this house.'

Jane refused to be goaded into the Emma argument so early in the day. Turning sideways, she stood up and walked across the kitchen to plug in the kettle.

'Why are you up so early anyway?' she enquired.

'The lads are going on a fishing trip this weekend. I've been invited to join them.'

'I see,' she said, woodenly. 'I thought perhaps we could have driven into Prestbury today to do some shopping. There isn't much food left in the house.'

'No chance. In any case, I don't intend spending my weekends out shopping with you. That's your job.'

'But I don't have the car, you use it for work.'

Then do the same as the other women. Walk up the hill and catch a bus.'

'For Christ's sake, Paul. It's over a mile to the main road up that steep hill. Pushing a pram up there is hard work.'

Her husband sneered defiantly at her, a reply being unnecessary as he had already made his feelings regarding Emma quite clear earlier on.

'I don't understand why you have to be so disagreeable these days,' she said unhappily.

'We have no family life at all anymore.'

'Look, Jane,' he said, swallowing the last mouthful. 'You're the one that is being awkward. You're the one that took Emma away from the hospital and brought her here against the wishes of the village. You consistently refuse to fit in with the way life is conducted in Ashingham and, as a result, you only have yourself to blame for your isolation. When Emma is adopted we will get on a lot better as husband and wife, but until then you must survive as best you can.'

'What if I leave you and take Emma with me?' Jane threatened.

'Emma will be leaving shortly, but you are not going anywhere.'

'You cannot make me stay against my will,' she replied, haughtily.

'Don't force it upon me. But rest assured that if it becomes necessary I will do so.'

A knock on the door interrupted the quarrel. Paul jumped up from the table and headed across the living room to answer it, picking up his fishing tackle on the way.

'Are you taking the car?' Jane screamed at him.

'Of course I am, you silly bitch. Wouldn't want to leave it behind as a temptation, now would I?' he said, before slamming the door closed behind him.

Jane looked around the kitchen at the untidy mess Paul had left behind him for her to clear up. Sitting down again at the table, she pushed the dirty plates across to the other side of it and buried her head in her hands. She allowed herself to wallow in self-pity until Emma started to cry again, reminding her mother that she had not been fed.

Later in the morning, Jane ventured into the front garden. The herbs she had planted several weeks earlier had taken root successfully, the tiny plants increasing dramatically in size day by day, as fine weather persisted over the northwest of the country. She settled down happily for the next few hours, carefully hoeing the beds to remove the ever-abundant supply of weeds which threatened the young plants. Occasionally she glanced across the wall at the neighbouring cottage, hoping to catch a glimpse of Susan, but nothing had stirred at the Hermitage by the time she finished her work and went back indoors to feed the baby again.

After lunch, Jane decided to spend the afternoon exploring the valley in more detail. With Paul away for the whole weekend she felt no need to rush home to prepare a meal. Her time was her own to spend as she pleased. With Emma securely fastened into her baby sling which Jane attached to herself around the waist, mother and daughter headed down the road towards the bridge. Crossing the river Jane turned to the left instead of right as she normally did when walking along the river bank path with the pram. Pushing open the gate leading to Heronsford Farm, she walked quickly across the farmyard towards the stile which lay beyond the barn at the far end of the house. She looked neither to the left or right, but doggedly straight ahead, fearful of being stopped and questioned. Fortunately there was nobody about in the yard, although she could hear men's laughter coming from the milking sheds behind the barn.

Quickening her pace she reached the stile and clambered over it to reach the open moorland. She felt safer now with the village behind her and she strode purposefully onwards in the direction of the woods, always keeping the river in sight, as a guide for the way back.

The flat valley floor stopped abruptly at the edge of the forest and inclined steeply up the wooded hill slopes. As Jane climbed steadily the river fell away quite dramatically into a ravine, hundreds of feet below her. A slight breeze gently fanned the bracken, carpeting the descent to the shimmering water. She thought the scenery in this remote sinister valley to be the most spectacular she had ever seen.

Totally unspoilt by the ravages of twentieth century technology, it remained quietly tucked away and forgotten, like the setting for an idyllic fairy tale.

Yet beneath this tranquil surface lurked an indeterminate evilness which slowly seeped into the very souls of the villagers, segregating them completely from the rest of civilisation.

Emma had fallen asleep, her tiny head resting on her mother's breast. It was only about thirty yards now to the crest of the hill and Jane could see the sun filtering through the branches of the last of the trees, before she stepped out into the full sunlight to look down upon the whole valley below. She flopped down on the grass to rest and gazed upon the sleepy village which appeared as empty as always, the only signs of habitation being the thin wisps of smoke from the cottage chimneys and a couple of full washing lines in the back gardens.

Suddenly, out of the corner of her eye she noticed something move between the trees at the forest edge. It was a blonde-haired young woman wearing a floral print dress. Jane felt sure the woman was Susan, even though she could only see her back. The dress seemed familiar. The build was about right as well. Jane called out to her. The woman turned round, startled, then darted into the shelter of the wood. Jane got up and hurried over to the trees, but the woman had vanished, the dense undergrowth providing superb cover for her flight. Jane and Emma walked back to the village without spotting the young woman at all on the homeward journey. Out of curiosity, Jane knocked on the door of 'Hermitage Cottage' but no-one came, not that she expected anyone to answer.

Sunday morning arrived, promising yet another fine warm day, but Jane had no inclination to get up and make a start to the inevitable boring day ahead. Instead, she made herself a cup of coffee, retrieved the newspaper from the letterbox and returned to the comfort of her bed. Only when Emma began to whimper from the other room did she realise how late it was and made the effort to get up and prepare breakfast for the two of them.

Later on Jane wheeled the pram into the back garden and settled Emma for a sleep. Then she went back indoors, only to emerge minutes later with a deckchair and a book she had borrowed from the mobile library earlier in the week. Arranging the chair so that she had a clear view of Hermitage Cottage, Jane sat down and began to read. The warm sun made her eyelids droop heavily and she dozed in and out of sleep until lunchtime.

By about four o'clock Jane felt like crawling up the wall. Life had better things to offer than boredom and isolation and it was up to her to reach out and help herself. But in her depressed state, galvanising herself into action was an uphill struggle. Indoors the telephone rang, but unfortunately the caller had rung off before she picked up the receiver.

Seeing the telephone reminded her of her mother's call and her promise to contact Dee.

Immediately she dialled the number. Dee sounded delighted to hear from Jane, and without hesitation accepted an invitation to come the following weekend and stay for a holiday. They chatted happily for some considerable time, but Jane carefully avoided answering Dee's questions about life in Ashingham, saying she must wait and see it all for herself.

The news of Dee's impending visit bolstered Jane's spirits no end. At last she had someone she could confide in. As an outsider it would be very interesting to see Dee's reaction to the valley, its inhabitants and perhaps most important of all, her reaction to Paul. Her spirits uplifted, the remainder of the day flew past and Jane retired happily to bed before Paul came home.

Paul sat down in front of the fire to open his mail, while Jane finished cooking dinner. On seeing a letter from the adoption society, he poured himself a large whisky before opening it.

The society had found a suitable couple to adopt Emma and had sent the final papers for the Richardsons to sign. Paul swirled the yellow liquid around in his glass while he thought of ways to get Jane' s signature on the documents. Without Emma, Paul hoped he and Jane might start afresh. It wasn't that he wanted to deprive his wife of children, but Emma had to go. The idea of having another baby, but one that would be conceived in the village, appealed to him. It would also make up for the loss of Emma. It was imperative that Jane understood his point of view and agreed to this adoption for both their sakes.

Jane called to him from the kitchen. Paul got up from his chair. With the papers in his hand, he shambled across to the table, not relishing the task ahead. He handed the documents to Jane who sat and read them quietly, leaving her meal untouched. Then she looked up and across at Paul in stony silence. He could hear the clock ticking as the seconds went by. Paul waited for her to speak. Feeling uncomfortable he shifted uneasily in his chair. The silence reminded him of the timespan between the flash of lightning and the roll of thunder that followed seconds later came the explosion.

Then 'You bastard,' she shrieked.

'Under no circumstances will I ever sign these papers.'

Paul was about to reply, but in a flash Jane had stood up, clutching the documents, and was heading towards the fire. He lurched forwards in an attempt to intercept her, but caught one foot in the chair leg and went sprawling. Jane turned to look at him and laughed as she tore the papers into shreds, dropping them into the flames.

'By the way, Paul,' she said, stepping over him to resume her place at the table. I completely forgot to tell you that Dee is coming up to stay for a holiday. I'm meeting her at Prestbury station next weekend.'

Her husband picked himself up and glared at her.

'Burning those papers doesn't mean anything. I'll ask for duplicates to be sent.'

'Get out, Paul. I thought I married a man, not some snivelling lap dog. You've certainly found your pathetic place in life, haven't you. You had better hurry across the road and report to your masters, or they will begin to think you're slipping.'

'Bitch,' he said, heading for the door.

The sound of her mocking laughter followed him down the path and across the street.

Little did Jane realise that the 'Castle Arms' provided no sanctuary for her husband at present. Formidable pressure from the two farmers weighed heavily on Paul's mind. They would not tolerate much more of his apparent ineptitude and it seemed inevitable that shortly one of them would personally deal with the problem. When that time came, Paul would lose all credibility in the village. He shuddered. By Christ, Jane would pay dearly for his humiliation, he thought.

Some time later Jane heard a knock on the front door. Outside darkness had fallen and she felt nervous about opening up to anyone at this hour.

'Who is it?' she enquired.

'It's Susan from next door,' whispered her neighbour. 'Please hurry up. I don't want to be seen.'

Shooting back the bolt, she opened the door, and Susan scuttled past her into the room.

'Where have you been?' asked Jane. 'Then, turning round she noticed Susan's face. Covered in hideous black bruises, her neighbour squinted painfully at her through one eye, the other completely closed by a gigantic swelling on her cheek.

'My God, what on earth has happened to you?' asked Jane.

'Do you mind if I sit down, I feel a little dizzy,' her neighbour replied, easing herself gently into the nearest chair.

Temporarily lost for words, Jane studied the damage to her friend's face. The bruising extended right across both cheeks, her nose swollen and purple, with crimson patches, where the blood from numerous broken vessels on the bridge of it weaved its way in all directions.

Susan's hands, clasped together in her lap, shook nervously and Jane noticed the purple bands of bruising around both wrists.

'You look as if you need a drink, and I don't mean tea,' she added.

Slowly, with the aid of a large brandy, Susan related the events that had taken place the previous Thursday evening.

Jane could scarcely believe the horrific violence that her neighbour talked about, the scenes depicted, being the sort you see in films, or read about in books.

'If the evidence wasn't staring me in the face, I would find it difficult to credit your story,' said Jane, tensely.

Susan didn't reply, but edged her chair closer to the fire in order to stop herself shivering.

'Why didn't you call the Police?'

'Impossible. Bert or Arthur always have to be consulted before anyone calls the Police down here, added to which Graham remained at home all evening, on Arthur's instructions, to make sure I didn't telephone anyone for help.'

Jane got up to refill Susan's glass, pouring one for herself this time.

'What are the problems you and Paul have to sort out?' enquired Susan.

'Paul has insisted we put Emma up for adoption. The problem is that I won't sign the papers. I get the feeling that Bert and Arthur are behind it all, but apart from the obvious fact that Emma is the only girl in the village, I don't understand why she has to be adopted.'

'Oh,' sighed Susan. 'It's all crystal clear to me now.'

'Enlighten me, please,' said Jane.

Without going into detail, Susan briefly told Jane about the village girl responsible for the annihilation of the male population three centuries earlier.

'You see,' she continued. 'Emma is the first female to be born into the valley since that time, and, unfortunately, the men have remained superstitious.'

Jane sat back in her chair. At long last she understood the hostility surrounding her. She also realised that Susan had been attacked for being her friend.

'What the hell are we going to do?' she asked her neighbour.

For a little while Susan said nothing in reply. She sat staring intently into the dancing flames as if seeking inspiration.

'I want us to remain friends. It's important to me,' said Susan, looking across at Jane. 'However, I don't think we should be seen in each other's company. It's not safe, and I am worried about Robert's safety. Like yourself, I can't trust anyone, not even my husband Graham.'

'Oh Susan. I'm so sorry for what has happened to you and I would not expect you to place your family at risk for my sake.'

'Don't misunderstand me,' Susan interrupted. 'I shall continue to remain your friend, but, from now on, under cover.'

The two women looked at each other, their eyes reflecting their thoughts as they both acknowledged, in silence, the eternal bond between them.

The clock chimed. Susan, startled, glanced up to see that it was ten o'clock.

'I must get home before Graham leaves the pub.'

'Yes, I agree. I don't want Paul to find you here either,' said Jane. 'Use the back door, it will be safer.'

In the kitchen, Susan turned to Jane.

'If I were you, I'd make plans to take Emma and return to London without delay.'

Jane nodded, opening the door quietly for her friend to leave.

'I'll try to come and visit you tomorrow,' whispered Susan. 'But, in the meantime, think about my suggestion. It's far too dangerous for you to continue living here. If I can he raped and beaten for just being a friend, what will happen to you and Emma?'

With that, Susan fled across the garden and disappeared into the darkness.

CHAPTER 10

The taxi glided to a halt in the station forecourt.

'Wait for me please,' Jane said to the driver. 'I'll only be a minute.'

Carrying Emma in her arms, she walked briskly into the station concourse in search of Dee. She was late. Thirty-five minutes late to be exact. Fortunately, only a handful of people were milling around in the entrance hall and she spotted her friend easily. Jane waved to attract her attention and Dee acknowledged with a beaming smile. 'Sorry I'm late,' said Jane apologetically. 'I'll explain later. I've got a taxi waiting outside.'

'You look rather pale and tired,' said Dee with concern, as she retrieved her suitcase and followed Jane through the swing doors.

'I'm OK,' she replied, pointing her friend towards the waiting vehicle at the kerbside.

The taxi pulled out into the main street.

'How far is it to Ashingham?'

'About ten miles,' Jane replied. 'I'm really pleased you could come up and stay. It's lovely to see you.'

'Thank you for inviting me,' said Dee. 'I've been dying to visit you, and I think the baby is absolutely gorgeous. Can I hold her for a while?'

'Of course,' said Jane, depositing Emma on to her friend's lap. 'I'm late because Paul went out and took the car just as I was about to come and meet you, and I had to call a taxi.'

'Don't worry about it,' said Dee laughing. 'It's not important'. 'Anyway,' she added, 'The train arrived late, so I haven't been waiting very long.'

Although she pretended to play with Emma, Dee was studying her friend closely. Jane had lost a remarkable amount of weight, even taking into account the fact she had been pregnant the last time the two girls had seen each other. In addition, her fresh, rosy complexion had completely disappeared, leaving an unbecoming sallowness, and the sparkling green eyes Dee remembered so well had sunk into dark shadowy sockets, from where they hauntingly reflected her innermost troubles.

Jane bent down to retrieve her handkerchief which had fallen on to the floor and Dee could not help but notice the numerous brittle grey streaks now running through her friend's rich auburn hair. In fact, everything about Jane looked tired and lifeless, and, considering only six months had elapsed, Dee found the changes alarming.

Jane broke the silence.

'How are things at work?'

'Oh. Fine. Running smoothly as always. Everybody sends their regards, and I've been asked to take back some photographs of you and the baby.'

The taxi turned into Boundary Road, giving Dee her first glimpse of Ashingham Castle. She shivered momentarily, then turned to Jane, raising her eyebrows in awe.

'We're nearly there now,' laughed Jane, as the car reached the top of the hill.

'I can't see the village yet,' said Dee, peering through the window into the valley below them.

'You will, soon enough!' replied Jane.

Dee stood quietly by the gate, soaking in the atmosphere, while the driver unloaded her suitcase. The road surface shimmered under the glare of the sun's rays, which beat down from the cloudless blue sky overhead, and yet, for no apparent reason, she felt a shivery sensation running down her spine. Instinctively, she rubbed her arms to dispel the goose pimples and slowly surveyed her immediate surroundings. She found the village enchanting with its solid stonebuilt cottages, each one unique in that it varied slightly from its neighbours, unlike the boring terraces of suburbia which she was accustomed to. Everywhere flowers grew in profusion, their heady scents mingling with the heat to such an overpowering degree as to make her feel light-headed. She leaned against the front wall for support and waited for Jane to pay for the taxi.

Apart from themselves, there was no sign of life anywhere. The taxi drove away, the sound. of its engine dying away in the distance. An uncanny silence descended, encircling them as they stood together in the deserted street. Dee shivered again.

She looked up at the grotesque castle towering above them and then across at the half-demolished mill. There was something about this village that frightened her, but, at the moment, she couldn't actually pin it down. Her instincts told her to leave, but she had only just arrived, for God's sake.

'Is everything alright, Dee?' asked Jane. 'Yes, fine,' replied Dee, smiling.

Inside Ivy Cottage a roaring fire blazed in the hearth and a delightful aroma of cooking wafted out from the kitchen. Dee's eyes lit up with pleasure on seeing the wealth of gnarled oak beams and the ancient inglenook fireplace. The overwhelming visual effect on her was one of hospitable cosiness in surroundings of olde worlde charm and character. But once again, she felt decidedly uneasy. Although on the surface the cottage welcomed you with open arms, she experienced strong undercurrents of hostility, and the interior seemed to be even colder than outside in the open air.

'This is ridiculous,' she thought, taking off her coat and following Jane into the kitchen.

'Dinner smells delicious,' she commented enthusiastically.

'I've put the kettle on,' said Jane. 'Why don't you take your things upstairs while I make some tea?'

The two girls sat together in front of the fire drinking their tea and playing with the baby. Jane noticed how close to the hearth Dee was sitting.

'You're cold, aren't you'?' she said.

'I'm afraid so. I haven't felt warm since I arrived. I couldn't stop shivering earlier on when we were outside.'

'It's funny you should say that. I've always found the cottage to be cold. That's why I light a fire every day,' said Jane.

Dee looked searchingly at her friend, her eyes prompting her to continue. This coldness was only the tip of the iceberg. There was far more that needed to be explained. But Jane had picked up the empty cups and was heading towards the kitchen. Dee refused to be fobbed off with such a limp excuse.

'Jane, come back here and sit down,' she demanded.

She returned somewhat meekly and perched herself on the arm of a chair, as if ready for the forthcoming interrogation.

'Now look, Jane. Whatever you might think of me, I'm not stupid,' said Dee, pacing backwards and forwards. 'From the first moment I saw you at the station, I knew something was wrong. There's something strange about this village and it's obviously having an effect on you.'

Jane glanced up to meet her friend's gaze.

'So you've noticed,' she said, lamely.

'Noticed?' exploded Dee. 'You've only been gone a few months and I hardly recognise you. For Christ's sake, Jane. What is happening?'

A car pulled up outside. Jane crossed over to the window.

'It's Paul. I can't say anything now. We'll talk later on when he goes out.'

Her husband breezed in through the door and headed straight towards Dee. He embraced her warmly and stood back holding her at arm's length.

'It's great to see you, Dee,' he said, beaming all over his face. 'We don't get many classy looking birds up here in the North. Wait 'til the lads meet you. They'll be green with envy,' he teased.

Dee giggled. Same old Paul, she thought. He hadn't changed a bit. Ashingham definitely agreed with him. He positively bounced with health and energy.

'Hey. I'm sorry I was unable to come to the station with Jane. Some urgent business cropped up at the last minute. 'What's for dinner, love?' he said, smiling sweetly at his wife. 'I'm famished.'

'Steak and kidney pie,' she replied stiffly, returning to the kitchen.

Paul and Dee chatted continuously throughout the meal. Jane quietly observed them across the table, waiting for her husband to slip up and show his true colours. At one point, Dee remarked upon Jane's appearance, but Paul cleverly skirted around the subject by saying that she was still recovering from a difficult pregnancy and delivery. He went on to declare that Dee's visit would be a tonic for Jane, as she had suffered from severe bouts of depression since Emma's birth.

Paul's friendliness appeared to relieve Dee's initial tension. She visibly relaxed as the meal progressed. Jane stood in the kitchen at the end of the meal, making coffee and listening to them laughing and joking· together as they had done so many times before in the past. She wondered whether her oldest friend would believe the story she would be hearing in an hour or two after Paul went out for the evening. Dee, however, being no fool, had decided to play along with him so as not to arouse any suspicions as to her true feelings about Ashingham and its effect on Jane. She compared Ashingham to a jigsaw puzzle - hundreds of different shaped pieces to be slotted together to complete the finished picture. So far none of the pieces connected up, but she resolved to crack it before the end of her stay.

Later on, after Paul had gone out, Dee settled down in front of the fire. Jane went upstairs to look in on the baby. With the curtains drawn to shut out the encroaching darkness and the soft glow from the lamps casting gentle pools of light around the room, Dee became lulled into a state of comfort and well-being. The flames from the fire produced dancing reflections on the white rough-plastered walls, highlighting the warmth of colour in the well-polished wood of the solid old furniture.

Suddenly a scratching sound attracted her attention towards the small door under the stairs. It sounded like the claws of a small animal requesting to be let in. Then she remembered Oedipus. The stupid cat must have got himself shut in the cupboard by mistake. As she slid back the bolt to let him in, she called up the stairs to Jane.

'The cat's shut himself in the cupboard. I'm just going to let him out.'

'Don't open. that door, for Christ's sake,' screamed Jane, flying down the stairs.

Pushing Dee roughly to one side, she rammed home the bolt, then sank to her knees and sobbed pitifully.

'Whatever is the matter?' asked Dee in alarm.

'It's not the cat. Oedipus is dead.'

Dee bent down and gently helped Jane to her feet and across to a chair.

'You look awful. Can I get you a drink?'

Jane nodded, pointing towards the drum cabinet standing in the corner.

'Ok. I think it's time you told me what's happening,' said Dee, returning promptly with two large tumblers of whisky. The scratching from the corner resumed again, this time accompanied by a dull moaning.

Jane got up and switched on the hi-fi to drown out the noise.

'Have you got an animal locked up in that cupboard?' asked Dee sharply.

'No. And it isn't a cupboard, but stairs leading to a cellar.'

'Go on,' she prompted.

By the time Jane had finished telling her about the discovery of the door itself and the horrors concealed behind it, Dee found herself perched on the very edge of her chair, spellbound with terror. Unable to glance at the door for fear of what might come hurtling through it at any moment, she asked Jane if she had any idea what this, as yet unseen, presence might be. Her friend shook her head.

'I've no idea. I can't tell how big it is, or, even if it's real.'

And although Paul repaired the wall down there, this creature has broken through into your cellar again?'

Jane turned down the volume on the stereo.

'What do you think?' she replied, as the clawing and moaning reverberated around the room.

'For God's sake, turn up the sound,' hissed Dee. 'Do you think there's any chance it might break down the door?

'Well, it hasn't as yet, but who's to say it won't happen in the future.'

Dee refilled her glass to the brim and drank it like water.

'You're mad to stay here. Why don't you pack up and come back to London with me?'

'There's more,' replied Jane, quietly.

'More!' said Dee hysterically, shakily refilling her glass for the third time.

Slowly Jane recounted the events of the previous months, pausing once or twice to brush away the stray tears that escaped and rolled down her cheeks, especially as she described the death of Oedipus. When she had finished the two girls sat in silence, each totally absorbed in their own thoughts.

At last Dee looked across at her friend.

'Please come back with me,' she implored.

'No. Not yet,' said Jane. 'Not until I fully understand what is happening in this valley.

'Is it that important to you?'

'Yes. To leave now would be admitting failure. And, not knowing the truth about Ashingham would torment for the rest of my life.'

'Would you like to go back yourself tomorrow? I'll fully understand if you say yes.'

'No,' replied Dee firmly. 'I'm not afraid to admit that this place bloody well terrifies me. But while I'm here I intend to fathom out this Godforsaken valley for myself, so that we can return to London together.'

It was well after nine o'clock before Dee surfaced the following morning. Wearily she raised herself on to her elbows to stare out of the window. It promised to be another fine day, with only the occasional cloud breaking up an otherwise clear blue sky. Downstairs Jane was bustling about in the kitchen, talking to Emma as she worked. Dee had slept fitfully during the night, tossing and turning, her mind continuously churning over the macabre details of Jane's experiences so far. Dee washed and dressed slowly as she grappled with the gargantuan task ahead.

They needed to devise a plan of action to take all aspects of the situation into account. There were so many factors to consider, the most important being, where to start?

'Hi, you two,' she announced, entering the kitchen with a grand flourish. 'Can I smell breakfast'?'

'Coming up,' replied Jane, laughing. 'You sound happy this morning.'

'Never rely on visual impression, said Dee. 'Underneath this jovial exterior lies a quivering mass of human jelly, and, my stomach is pretending to be the Bay of Biscay on a bad day.'

'In that case I presume coffee will suffice for breakfast?' quipped Jane.

'Too right! Seriously, though,' said Dee. 'In spite of my fragile nervous system, we must endeavour to make a start today.'

'I agree. Have you any ideas?'

'Well. For starters, I'd like to wander around the valley for a couple of hours, just to get the feel of the place. Until I'm more familiar with the area, I can't put anything into perspective if you see what I mean?'

'What about the cellar?' asked Jane.

'Don't mention it. Can't you see I'm scared to death already?'

'Are you sure you wouldn't rather go home?'

'Will you come as well?'

'No,'

'Then said Jane, vehemently.

you already have the answer, don't you,' replied Dee, gazing steadily into her friend's eyes.

'Shall we take Emma with us?' asked Jane.

'Yes. That's a good idea. The last thing we want to do is arouse suspicion. Taking Emma for a walk will provide excellent cover.'

Half an hour later the three of them strolled leisurely down the road towards the bridge, Emma securely fastened to her mother's waist in a baby sling.

'I get the distinct impression we're being watched,' said Dee casually.

'You'll get used to it,' replied Jane, with a nervous laugh.

They stood side by side on the bridge looking out across the Valley.

'Stupendous scenery,' remarked Dee, subjecting the surrounding landscape to close scrutiny. Her eyes came to rest on a large hole in the river bank about fifteen yards away from where they were standing.

'Jane. What's that large hole for?' she enquired, pointing towards the gaping chasm just above water level.

'It's the tunnel from the mill. After all the brouhaha surrounding the surveyor's death, nobody bothered to reseal the entrance.'

'Right, let's take a look at it,' said Dee, delving into the pockets of her anorak to check she'd remembered everything. Torch, candles, matches – yes, not much but enough to make a start.

'Come on,' she shouted over her shoulder as she strode purposefully along the path.

The size of the opening surprised Dee. From the bridge it appeared to be much smaller. Not a single ray of light penetrated the interior. Dee produced the torch from her pocket and shone it into the opening. A flight of steep stone steps led down into the blackness. A sudden movement behind her made her spin round in alarm. Jane had finally caught up.

'For Christ's sake, don't creep up on me like that,' said Dee, her heart thumping wildly. 'Come on, follow me. And be careful, these treads are slippery.'

At last Dee felt ground level under her feet. She turned and helped Jane descend the last few steps to the bottom.

'Right. Stay where you are. I'll light a candle for you.'

Jane stood shivering, while she waited for her candle. The temperature in the tunnel was considerably lower than outside in the strong sunlight. A familiar rank odour of dampness and decay, similar to that in the cellar at Ivy Cottage, permeated the atmosphere, making it unpleasant to breathe normally.

Raising her candle into the air, Jane's gaze focussed on the furry green mould and fungi covering the passage roof a few inches above her head. Rivulets of water coursed down the walls into deep gulleys, draining away somewhere below floor level.

With care the two women moved forwards into the murky gloom, their vision restricted to roughly ten feet. Suddenly, and without warning, the passage floor dropped sharply, catching them both off-balance and they stumbled awkwardly into a large cavern.

In her struggle to stay upright, Dee dropped the torch she was carrying, leaving them only the benefit of Jane's candle. She lit another and held it aloft.

They found themselves in a large natural cave with several passageways leading off it. Jane's thoughts flashed back to the day she and Paul explored the cellar and tunnels under their own cottage.

'Let's go back,' she said, tugging at Dee's sleeve.

'No, not yet. I'm going to have a look around first.'

Over to the right, in a small niche cut into the stone wall Dee found a pile of electronic equipment covered by a sheet of tarpaulin.

'Come and see what I've found,' she shouted.

Carefully pulling the sheet away, Jane recognised the equipment the surveyors had been using at the mill.

'It belongs to Nick. He spent a whole day down here.'

Dee didn't bother to listen to Jane's explanation. At the same time as she stood looking at their latest discovery, her brain was receiving strange telepathic signals, urging her to explore further into the tunnels leading away from the main cave. Jane, still talking, watched her friend turn slowly to face one of the exits and move mechanically towards it.

Beads of perspiration formed on Jane's forehead as a warm clammy vapour began to swirl around her.

'Dee. Come back,' she shouted.

The moisture from the atmosphere extinguished her candle with a hiss as it formed a cocoon firmly around her, barring any attempt at escape. Dee had almost reached one of the tunnels, her candle flame flickering unsteadily as she moved across the uneven floor. Jane, now plunged into total blackness and struggling to break free from her invisible bonds, screamed at her friend to attract her attention.

Her mother's frenzied agitation woke little Emma with a jolt. The baby's senses prickled as she became aware of her surroundings and the imminent danger facing the three of them. Unlike her mother, Emma's eyes were capable of normal vision in the dark.

And, although Jane instinctively knew they were not alone in the cave, Emma clearly saw the evil apparitions encircling them. She also saw Oedipus, the cat who once belonged to her mother, mewing plaintively at her, his enormous luminous eyes, appealing to her for help. The paralysing web of swirling vapour which trapped them flowed freely from the gaping mouths of these hideous protoplasmic spectres.

Emma's gaze latched on to one creature which stood apart from the rest, transmitting telepathic messages into Dee's brain. Held in a trance, her mother's friend was allowing it to gently guide her to the tunnel entrance. Inside Emma's tiny body, a tremendous power force surged into action, as she prepared to attack and destroy the invisible creatures threatening them.

Her pupils dilated to form two huge ebony pools from whose depths she released a multitude of deadly lasers that ripped into the cavernous mouth-like orifices, exploding violently on impact. Then, turning her attention to their leader, Emma fired a surge of electrical current into the grey mass of flesh above its eye sockets to penetrate the brain. The eruption which followed, splattered the putrid organic matter in all directions. The paralysing spell broken, Jane hurried over to Dee, who was rubbing her eyes in an attempt to clear her head.

'What happened?' she asked Jane in bewilderment.

'I'm not sure. You were heading towards this tunnel. I tried to stop you but my feet wouldn't move. It was almost as if someone had glued me to the spot.' She continued. 'Didn't you hear me shouting at you?'

Dee struggled to remember. Finally she shook her head.

'The only thing I recall is experiencing a tremendous urge to explore further along the tunnels.'

'I think we should go back,' said Jane. 'It's evil down here. My instincts tell me that something in this cave endeavoured to separate us.'

'Did you see anything?' Dee enquired.

'No, but I'm sure we're being watched. I felt the same sensations when Paul and I explored the cellar and passages under Ivy Cottage. They probably all interconnect.'

'It wouldn't surprise me in the least,' said Dee. 'OK, let's go back.'

Baby Emma remained awake on the journey back, to ensure their safe return. Oedipus diligently led the way, invisible to everyone except herself. As they approached the flight of steps leading to the surface, he looked back at Emma in warning before he ascended to the top and disappeared out of sight.

Dee stepped out into the bright sunlight and flopped down on the bank to wait for the others. A shadow fell across her, blotting out the warmth from the sun, and she twisted her head round, expecting to see Jane and the baby.

The figure of a tall, powerfully built man towered over her as she lay full length and defenceless on ·the grass. All attempts to get up were foiled by the force of the man's boot shoving her backwards on to the ground.

'Who the hell are you?' she gasped, struggling for breath.

'Bert Grimshaw,' was the surly reply. 'Now see here, young lady. We don't like strangers in Ashingham, especially nosy ones. If I catch you snooping around here again, you'll be sorry. So be warned and clear off.'

'Get away from her,' a woman's voice shouted from behind him. He half turned to see Jane and the baby emerge from the tunnel entrance. With one foot firmly pinning Dee to the ground, he waited for the other woman to approach.

Suddenly his knees buckled, forcing him to release his victim. The scenery swayed in front of his eyes. The nearer Jane came, the dizzier he felt. He staggered backwards a few steps, fighting to remain upright. Black spots danced in front of his eyes. He blinked, trying to focus on Emma, when a blinding flash hit him full in the face, sending him reeling to the ground.

Neither of the women spoke. Not understanding what had caused the farmer to collapse so dramatically, they both watched in amazement as he crawled several yards away from them before raising himself, somewhat unsteadily, on to his feet.

'You'll pay for this, the pair of you,' he stammered, still winded and badly shaken from his unexpected fall.

With accurate precision, Emma aimed a second wave of current at the man's stomach, creasing him double with pain. In bewilderment, he retreated, his hands clutching his abdomen. As he stepped on to the bridge, he looked back at Emma, obviously puzzled. Then with head bowed, he crossed over to seek sanctuary at Heronsford Farm.

Jane and Dee watched him limp away until he finally disappeared into the farmhouse.

'Well, what do you make of that?' exclaimed Jane.

'Come on,' said Dee. 'Let's grab some lunch. I've got plans for this afternoon, and time is of the essence.

CHAPTER II

O ver lunch Dee scanned the local timetable.
'We'll catch the two o'clock. It only takes half an hour.'

'What about getting back?' asked Jane, apprehensively.

'Don't worry. We'll make sure we arrive home before Paul comes in. He'll never know.'

'And the locals?'

'No problem. With Emma in her pushchair, it'll look as if we're out for a walk.'

Not entirely convinced, Jane reluctantly collected her cardigan and handbag, before carefully locking the door behind them.

On the walk up the hill to the bus stop on the main road they saw nobody from the village. And, thankfully, no-one was waiting for the bus either. The little single-decker arrived promptly, stopping only the length of time it took them to board before continuing its run to Prestbury.

The handful of passengers already on the bus occupied the seats at the front, near the driver. Dee, carrying the folded pushchair, edged her way down the central gangway towards the back.

'You haven't told me why we're going to the library?' whispered Jane.

'It's very simple. I'm going to see if I can find anything on the history of Ashingham.'

'What for?'

'I think the history of the valley may well play an integral part in the behavioural patterns of the villagers.'

'Sounds feasible.'

'Well, it's only a theory, but I'd like to follow it through.'

Jane nodded, thoughtfully. 'Anything specific in mind?'

'Yes. After what you told me last night, I want to discover exactly what happened during the Civil War to result in the extinction of the female line.'

By this time the bus had reached the outskirts of Prestbury. At the next stop an old couple alighted before the final stage of the journey to the bus station.

The library, a building of magnificent architectural construction was prominently sited in the main square, directly opposite an equally statuesque Town Hall. The two women, Jane carrying Emma in her arms, climbed the fan-shaped flight of steps and passed under a splendid portico to enter the large marble-floored entrance hall. Immediately to their to their left, through a pair of open double doors they saw the art gallery, which formed part of the literary complex, while, in front of them, at the far end of the hall, an elegant sweeping staircase ascended to the first floor.

Dee headed towards the enquiry desk in the far corner, where a slim, curly-haired young woman was busily making notes following a telephone call. The receptionist nodded in reply to Dee's enquiry and pointed towards another set of double doors to the right.

'Ask for Mr Green, the Archivist,' she said, cheerfully. 'I'm sure he'll be able to help you.'

Following the directions they'd been given, Dee and Jane found themselves in a long narrow room, identical to the one housing the art gallery on the opposite side of the entrance hall. Several glass topped display cabinets, containing exhibits of local historic interest, lined the wall beneath the windows, which overlooked the square. To the left, bookshelves, literally bulging with pamphlet boxes and dusty old tomes, ran the entire length of the room from floor to ceiling. At the far end, raised up on a wooden dais, stood a large cluttered and rather battered old-fashioned desk covered in paperwork and reference books. The whole place smelled of old leather and floor polish.

Dee rang the brass bell, precariously positioned to act as a paperweight on one of the untidy piles.

'Coming,' boomed a voice from beyond an open doorway to the left.

The man that emerged from the inner office was the epitome of the profession he represented. Attired in a tweed sports jacket with well-worn leather elbow patches, cavalry twill trousers, check shirt and obligatory woollen tie, the medium height, medium built librarian walked towards them, his shoes making no sound whatsoever on the highly polished wooden floor. Dee judged him to be in his early thirties.

'Good afternoon,' he said, with a broad beam.

'Mr Green?' enquired Dee.

He nodded. 'How can I help you?'

'We're interested in looking at anything you may have on the history of Ashingham village,' said Dee.

'Do you require a light history, or is this a research project?' he enquired.

'We'd like as much information as possible please,' said Dee.

Jane interrupted at this point. 'It's rather urgent, Mr Green, we have a deadline to meet.'

'I see,' he replied. 'In that case let me jot down some more details.'

He cleared a space at the desk, by pushing the various piles of paper further to the edge and from the right-hand drawer he extracted a large notepad and pen.

'Right,' he said. 'Now then, I presume you would like me to trace back to the earliest records we have?'

'Yes please,' said Dee.

'Fine. Actually, if I remember correctly we received the bulk of the records from Sir Francis Ashingham Castle.'

'How long will it take you to gather together all the information we need?' asked Jane.

'I don't know, but I will make a start immediately.' He stopped writing for a moment and looked up, beaming.

'If you could let me have your address and phone number, I'll ring you as soon as it's ready.'

'Thank you very much,' said Dee.

'Not at all,' replied Mr Green, rising from his chair.

He shook hands with both Jane and Dee and then escorted them back to the entrance hall.

'Charming man,' remarked Dee, as they made their way back down the flight of steps to the square.

'Yes,' said Jane. 'I'd almost forgotten what they were like,' she added, somewhat cuttingly.

'What a stroke of luck the library obtaining the Ashingham papers,' said Dee, as they boarded the bus for the return journey. 'Any chance of visiting the castle?'

'No,' replied Jane. 'It's not open to the public. We would never have been given permission to look at the records either,' she added. 'The old baronet is a recluse, I believe.'

'That's not surprising. With neighbours like he's got, who would want to socialize,' she quipped.

In good spirits, they got off the bus at Boundary Road, strapped Emma into her pushchair and sauntered slowly towards the village. In the field to their right, the cows had congregated along the fence, as if to welcome them back.

'It's difficult to believe that such a beautiful place can harbour so much evil,' reflected Dee, patting one of the beasts on the nose. She lifted her gaze towards the castle.

'I wonder what Sir Francis is like?'

'Come on,' said Jane. 'Let's get home.'

The warm afternoon sun filtered gently through the canopy of trees at the bottom of the hill, creating a dappled pattern on the road in front of them rather like a carpet. The two Collies from Half Acre Farm bounded out of the cowshed, across the farmyard and into the lane, barking loudly as they chased up and down in front of the pushchair. Something about the way the dogs were barking disturbed Dee. She wondered whether it might be some kind of signal to the village that they had returned. This thought had obviously not occurred to Jane, however, who had bent down to fondle them. Dee stared hard at the cottage windows.

'What's wrong' asked Jane, standing up.

'Nothing,' she replied untruthfully.

The dogs responded instantly to a distant whistle and disappeared back into the cowshed. 'The girls walked up to the front gate of Ivy Cottage. While Jane bent down to lift

Emma out of her chair, Dee scanned the village street. Now that the dogs had gone, they seemed to be surrounded by an eerie silence.

It was strikingly cold in the cottage. Jane hurried across to the dog-grate to light the fire. Dee wandered into the kitchen to make tea.

'I've put the kettle on,' she shouted through the open doorway. As she spoke, her breath visually trailed away into the air. Considering the temperature outside it was ridiculous to be so cold in here. Her eyes darted around the room. Everything appeared to be exactly the same as before, and yet, she had the uncanny feeling that someone had been in the cottage during their absence. Behind her the kettle reached boiling point. She turned round to switch it off. The lid was jumping up and town as the steam spiralled upwards to the ceiling, covering the window in the chilly room with a fine layer of condensation. An icy draught ran up her legs. There was no question about it. Ivy Cottage was possessed. She hurriedly carried the cups into the living room and stood in front of the fire to warm her legs.

Unable to settle she walked across to the window and looked out into the garden. Several bees were hovering around the flowers, collecting the last pollen of the year. The sun went in, throwing the garden into deep shadow. Looking up at the sky, she saw thick banks of cloud drifting across from the west. The telephone rang. Jane got up from her chair to answer it. Still feeling cold, Dee went upstairs to change into warmer clothes.

Surprisingly enough, the room she was sharing with the baby felt warmer than downstairs. She relaxed, soaking in the heat. This room remained free of the unhealthy atmosphere in the rest of the cottage. Dee looked over to the cot where Emma lay fast asleep, seemingly oblivious to the underlying currents of unrest. She smiled fondly at her, gently opened the door and tiptoed out on to the icy landing.

Downstairs, she found Jane setting the table for dinner.

'That was the Archivist on the phone,' she said excitedly, arranging the napkins neatly on the side plates. 'Apparently he has amassed a considerable amount of information for us.'

'That's great,' said Dee. 'I knew he'd come up trumps. When does he want us to call at the library to collect it?'

'Well, actually he suggested I drive over to his house and pick it up, since we need the material urgently. He lives in Hanslope, a village about five miles from here.'

'Did you agree?'

'Yes, I thought it would save a lot of time.'

'Good. Now don't worry about Emma. I'll stay here and babysit for you. I take it that Paul will be going to the pub as usual?'

'Can't think of any reason why not. We lead totally separate lives now, so he's hardly likely to spend the evening at home with me,' she added bitterly.

By the time her husband arrived home from work, Jane had fed, bathed and put Emma to bed for the night, and the meal was ready to be served. Much to her irritation and Dee's amusement Paul played the perfect host and loving husband for the second evening in a row.

Dee, fully aware of the true situation between them, acted out her role brilliantly. She laughed at his jokes, teasing him unmercifully in return, until the tears rolled down their faces. Watching them across the table, Jane wished the laughter and merriment could be genuine. She wondered if there was any possibility of Paul making a complete recovery if he returned to London with her and the baby? Away from the influence of the place it might happen. She desperately wanted him to have the chance.

Up to a point, Jane held the village responsible for the breakdown of her marriage. Before moving to Ashingham they had lived together in perfect happiness, the foundations of their union, rock-solid from the outset. To say Paul was over the moon on learning his wife was expecting a baby would not be an understatement. Indeed, the pregnancy had been planned, Paul wanting them both to start a family. She remembered him saying he didn't care whether they had a boy or a girl. As long as the baby was healthy, it didn't matter. With a successful marriage to bolster them, a baby on the way and a new job on offer, what more could any young couple want from life. They were fortunate and they knew it.

To a certain extent, however, Jane held herself partly to blame for what had happened, in her decision to buy Ivy Cottage. She remembered the day they had driven up to look at it, and how, captivated by its beauty she had lightly brushed aside the fact that the interior seemed unnaturally cold and sinister. On mentioning the chilly atmosphere in passing, Paul had laughed at her, insinuating she possessed a vivid imagination. Had she forgotten it was the middle of winter, blowing a gale outside and, moreover, threatening to snow at any minute? Jane had accepted his derision with good grace, laughing at herself. But now, on reflection, she wished she had taken her initial observations more seriously.

Another factor also dismissed at the time was the hostile reception from the villagers they had encountered that day, both at the general store and in the 'Castle Arms'. The overwhelming desire to own Ivy Cottage and live in Ashingham had clouded their judgment to exclude all the other considerations. Without thought or hesitation they had grabbed at the chance to settle in this idyllic valley, for which mistake both she and her husband were now paying the price, each in their different way.

She looked sadly across the table at Paul. Feeling her eyes on him, he coloured slightly and smiled awkwardly in return. Yes, she decided, he deserved the chance to escape from this living hell and its stranglehold on him as much as she did. Perhaps Dee could come up with some ideas.

Jane got up and began to take the dirty dishes into the kitchen. Dee followed her example and Paul disappeared upstairs to change.

'When the time comes to leave Ashingham I'd like to take Paul with me,' said Jane in a low whisper.

'I know,' replied Dee softly. 'You still love him, that's obvious and you're not the sort of person that lightly throws away a marriage. But, if you don't leave soon, it may be too late,' she added, gravely.

'I'm off now,' Paul said, cheerfully, popping his head around the door.

Caught unawares, both girls jumped. Dee, the first to recover, turned towards him with a forced smile.

'See you later then. Have a good time.'

Jane, her back to him, continued to wash up, not bothering to acknowledge his departure. Only the tears that silently trickled down her cheeks showed how much she really cared.

Shortly after eight o'clock, Jane left Ivy Cottage to drive over to Hanslope. Torrents of rain swept along the street, carried by strong winds that had whipped up during the previous hour or so. She made a quick dash to the car, fumbling awkwardly with the door lock in her haste to avoid the heavy downpour. Seconds later the engine roared into life and she drove quickly out of the village.

In the darkness, and in her hurry to leave, Jane failed to see Dorothy's husband on the other side of the unlit street. Reuben Haresnape on his way to the 'Castle Arms' for the evening slipped stealthily into the deep shadow of the mill the moment he saw Jane leaving the cottage. Unobserved, he watched her get into the car and drive away. When the taillights finally disappeared on the bend he stepped out from his hiding place and walked to the pub. Once inside, he elbowed his way across the crowded room to the bar, looking for either Arthur or Bert. He was relieved to see Farmer Briggs chatting to the landlord, Terry Smith. The thought of having to traipse over to Half Acre Farm to find him in this foul weather didn't appeal to Reuben one bit.

'Usual?' Terry asked him, reaching under the counter for a pint glass.

'Yes please, Terry,' he replied. While he waited for this drink he turned to face Arthur. 'Can I have a quick word with you?' he asked, furtively.

The other man nodded.

'I've just seen Jane Richardson driving out of the village. She seemed in quite a hurry.'

'Interesting,' replied Arthur, scratching his chin. 'With the friend who is staying with them?'

'No, she was alone.'

'Thanks, mate,' he said, patting Reuben on the shoulder like an obedient lap dog. 'Leave it with me.'

Arthur beckoned to the landlord, who was serving another customer.

'Terry, is Paul Richardson in the bar tonight?'

'Yes, I only served him a few minutes ago. He's playing pool with several of the lads in the back room.'

'I want to see him in your office upstairs, Terry.'

'OK,' replied the landlord, touching his forelock. 'I'll send him up straight away.'

'Come in, 'shouted Arthur in reply to Paul's knock on the door. The farmer wagged a finger impatiently in the direction of a vacant chair. Paul sat down, apprehensive at the unexpected summons. The palms of his hands felt wet and clammy. He rubbed them on his trousers while he waited for the other man to speak. Arthur studied the younger man's face closely for a few moments. Paul Richardson differed from the other men in the village in that he visually portrayed his nervous character. As a man, Arthur disliked him intensely. He expected certain standards in the village which Paul failed to achieve, even with guidance. His general eagerness to please and his nervous disposition irritated Arthur, who much preferred the dour, surly attitude of the other men. At least they retained control of their households, unlike the quivering mouse sitting in front of him.

Ever since the Richardsons had purchased Ivy Cottage and moved into the valley, both he and Bert Grimshaw had been burdened with problems. To begin with the villagers detested strangers which boded trouble from the start. In addition, Mrs Richardson's advanced pregnancy naturally aroused a great deal of alarm, culminating in a flood of hysteria when she produced a baby girl, a child which, despite all the pressure on her father to have her removed, still remained in the valley.

Not content with the damage inflicted thus far on the community, Mrs Richardson went on to befriend he neighbour Susan Entwhistle, who, in consequence, had to face a stiff penalty for succumbing to temptation. Having successfully thwarted her endeavours to make friends in the village, Mrs Richardson fought back by inviting a girlfriend to stay. Bert Grimshaw had already given Arthur a detailed account of his brief encounter with the two women on the river bank that morning.

The whole situation regarding the Richardson family was becoming difficult to handle and Arthur, at the end of his tether, resolved to settle the matter once and for all. The farmer coughed several times to clear his throat.

'Where is your wife this evening, Paul?' he asked, gravely.

A look of astonishment flashed across the younger man's face. What sort of silly question was this? he thought to himself.

'She's at home, as usual, Arthur,' he replied, breaking into a nervous laugh.

'I'm afraid you're wrong, Paul,' he said. 'She was seen driving your car out of the village earlier this evening.'

'Was she with her friend and the baby?' he asked shakily.

'No, your wife left on her own.'

'Well,' Paul stammered, racking his brain for an answer that he didn't have. 'I'm sorry, but I've no idea where she can have gone.'

'I thought as much,' Arthur muttered. 'You've no control over your domestic affairs at all, have you?'

Paul looked down at his knees, unable to face the penetrating glare of the man opposite him.

In exasperation the farmer abruptly pushed his chair backwards and stood up. He crossed over to the window that overlooked the main street and peered out into the darkness.

'Listen carefully to what I have to say, Paul. I am not going to repeat myself,' he said, without turning round.

'I want you to return home immediately and deal with that interfering girlfriend you have staying with you as well as that accursed child of yours.'

'How do you mean 'deal with'?' enquired Paul, edgily.

'Kill them,' replied Arthur, spinning round dramatically to face the terrified man.

'No, I couldn't bring myself to kill anyone, least of all my own flesh and blood,' he stammered, devastated by the other man's demands.

'You will, Paul. You will carry out my instructions to the letter.'

'What about my wife?'

'Leave her to me. I'll deal with Jane when she returns,' said Arthur, with a broad beam.

Paul stood up. His legs felt like jelly. He grasped the table for support.

'I can't do this,' he pleaded.

Arthur's face became rigid with anger.

'Let me know when the task has been carried out. By the way,' he added. 'If you fail to report back, I'll have you hunted down. Do you understand?'

Paul nodded and left the room, quietly closing the door behind him.

CHAPTER 12

D ee stood at the front window to wave goodbye, as Jane set
out on her journey to Hanslope. The torrential rain made
it difficult to see through the glass as a constant stream of
water coursed down the window from the overhead guttering
which was unable to cope with the deluge pouring off the roof.
A violent gust of wind and rain lashed against the leaded panes
exhibiting the defiant mood of the storm. Dee replied, equally
defiantly by grasping the curtains and dramatically sweeping
them together to shut out the encroaching elements.

Despite the roaring fire, the warm glow from the heavy
wooden furniture and the inviting comfort of the soft
furnishings, the cottage was chilly. The firelight danced
against the white-washed walls in the soft lamplight, the
brass and copperware decorating the inglenook shone brightly,
reflecting the glow of the flames, yet for some inexplicable
reason, Ivy Cottage remained without warmth, or indeed any
atmosphere of contentment. Dee shivered, as an icy draught
wafted around her feet. She moved towards the fire, pulling
one of the armchairs as close to the hearth as possible. With
her legs curled up beneath her, she casually flicked through
one of the magazines Jane had left lying on the coffee table.

The clock on the mantelpiece struck the half hour, interrupting her concentration. She was not in the mood for reading anyway. Dee stood up and bent over the fire to warm her hands. Suddenly the temperature inside the cottage dropped rapidly as a deathly coldness descended from nowhere. She spun round, fearing the worst, only to find herself quite alone. Or was she? Were these icy draughts genuine or were they caused by the movement of unearthly spirits haunting the cottage? Whatever the answer, the cold had become so intense by now, her breath was clearly visible in front of her face.

Then the scratching started from the cellar. Dee stood, literally frozen to the spot, from both fear and cold, her eyes riveted on the door under the stairs. Her senses prickled like static electricity in the presence of the invisible phenomena that swirled around the room, and she could feel her heart pounding as the clawing became more insistent.

On a sudden impulse Dee crossed the room and bolted up the stairs, two at a time. The baby – she had to make sure Emma was OK. She grasped the door handle firmly enough, but her legs wobbled like jelly as she hesitated momentarily on the landing to catch her breath.

She entered the room on tiptoe and quietly closed the door behind her. The small night light on the table beside her bed glowed softly, enabling Dee to glance around without switching on the main light. Emma lay fast asleep in her cot, undisturbed by the evil influences permeating the rest of the cottage. This little sanctuary remained in splendid isolation, out on a limb, so to speak, rather like a secure unit. Dee pondered the reason for this as she basked in the cosy atmosphere. The temperature in Emma's room appeared to be fairly constant, no matter what the time of day or night, almost as if it was permanently regulated. The baby stirred, turned over and slept on. At least she's safe in here, thought Dee, picking up a cardigan before returning downstairs. The conjecture that perhaps ghosts dislike babies enough to leave them in peace made her smile to herself, although inwardly she prayed it might be a true statement.

Before sitting down again, Dee manoeuvred the armchair into a position from where she had a clear view of the cellar door.

'There is absolutely no way I am going to sit with my back to the stairs,' she muttered vehemently to herself.

The scratching, which had abated during her absence upstairs, recommenced.

'Oh. For Christ's sake,' Dee said in exasperation. 'Why don't you piss off and frighten someone else?'

The clawing and moaning immediately crescendoed into a mind-bending, excruciating cacophony that forced her to raise both hands to cover her ears. It was almost as if whatever was behind the door understood her remarks and decided to apply more pressure. Incensed, she reached across to the television and switched it on.

'OK, smart-arse. Beat this,' she said, twiddling the dials to find a channel broadcasting music.

What on earth had possessed Jane to buy this godforsaken cottage with its rent-free lodgers. Looking round the room Dee quite expected to see spectral apparitions stepping out of the woodwork at any moment. The TV programme failed to hold her attention. The music served only to drown the battering against the door, and, quite frankly, it fought a losing battle as the violent thrusts strained the bolt to its limit. The last threads of Dee's confidence snapped. If the creature in the cellar broke free, it was impossible to predict what would happen, and she, for one, didn't want to accommodate it by being its first victim. Also, whatever it was, breaking down the door, possessed an intelligent mind, in that it only tormented people when it knew someone was in the room. With any luck it might stop if she went upstairs, as it had earlier, when she looked in at the baby.

Dee placed the guard in front of the fire, switched off the lamps and retreated upstairs to the safety of Emma's bedroom. In the event of the creature breaking the lock, she felt it unlikely that it would violate the sanctity of this room. She undressed quickly and quietly to avoid disturbing the baby, before slipping into bed, where she lay, silently reflecting on the day.

Paul emerged from the 'Castle Arms' with a heavy heart. The task ahead of him required a cold, calculating mind, a mind that felt no fear or pity for his impending victims. Even though he was aware of, and accepted, the mental change he had undergone since moving into the valley, Paul found it difficult to believe he had been instructed to murder his own child. OK, so the baby frightened him, for reasons unknown to the villagers, but he had never considered killing her.

He stood in the shelter of the porch, numbed with shock, hardly noticing the driving rain that stung his face like a thousand tiny pinpricks. There had to be a way of dealing with the situation without resorting to murder, but, for the life of him, he couldn't think of anything on the spur of the moment. Arthur hadn't even given him time to formulate a plan. The man plainly expected him to walk into his own home, as bold as brass, eliminate two people and report back.

Paul had the distinct impression that this was his last chance as far as the two farmers were concerned. If he loused this up, he would certainly pay the price, whatever that might be. He shuddered as if someone had walked across his grave.

The downpour showed no sign of abating. The gale force wind swept eroding sheets of rain along the street, battering on impact anything in its path. Paul looked down at his shoes, completely saturated now from the perpetual backlash of water. The car had gone from outside Ivy Cottage. He racked his brains trying to think where Jane had gone. She never ventured out at night, but there again, she didn't usually have the luxury of a resident babysitter. He'd have to ask Dee. There could be a perfectly legitimate reason for her going out. Everything hinged on Dee's explanation. If it was satisfactory he would try and smuggle both her and the baby out of the village, as well as contacting Jane, if at all possible, to warn her not to return. With any luck the three of them could escape to London. He would return to the pub, tell Arthur that Reuben had been mistaken in thinking that Jane had gone out alone and that the cottage was empty. Then, when the hoo-haa had died down, he would quietly leave the valley and re-join his family in the south.

If, however, talking to Dee proved to be a waste of time, he'd have to follow his immediate instincts in deciding what action to take. He didn't have the time to make a list of alternatives now, and standing outside the pub wasn't exactly the most pleasant occupation on such a wretched night.

Paul hurried across the road, lifted the wet gate latch and sought the shelter of his own porch. He entered quietly, and was surprised to find the cottage in darkness, the fire providing the only light inside the living room. Perhaps Reuben had been mistaken after all. Perhaps the girls had made a bolt for freedom. He hoped they had – it would relieve him of a most gruesome burden. Paul switched on the table lamps, then pulling the guard away, stood in front of the fire to dry out his clothes.

Upstairs, Dee woke with a start. There was somebody moving about downstairs. She was sure of it. She lay tensely, holding her breath hard, and recognised the scraping sound of the lamps being switched on. She reached over to the bedside table in the dark to retrieve her watch. It was difficult to see, but gradually she was able to make out the time. Half past nine. Who on earth could it be? Paul never came in before midnight. Had Jane come home early for some reason? Pulling her dressing gown around her shoulders, Dee got out of bed and groped her way across the room. She found the wall switch and turned on the light. A chilly draught swirled around her legs as she stealthily crept onto the landing and peered through the bannisters into the living room below.

Dee saw the figure of a man bending low over the fire. For a moment or two she was unable to identify him as he had his back towards her. But after a short interval he stood up and turned. It was Paul. Thank God. The pounding in her heart eased significantly. She hurried down the stairs to greet him. Still pretending to be in ignorance of the true situation she smiled warmly at him.

'Hello Paul. You're back much earlier than usual?'

He looked startled to see Dee. His hopes of finding the cottage empty were dashed. He quickly recovered his composure and smiled back.

'I'm rather tired this evening, so I thought I'd have an early night. By the way,' he added, almost as an afterthought, 'I noticed the car's not outside. Has Jane gone out?'

'Yes,' replied Dee, carefully. 'She won't be long. I'm going to make a cup of tea. Would you like one?' she said, deliberately steering the conversation away from Jane and her absence.

In the kitchen Dee filled the kettle and switched it on.

'Where has she gone?' he shouted from the other room.

'Sorry, can't hear you. Just hold on a minute.'

While she made the tea Dee ran through all the questions she was likely to be asked and, satisfied with the answers she would give, picked up the tray and returned to the living room.

'Sit by the fire, Paul,' she said coaxingly. 'You're wet through.'

She handed him a cup and sat down in the chair opposite his, waiting for the questioning to commence.

'It's most unusual for Jane to go out at night. Has she gone anywhere special?'

'Yes, she has, as a matter of fact,' replied Dee evenly. 'Mr Green, the county archivist, telephoned earlier and asked her to pick up some research materials for the project she is working on.'

Paul stared at Dee as if she was mad.

'Project, what project? I've no idea what you're talking about,' he said, a hint of agitation creeping into his voice.

'I'm sorry. I thought you knew all about it. Surely Jane has mentioned it?' replied Dee casually.

'No, she hasn't. What's it all about?' he asked, trying to remain calm.

'Well, it's quite simple really,' said Dee, smiling at him. 'She's decided to write a book on the history of the valley and

Mr Green is supplying her with relevant material from the archives.'

'No. It's not true,' stammered Paul, his face turning ashen grey. 'I don't believe you. You're lying to me.'

For the first time since she had arrived, Dee saw the real Paul emerge from behind the mask he had worn to deceive her. His face became taut with repressed anger, his eyes narrowing to the merest slits. He reminded her of an eagle ready to pounce and tear its prey limb from limb.

'Paul, I'm not lying to you. I'm telling you the truth,' she said nervously.

The whole of Paul's body began to shake uncontrollably, his white knuckles clenched tightly in his lap. He didn't appear to have heard what she said. Instead he had become introverted and was fighting some sort of raging internal battle. The unintelligible spitting and hissing sounds that spewed out from between his bared teeth frightened Dee and she hurriedly vacated her chair.

The sudden movement made him look up at her.

'You lying bitch,' he said, deliberately rising from his chair. 'You're in this together, both of you intent on destroying me and everyone else in the village I shouldn't wonder. Well you made the biggest mistake of your life the day you decided to come and stay here.'

As Paul spoke, Dee was slowly backing away from him. She felt the bannister rail behind her and grabbed it for support. Paul moved towards her, his piercing eyes boring into her as he came closer and closer.

'Keep away from me,' she warned. 'I'm Dee, your friend. I've done nothing to harm you.'

He appeared to be in a trance. Her pleas went unheard. One more step would bring him too close for comfort. A hand swung out to grab her. She ducked and charged up the stairs. In her flight she could sense he was only one pace behind her. Having reached the landing she saw the bathroom directly ahead, the door slightly ajar. She hurled herself towards it, desperate for sanctuary behind its lockable door.

At that moment Paul grabbed her ankle and she went sprawling. As she fell her head hit the washbasin with a resounding crack. Stunned by the blow her body went limp. Paul took full advantage of this and dragged her back on to the landing.

Dee rallied almost immediately, adrenalin pumping through her veins as if her life depended on it.

With both hands fastened around her throat, Paul continuously battered her head on the floor. In her struggle to remain conscious, Dee felt something wet on her face. She stared up at him in terror. He slavered freely from the mouth like a rabid dog as he shouted at her, still demanding to know where his wife had gone. His thumbs pressed hard against her windpipe, making it impossible for her to speak.

In a last ditch attempt for freedom, Dee took a deep breath, tensed her muscles and thrust her feet into Paul's stomach. The force of the impact winded him and he let go of her throat. She rolled away from him as he doubled up, clutching himself.

Woken by the noisy scuffle outside her door, Emma began to cry. Dee ran into Jane' s bedroom in search of anything she could use to defend herself. A fraction of a second later Paul followed her, slamming the door closed behind him. Dee could hear the baby crying and rattling the bars of her cot.

'For God's sake, Paul. You've woken Emma,' she said.

He ignored her and advanced slowly. She backed away until the bed lay between them. He laughed mockingly at her. She was trapped, he knew it, she knew it. Her only means of escape stood firmly closed behind Paul. He edged around the bed. In panic she grasped the bedside lamp and hurled it at him. He ducked. It smashed into the dressing table mirror, the explosion showering thousands of tiny broken shards everywhere.

With out further hesitation, Paul pounced on her. Using one hand to pin her firmly against the wall, he curled the other into a tight fist and repeatedly smashed it into her face. He stopped to catch his breath and stared down at his bloodied hand. In his bewilderment he didn't know where the blood had come from. Dee, seeing the mesmerised expression on his face, realised the man was insane and not responsible for his action. Clearly, both she and Emma were in mortal danger from this maniac, no longer Paul, but a mechanical destruction machine. Her strength was failing while his increased as he rhythmically rained blows into her body. In one last attempt to evade him Dee kneed him in the groin and made a dive for the door. Paul's fingers grabbed the belt on her dress, causing her to twist awkwardly against him. She lost her balance and fell crashing to the floor and lost consciousness.

In the bedroom cross the landing Emma stood in her cot screaming hysterically. Paul glanced vaguely towards the door, then bent down to examine his victim. His hand felt bruised and sticky. He delved into his pocket for a handkerchief. Unable to find one, he used the edge of the counterpane. The screaming from the other room continued.

Wearily, he stood up, wiped his face on his sleeve and shuffled towards the noise. He looked back at Dee. She hadn't moved. Perplexed, he gazed down at the limp body of his wife's friend. Why was she lying on the floor? He couldn't remember. His mind a total blank, he shrugged his shoulders and left the room.

The crying from Emma's room irritated him. With robotic precision he grasped the door latch and walked in. Unable to see in the dark he groped for the wall switch and turned on the light. Although as yet too young to stand up, the baby had pulled herself upright with the aid of the bars. Her tiny fingers gripped the top rail as she clung on, screaming for all she was worth. The moment the light went on she stopped, blinking at the sudden brightness.

'Ssh. It's only Daddy,' he whispered, soothingly from the doorway. 'Now, what' all the noise for?'

He tiptoed softly towards the cot, smiling warmly at his daughter. 'Come on, let me tuck you up,' he said, gently easing her fingers away from the bars.

Emma stared hard into her father's face. She didn't return his smile or relax her tense muscles as he laid her beneath the warm blankets, but remained quite rigid and tightly sprung, ready to defend herself.

'Close your eyes, Emma and go to sleep,' he coaxed. Daddy will sit here with you for a little while.'

He sat down on Dee's bed and prepared to wait, observing the baby closely. Emma closed her eyes, feigning sleep and also waited. The cottage was so quiet you could have heard a pin drop.

After a few minutes Paul glanced at his watch. Time was getting on. He looked over at Emma. He saw the gentle rise and fall of her chest as she breathed evenly, apparently fast asleep.

'It's now or never,' he muttered under his breath. He inhaled deeply and stood up. Emma, listening intently, recognized the first warning signal. Paul approached the cot and bent over the bars. His shadow fell across Emma's face as his body blocked out the light overhead. The second signal. Her powers of extra sensory perception warned her of impending attack. She braced herself and waited until she could feel the shimmering warmth from his hands in close proximity to her body.

The moment arrived. Paul's fingers encircled Emma's throat, gently at first, then tightening as he applied pressure with his thumbs in an attempt to choke her to death.

In a flash she opened her eyes, catching Paul off-guard. An expression of horror crossed his face. He stared down into the twin pools of fathomless ebony liquid, mesmerized by the veiled mysteries concealed in their depths. Their eyes locked together and Paul experienced the same power transmission as before, during the last confrontation between them on the fateful day Jane brought Emma home from the hospital.

He increased the pressure on her throat, only to find his hands paralysed. At the same time, an attempt to avert his gaze from the searing bolts of electrical current proved futile. Totally transfixed and at her mercy, Emma held him in suspension, her own face covered in the salty liquid flowing freely from her father's tear ducts. In excruciating agony he writhed about, trying to protect his brain from the damage being inflicted by the electrical shock waves passing relentlessly through it. He felt several small explosions inside his head as numerous blood vessels erupted under the strain. His tears turned pink, then red. Paul gagged, watching helplessly as his life blood trickled, not only from his eyes, but also from his nose and mouth, spattering the baby and soaking into the cot sheets.

Emma took a deep breath and thrust her tiny clenched fists at her father. An immense power surge emanated from the tiny body, hurling him across the room. He smashed into the opposite wall and hit the floor like a ton weight, badly winded. The spell broke.

Paul lay in a crumpled heap, panting for breath. Emma hauled herself back to a standing position and waited. He glanced up to meet her piercing eyes, then looked away quickly.

Defeated, he staggered to his feet, avoiding her gaze and hobbled to the door. He knew, without doubt, that his left ankle was broken. Before he could grasp the latch, the door swung open and he collided with Dee. Paul blindly struck out at her, sending her reeling backwards, then threw himself down the stairs. At the bottom his ankle gave way and buckled under his weight. Dee heard him cry out in pain. Then she listened to the sound of furniture being overturned in his struggle to reach the door and the fury beyond.

CHAPTER 13

The wipers had little effect against the rain pounding on the windscreen. Jane flicked the switch to fast speed wipe and hunched herself over the steering wheel, straining to see the road ahead. Her journey to Hanslope was all the more difficult, the route being directly across country on unlit minor roads. At the next signpost she stopped the car and glanced briefly at the map spread over the passenger seat. Not far now, only another mile or so according to the atlas.

As the village loomed up ahead, she dipped her headlights and drove slowly along the main street. Unlike Ashingham village, Hanslope had the advantage of street lighting, making the Archivist's house quite easy to find at the end of an imposing terrace of fine three-storey Edwardian town houses. Peter Green, who had spotted Jane's car draw up outside, stood at the front door waiting to greet his guest.

'I would never have suggested that you drive over here had I known we were in for such a storm,' he said, ushering Jane into the hall and closing the front door. 'Please let me take your wet coat.'

'After all the trouble you've gone to on my behalf, I'd have come, no matter what,' she replied, smiling at him. 'It's very kind of you to invite me this evening, Mr Green.'

'Peter,' he insisted, warmly correcting her. 'Now, follow me.'

He led the way into the large, elegant front room. A tall, extremely attractive lady, with shoulder-length natural blonde hair, stood with her back to the fireplace, warming her legs.

'Sally, this is Mrs Richardson.'

His wife smiled pleasantly and stepped forward to shake Jane's hand.

'Hello Mrs Richardson. I'm pleased to meet you.'

A feeling of warmth radiated through Jane as she clasped the other woman's hand. She relaxed immediately and returned Sally's smile.

'Thank you for inviting me, and please call me Jane.'

'Why don't the two of you sit down and get started, while I make some coffee?' suggested Sally.

'Sounds fine,' replied Peter. Jane nodded in agreement.

'Right. I won't be long.'

She glided gracefully out of the room, leaving the two of them alone.

Peter guided Jane towards a deep wing chair, unholstered in rich ox-blood leather situated on one side of the fireplace and sat in one identical opposite. On a long highly polished mahogany coffee table between them lay a pile of reference books and pamphlets to be tackled during the evening.

'Looks formidable, doesn't it?' he said, grinning. 'But don't worry, I've leafed through them already and marked up the relevant sections.'

He leaned forward and selected a book from the top of the pile. 'Have you brought anything to take notes in?' he enquired.

'Yes,' she replied, extracting a large writing pad from her shoulder bag.

Jane studied the librarian as he deftly flipped through the ancient leather-bound volume. He had changed out of his tweedy working clothes and into a pair of casual corduroy trousers and a roll-necked sweater. She thought he blended in rather well with his surroundings, like a chameleon. The man obviously possessed the most excellent taste, and no expense had been spared in selecting the furnishings for this particular room, which to her mind created the perfect balance between homely comfort and refined luxury. She wondered how he could possibly afford it on his salary. Perhaps his wife had money?

The archivist cleared his throat and Jane returned her attention to the business in hand.

'Well,' he said, pushing back the stray forelock of hair which had fallen over his brow as he studied the text. 'The earliest records pertaining to the valley are somewhat patchy as you can imagine, but I've managed to trace back to William the Conqueror.' He leaned across the coffee table and handed Jane a photocopy taken from an ancient document.

'As a matter of interest, the original parchment scroll is still in the castle vault,' he explained.

She perused the document carefully. It stated that one, Philipe Dupont, General, was granted the Manor of Ashingham for allegiance and services rendered to the Duke of Normandy during the Conquest of Britain. Witnessed by a dozen hands and bearing the King's Seal, it was dated 10th July, 1068. Jane glanced across at Peter and he handed her the book containing a marked text. It confirmed the facts laid down in the deed and went on to mention a further accolade that was bestowed on the family a short time afterwards when Philipe received a Knighthood and became the first Baronet Ashingham.

As she read on she learned that the original estate boundaries stretched across twenty miles of rolling countryside from the West Coast to the County of Yorkshire, but had shrunk considerably over the centuries to pay off enormous gambling debts, a penchant which appeared to be almost hereditary within the family, until by the late eighteen hundreds only the valley and the castle itself bore witness to the royal bequest.

Jane closed the book, deep in thought as she imagined what life must have been like in medieval times when the Ashingham estate prospered and everything visible to the eye in all directions from the castle ramparts belonged to the Lord of the Manor. A movement broke her fantasy. Sally entered the room carrying a tray of coffee and sandwiches. Her husband hurriedly cleared a space for her to set it down on the low table, moving several piles of books to the floor by his chair.

'This is very kind of you,' said Jane, smiling warmly at her hostess.

'It's my pleasure,' Sally replied as she sat down on the fine leather chesterfield that completed the sumptuous three-piece suite. 'In fact I'm very interested in local history myself, so this evening will be of immense value for me as well.'

'Sally lectures in history at the university,' announced Peter proudly as he passed around the plate of neatly cut sandwiches.

'Are you researching a book by any chance, Jane?' she enquired.

Jane smiled, carefully formulating her reply before speaking. 'No, not exactly. I'd say it's more of a research project for my own personal use really. But I will admit that if I find what I'm looking for, it may well end up as a book. It just depends.'

'What are you looking for?' Peter asked, fascinated by her reply.

'To be perfectly honest I'm not sure at present, but the moment we uncover it, I'll recognise it.'

'Sounds most intriguing,' Sally chuckled. 'Have you lived in Ashingham very long?'

'No, only a matter of months. My husband Paul has recently taken a job in Prestbury and we've moved up here from London.'

'In that case you must find village life very different to the never ending bustle you've been used to. How are you coping with the change?'

'It's difficult to make a true comparison. You see, I've just had a baby, so I'm adjusting to a new role as a housewife and mother in the country, whereas in London I had a full-time job.'

Peter glanced at Jane's empty cup.

'More coffee?' he asked.

'Yes please,' she replied. 'Do you know Ashingham at all, Peter?'

'Not really. Sally and I have only lived in the North-West for about a year. We both originate from the West Country.'

Lifting his eyes to the ceiling he thought for a minute.

'The only time I had cause to visit Ashingham was when I called at the castle on my way home one evening to pick up the archives about six months ago.'

Jane perked up immediately. 'Did you meet Sir Francis?'

'Yes, or rather what was left of him.'

'I beg your pardon?' she said, somewhat startled by his strange remark.

Sally interrupted at this point. She turned to face Jane, her expression sombre.

'When Peter arrived home that night he looked as if he'd seen a ghost.'

Peter confirmed this statement with a nod.

'Yes, it's true,' he said sadly. 'The baronet was confined to a wheelchair, a very sick man and obviously dying from a wasting disease according to his housekeeper. Sir Francis made it very clear to me that his decision to transfer the archives had not been taken lightly. The deciding factor lay in the harsh reality that he was the last of the family line and afraid the Ashingham papers would fall into the wrong hands on his death. His parting words to me were to guard them with my life.'

'Rather a strange thing to say, don't you think?' Jane commented, looking questioningly at Peter.

'Yes, I thought it most odd myself at the time.'

'Right,' said Sally standing up. 'If everyone has finished, I'll clear away.'

She gathered together the dirty crockery, heaped it on to the tray and headed for the kitchen.

'Would you like any help?' Jane volunteered.

'No, I'm fine. Carry on without me. I won't be long.'

Peter replaced the books he had moved back on to the table while Jane busily made notes on the information they had assimilated so far.

'When you've finished, I'd like to take a look at this chapter,' said Peter, slipping across the table towards her a slim, dark blue leather-bound book. 'It's a reasonably concise account of events on the estate until the outbreak of the Civil War.'

Jane reached across and picked it up, audibly admiring the exquisite gold tooling on the cover as she settled back in her chair.

Although the subject matter contained within the book covered the history of the County as a whole, one chapter dealt solely with the affairs of Ashingham itself. It gave an explicit, if rather boring, everyday account of the feudal system operational during this period, describing at length the typical three-field agricultural rotation commonplace throughout Britain. Generally speaking, it seemed that nothing worthy of note had occurred between the setting up of the Estate and the onslaught of the Civil War which ultimately rocked the foundations of every landed family, and indeed every ordinary household, the length and breadth of the country.

The original fortified manor house, perched high on its cliff top, and replaced in the twelfth century by the present gloomy and formidable castle, represented the nucleus, the focal point on which the entire estate hinged. Everything contained within its boundaries belonged to the feudal lord. The villagers, or serfs, as they were more usually known, worked the land in return for a roof over their heads and a few meagre strips of ground on which they struggled to produce enough food to feed their families.

However, in times of trouble, the men ceased to be labourers and instead became soldiers, duty bound to answer any call-to-arms from their lord, or in the case of national emergency, their king and country.

Turning the page, Jane came across a transcription taken from part of an old map of the area. She saw at a glance that very little had altered in the valley over the centuries. The fields on the old map were fewer and larger, and, of course, the present cotton mill was missing, although she did notice a small grain mill clearly marked on the same site. There was no sign of Heronsford or Half Acre Farm either, the land occupied by the present farm buildings being divided into open strips for the peasants' own personal use. But apart from these differences, everything else appeared to be much the same as present day, even down to the number of cottages, indicating a stable equilibrium in the population.

Jane closed the book and placed it on top of the volume she had previously looked at.

'Finished?' enquired the librarian.

She nodded.

'Good,' he replied. 'Now, while you've been acquainting yourself with the general set up, I've ploughed my way through the years immediately preceding the Civil War.'

At this point, Sally quietly slipped back into the room and re-joined them both.

'Anything interesting happened while I've been away?' she laughed.

'Well, I think you've arrived in the nick of time, as a matter of fact. From 1600 onwards, several significant events are recorded in the archives.'

He glanced across at Jane.

'You'll need your notebook at the ready.'

'Oh. For heaven's sake, come on, Peter,' his wife said. 'You're keeping us in suspense.'

He grinned at her, a mischievous smile curling around the edges of his mouth. Sally broke into peals of laughter at his impish expression and their eyes met and locked together in mutual love and affection. Jane felt a lump forming in her throat as she reflected on her own marital relationship. In the past similar endearing moments had passed between Paul and herself. But those times were long gone, leaving only the memories.

'Right, to business,' said Peter, aware of Jane's embarrassment. He began to quote verbatim from the text in front of him.

'In April 1602 a number of women from within the county arrived at Ashingham Castle under heavy guard and were subsequently held in the dungeons awaiting trial on charges of witchcraft.' He looked up to ascertain the general reaction to his statement and saw, to his satisfaction, two pairs of eyes regarding him intently, silently urging him to continue. Jane sat on the very edge of her chair, the hand holding her pen, poised in mid-air as if uncertainty prevented her committing pen to paper. He coughed to break the illusion. Both women jumped slightly, then relaxed and laughed at their nervousness.

He continued.

'The trial, held later in the year, received tremendous publicity and people flocked from every town and village to witness the proceedings.'

Peter stopped reading and glanced across at Jane, who this time was busily scribbling notes. She looked up to meet his gaze. 'You see,' he explained. 'This county was renowned for the practice of witchcraft. In fact, even today it is still flourishing in the more remote areas. At that particular time, however, public feeling regarding the black arts ran high, the common people living in constant fear of witches' curses and the like. Whether the accused women actually practised magic or were merely dotty old crones mattered little, just the fact that charges of witchcraft had been brought against them was enough to seal their destinies.'

He resumed quoting from the text.

'The prisoners, closely manacled together, were brought before the court, charged and duly found guilty of their heinous crimes, no defence being submitted on their behalf. The judge passed sentence, condemning them all to be burnt at the stake within the confines of the castle. News of the death penalty was publicly broadcast to the masses waiting patiently outside the walls, who rejoiced at justice having been seen to be done. Celebrations and feasting followed and continued for a full seven days, only pausing briefly to enable the crowds to watch the executions carried out on the fifth day.'

Peter closed the book and added it to the ever-growing pile. While her husband had been reading aloud, Sally had spent several minutes studying Jane, her intuitive mind quite unable to accept at face value the reasons for the research, and she felt quite sure there was far more to the woman opposite her than initially met the eye. Suddenly she became aware that both Peter and Jane were staring at her.

'Shall I make some more coffee, or would you rather wait until later?' she asked her husband.

He glanced at the clock and then over to Jane.

'I think we'd better press on for a bit longer. What do you think, Jane?'

She nodded. 'Yes, it's getting rather late.'

Peter fished out yet another ancient tome.

'This book covers the Civil War in the County, and once again Ashingham has been considered important enough to warrant a whole chapter, which makes our research much easier.'

Somewhere in the house a telephone rang. Sally got up and left the room, closing the door behind her. Jane selected a clean sheet on her note pad while she waited for Peter to begin.

'It's for you, dear,' called Sally.

'I think perhaps you had better make a start on this chapter yourself,' he suggested to Jane as he strode across the room.

She picked up the book and submerged herself in the gripping narrative as if she were a part of the drama, witnessing at first hand the frenzied activities of the villagers as they prepared for battle in the face of such grim and overwhelming opposition.

The Ashingham family, staunchly loyalist, had fought many campaigns throughout the country, as well as returning periodically to defend their own castle and estates. Royalist victories, however, were few and far between, the King's army weary and depleted, marching from battle to battle, for the most part on foot, with no rest and little food. Already two of Ashingham's sons, Walter and Richard, had perished at the hands of the Parliamentarians, total collapse lay on the horizon and it was only a matter of time before Cromwell seized power.

Sir Francis Ashingham knew the time had arrived to return home for the last time to defend his own castle. Several earlier assaults on Ashingham had constituted little more than minor skirmishes, easily dealt with by his own soldiers. But Sir Francis acknowledged, in the depths of his heart, that the next attack would be the last, even though he was determined to defend his own stronghold down to the last man.

The defence strategy, employed in the past so successfully, remained unchanged. When under siege it was common practice to send a company of troops down a secret tunnel, leading from within the castle itself as far as the river bank in the valley below. The soldiers would emerge into the open behind the enemy lines, effectively cutting off any means of retreat for the attacking army. The plan always achieved its aim, and, as yet, no-one outside the valley knew of the tunnel's existence.

The estate prepared for attack. The harvest was reaped in haste, women and children assisting the men in the arduous task of loading up wagons with corn and wheat ready to be taken and stored in the large granaries inside the castle. Next all the livestock was rounded up and herded into temporary pens, hurriedly erected outside the perimeter walls, near enough to be moved into the outer bailey at a moment's notice.

After only two weeks, the preparations were complete and Ashingham Castle, with enough munitions and food supplies to withstand a lengthy siege, grimly towered above the surrounding countryside and awaited the arrival of the enemy. With little time left, the villagers returned to their cottages to pack up their own goods and chattels, many of them burying anything of value deep in the ground. In only a matter of hours, reports reached Sir Francis of a large army one day's march away to the south. Immediately a messenger was despatched to alert the village. All movable possessions were hastily piled on to hand carts and the entire population trundled back along the road to the castle and the sanctuary provided within its walls.

On arrival, the enemy forces camped in the valley basin between the river and the castle, much to the delight of the baronet. For the rest of the day, the soldiers patrolling the battlements, passively surveyed the activity below, as officers-in-charge organised troops, horses and artillery.

Darkness fell. Inside the castle Sir Francis held a final consultation with his troops in an atmosphere of hushed optimism, the assembled company firm in their belief that good must ultimately prevail over evil. Even inside the great hall as the men stood to receive the last orders for battle, they could hear the bawdy drunkenness from the enemy camp wafting over the ramparts in the balmy night air. The castle retired to bed early, leaving the Roundheads to celebrate into the early hours.

The initial bombardment commenced at dawn and continued solidly throughout the day. Sir Francis made several appearances on the battlements to assess the situation and speak to his commanding officers. That night, in conference, it was agreed to put the well-tried plan into operation on the following day, the baronet not wishing to become entrenched in a position of siege for any longer than necessary.

Dawn the following day heralded the revival of the assault. After only a few hours, reports reached Sir Francis of considerable damage to the north tower. Deciding the time had come to implement his plan of campaign, he gave the order to open the valley tunnel. Within minutes a handpicked detachment of soldiers were making the journey along the dark, evil-smelling passage, passing under the enemy lines and on towards the river bank.

Then disaster struck. After toiling for over a mile along the tunnel, only three feet high in some places, which meant crawling on hands and knees in several inches of stagnant water with their muskets and flaming torches held aloft for safety, they reached an impenetrable barrier. To their horror, they found that the entrance had been sealed up with several large stone boulders. Unable to proceed further, the soldiers had no alternative but to return to the castle with all speed to report that the enemy had discovered the tunnel and, no doubt the mission they were engaged upon.

However, while the special detachment were occupied below ground, events on the surface had progressed dramatically in favour of the parliamentary forces. The continuous artillery bombardment had at last succeeded in demolishing part of the north wall and the enemy were pouring into the outer bailey under covering fire from their own cannon.

Inside the castle the hand-to-hand fighting escalated as the Royalists vainly struggled to defend their positions against the ever-increasing number of Roundhead soldiers entering the breach. Hopelessly outnumbered, they fought on until they found themselves completely surrounded, the ground littered with the bodies of wounded and dying men. The day lost, Sir Francis surrendered the castle on behalf of the King to General Fairfax and the hostilities ceased.

During the heavy fighting inside the castle, a small reconnoitring party sought out the entrance to the secret tunnel, whereupon it was hastily sealed up, condemning its imprisoned occupants to a long and painful death by starvation.

Jane had become so absorbed in the text, she didn't notice Peter come back into the room. Only Sally's entrance with another tray of coffee interrupted her concentration enough to draw her attention away from the riveting account.

'Nearly finished?' Peter asked.

'Just one more paragraph,' Jane replied, returning to the text.

Under arrest, Sir Francis was taken to London to await trial. Ashingham Castle was garrisoned by a contingent of Parliamentary troops for the remainder of the war, whereupon the soldiers disbanded, many of them drifting into the village, marrying the widows and daughters of the dead men, whose bodies lay rotting in the underground tunnel. The country restored to peace, Ashingham village settled down to its former sleepy existence.

Jane picked up her coffee cup and sank back into the comfortable armchair.

'Those poor men. What a horrible way to die,' she said with a prolonged sigh.

'It's no worse than the fate of prisoners-of-war throughout history, Jane,' said Peter, reflectively. 'You only have to look back thirty years or so to World War II for atrocities, and even less if you think about Vietnam.'

'Yes, you're quite right,' she agreed.

Her eyes strayed up towards the clock. It was already five past ten. Peter followed her gaze.

'It will take about half an hour to finish this lot. Do you want to continue?'

Jane nodded. 'Yes, if it's OK with you?'

He picked up another book, opened it and scanned several pages. 'Apart from the restoration of the estate to the family during the reign of Charles II, there's nothing of historical importance relating to Ashingham until the Industrial Revolution,' he said. 'Most of the landed gentry abhorred the whole idea of trade and

172

industry, the wealthiest refusing to acknowledge its existence at all, unless they reaped any personal gain with which to extend their already immense fortunes. Sir William Ashingham, however, welcomed this new era with open arms. The estate was struggling for survival as the family fortune dwindled away in the face of ever-increasing gambling debts. Every surplus acre had been sold off, leaving only the castle and valley intact.

The baronet carefully observed the growth of a flourishing textile industry within the county and, realising the potential of the natural resources upon his own estate, sold the valley to the highest bidder, thereby saving himself from financial ruin.

The new owner, a Mr. Edwin Arkwright from Manchester, immediately set about redeveloping his newly acquired land for maximum efficiency. At the far end of the valley he constructed a weir to increase the flow of the river and cut a channel out of the back at the base of the fall to create a mill race across the valley floor. This led directly to the wheel of the new textile mill situated at the far end of the village, the surplus water draining into a pond and back into the main stream again by means of a narrow gully. As far as the rest of the village was concerned, Mr Arkwright made very few changes. The original daub and wattle huts had been replaced by sturdy stone-built cottages soon after the Civil War, and for the most part, remained solid and in good repair, requiring no alterations. Only a pair of dilapidated dwellings at the foot of the hill needed to be restored, and these he had converted into a general shop for the use of the community.

The outlying fields were divided into two separate lots together with their existing buildings, the respective freeholds being purchased as farms by the Briggs and Grimshaw families, the wealthiest members of the community. The cottagers shed their agricultural traditions to become mill workers. The newly opened village store and the produce from the two farms supplied all the provisions necessary to sustain the inhabitants, and with trade booming, the valley virtually self-sufficient, the village settled happily into its new lifestyle. Mr Arkwright prospered, farmers Grimshaw and Briggs prospered, and Ashingham prospered.'

Peter closed the book and looked across at the two women.

'All that's left now are newspaper cuttings to bring the archive up to date.'

He exchanged the book for a buff folder from which he selected a couple of clippings.

'According to the Prestbury Chronicle, the last member of the Arkwright family died in 1972 leaving no heir, and the present Briggs and Grimshaw families raised enough capital to buy the valley from the mill estate.'

'Yes, I already know that,' said Jane. 'Funnily enough, however, Ivy Cottage, the house my husband and I bought recently, somehow slipped through the net.'

Sally looked up abruptly at this snippet of information, but her husband just smiled and continued to the next cutting.

'Finally, as you already know, Sir Francis Ashingham, last of his own line, still lives up at the castle, in complete isolation.'

He sat back, obviously exhausted, but at the same time extremely pleased with the amount of research completed during the evening.

'I read somewhere that one of the local societies intended to restore the old mill and turn it into a museum,' said Sally. 'Has anything happened yet?'

'Yes,' replied Jane. 'A short time ago a local firm carried out a survey on the building, but the results showed the structure to be in a dangerous condition and commended it be demolished.'

'What is the employment situation in the valley now that the mill has closed down?' asked Peter.

'Well, you could say events have turned full circle,' Jane said.

'Everyone in the village works for Arthur Briggs or Bert Grimshaw apart from my husband Paul.'

Before Sally could ask any more personal questions, Jane glanced at the clock and stood up.

'Good gracious. Is that the time? I really must be going.'

Peter hurried out into the hallway to fetch her coat.

'Thank you for all the work you have done. I really am most grateful,' she said, shaking hands with both Peter and Sally at the front door.

Outside the rain still swept down the street in torrents.

'By the way. Have you found what you are looking for?' asked Peter.

'Partly,' Jane replied. 'But my intuition tells me to dig even deeper, if that's possible.'

'Well, good luck,' said Sally. 'And do be careful, won't you?' she added warily.

'I'll try. Thanks for a lovely evening.'

She turned and ran quickly towards the car.

Sally Green carried the tray of dirty cups into the kitchen. She wondered what Jane was searching for. Several times during the evening she had noticed the tension on the girl's face, the taut lines furrowing her brow, the delicate hand gripping the pen just a little more tightly than normal. And why did she need the information so quickly? Was Jane in some kind of danger?

Sally decided to telephone her friend Claire first thing in the morning before leaving for the university. Claire would know what to do.

CHAPTER 14

Paul stood outside the cottage for several minutes, his brain reeling in a mixture of pain, shock and terror. He clung to the front gate for support, the full weight of his body balanced on one leg. The driving rain bit into his face and water droplets freely trickled from his matted hair on to the already saturated clothes he wore.

In truth, the fact that he was wet through and shivering uncontrollably didn't seem to bother him unduly. What did bother him, however, was the total failure of his assignment. He concentrated hard, trying to recall what had happened, and, more to the point, what had gone wrong. Paul remembered seeing Dee slumped on the bedroom floor, and yet, somehow she had managed to confront him minutes later in Emma's room. Obviously he had bungled the whole thing. He should have checked to make sure she was dead, instead of just assuming it. The cock-up rested fairly and squarely on his shoulders, he had no excuse. None whatsoever.

On the other hand, Emma was a different matter altogether. His confrontation with the baby now confirmed his worst fears. His daughter possessed supernatural powers against which he was unable to defend himself, let alone seek to harm her in any way. Emma not only had the ability to indefinitely immobilize people but also sufficient power to kill. Although outwardly she appeared to be a normal, healthy child, the tiny body concealed a deadly powerhouse capable of generating sufficient electrical energy to destroy anything. In addition, her natural gift of extra sensory perception rendered his position hopeless. As far as Paul was aware, no-one in the village had any conception of his daughter's far-reaching mystical talents, but he wondered how much longer this ignorance could possibly last.

He looked down at his badly swollen ankle. If he didn't remove his shoe soon, it would never come off. The continual throbbing made him feel sick and the blood he had swallowed earlier on, refusing to mix with the rest of the contents of his stomach repeatedly surged up into his throat.

Despite these painful injuries, Paul couldn't help but chuckle to himself as he opened the gate and hobbled across the road to the pub. Let Arthur get some other village idiot to carry out his dirty work. Nobody stood a cat's chance in hell against Emma, but the attempt would be worth watching. He chuckled again, with more confidence this time. If any man thinks he can do better, then give him the chance, he thought. With that, he pushed open the door and stumbled inside.

A deathly hush descended over the crowded room. Two dozen pairs of eyes were solidly fixed upon Paul. Nobody moved. Wide-eyed with disbelief the villagers gazed at the dishevelled figure hovering in the doorway. The harsh strip-lighting highlighted the livid purple bruising on his face, caused by the eruption of numerous capillaries beneath the skin's surface. The man's eyes, gorged with blood, stared blindly at the shadowy outlines wavering in front of him. At first they failed to recognize him. Then a shout went up.

'It's Paul Richardson. Call Arthur, he's somewhere out the back.'

'Get out of my way,' shouted Terry Smith, as he marched across the bar, shoving aside the gawping onlookers barring his path. 'Will someone fetch a chair for the lad to sit on, for Christ's sake? Reuben, get a bowl of hot water.'

'What seems to be the problem, Terry?' enquired Arthur irritably, pushing his way through the melee.

'It's Paul Richardson. Looks as if he's met with some kind of accident.'

Reuben returned, armed with a steaming bowl of water and a sponge, whereupon he attempted to clean up Paul's battered face.

Although inwardly shocked by the mutilated and crippled human being slumped in the chair, Arthur's expression hardened the moment the young man painfully lifted up his head to peer blindly at him.

'Well?' demanded the farmer, bluntly, without making any reference to Paul's appearance.

Paul shook his head lamely and remained silent.

'I might have known,' sneered Arthur, sarcastically. 'Haven't you got anything to say?'

Paul nodded. 'I tried, Arthur. Honestly I really did my best.'

'And failed miserably, as always,' replied the farmer, finishing the sentence for him.

Paul hung his head in defeat. What could he say? If he told them the truth they wouldn't believe him. It really didn't matter to him anymore. From now on his family was their problem, to be dealt with in any way they thought fit, and as far as he was concerned, they were welcome to it.

He sank back into the chair and succumbed to the convulsive shafts of pain which racked him from head to toe. Every bone in his body ached and the intense throbbing in his temples made him giddy and nauseous. He tried to concentrate on the indistinct murmurings around him, but found it impossible to decipher clearly what was being discussed.

Suddenly it dawned on Paul that his injuries might well be more extensive than he had at first anticipated. He wondered whether the blood from the shattered vessels in his skull had caused permanent damage to any vital organs. He looked straight ahead, straining to hear and see clearly, and found, to his alarm that the earlier blindness he had experienced had not improved at all and that his hearing was incredibly fuzzy, as if his ears were jammed full of cotton wool. Paul's imagination began to run riot, conjuring up all sorts of crippling disabilities. The suggestion of brain damage and its appalling implications flashed through his mind. He shuddered, suddenly feeling very cold and insecure. What did the future hold in store for him? Had fate decreed that he pass the remainder of his life as a vegetable? Never before had Paul experienced such fear and loneliness. He stared up at the obscure figures towering above him, silently hoping for a miracle, to wake up from this nightmare of a dream. He heard a sudden clamouring, followed by an appeal by Arthur for order to be restored.

Arthur Briggs turned away from his audience and addressed Paul. 'From the very first moment your wretched family moved into Ivy Cottage, everyday life in this peaceful village has been constantly disrupted. For generations, the inhabitants of Ashingham have succeeded in living and working together in friendship and harmony following a few simple guidelines laid down by our forebears for the general benefit of the community. Yet despite all the guidance we have offered, to enable you to slot easily into our fraternity, your household, like a putrid festering sore, continues to undermine everything we believe in. Such an embarrassment cannot be tolerated any longer, and to this end, we intend to relieve you of the burden of your wife and child and remedy the situation ourselves. As for yourself, we have agreed unanimously that you are to be considered persona non grata and expelled from the village.'

Paul opened his mouth to speak, but Arthur slapped him down. 'I order you to leave Ashingham immediately and take nothing with you. Is that understood?'

Paul nodded.

'Don't ever try to return. Your life is at stake if you do.' Arthur gestured towards John Mallen and Daniel Booth, two of the burliest men standing close by.

'Get this miserable little person out of my sight.'

Paul felt himself hauled out of the chair and dragged across the floor towards the door. Seconds later he was outside, lying face down in the gutter.

The driving rain beat down on his back, soaking through his damp clothes in seconds. He raised his head weakly and glanced at Ivy Cottage, his home, unaware that Arthur's two lackeys stood silently in the shelter of the 'Castle Arms' porch waiting for him to pick himself up and depart.

'Don't even think about it,' shouted John Mallen in an acidic tone. The other man laughed mockingly.

'Come on, damn you. Get up and bugger off. We're wasting precious drinking time standing about out here.'

With some difficulty, Paul heaved himself into an upright position, his total bodyweight balanced precariously on his one good leg. He half turned to look at the two men, then hobbled slowly away into the enveloping blackness.

Jane switched on the interior light inside the car and glanced quickly at her watch. The return journey to Ashingham was taking much longer than she would have liked, but the road conditions had worsened considerably during the last couple of hours. She saw little point in stopping, the rain had no intention of abating and it was nearly midnight. Another blanket of water completely doused the car as one of the front wheels hit another large puddle, blinding her vision for several seconds. Easing her foot slightly off the accelerator, Jane reduced her speed to a steady thirty miles an hour and ploughed on, avoiding the occasional potholes as best she could. Luckily she encountered no other traffic on her route along the winding country lanes, flanked for the most part by deep unfenced ditches, a motoring hazard for drivers even in the best of weather.

The night sky spread its sombre funereal cloak across the heavens, a barrier too awesome for either moon or stars to dare penetrate. Only the glare from the car headlights cut into the blackness, illuminating the way ahead, and fleetingly silhouetting both the dense undergrowth beyond the ditches and the tall slim trunks of the pines in the woodlands on either side of her. The trees thrashed violently in the gusting wind and the debris strewn across the road clearly emphasized the violence of the storm directly overhead.

Swerving to bypass another pool of water, Jane ran over a large branch and the car went into a skid, careering sideways along the slippery verge for about twenty yards until she managed to regain control of the steering. The shock of the ordeal agitated her sufficiently to brake to an abrupt halt in order to calm herself.

The atmosphere inside the car was becoming oppressive and Jane began to feel claustrophobic, imprisoned in such a confined space. She rubbed her clammy hands on a duster she found in the glove compartment and set about wiping the condensation off the inside of the windscreen. A sense of vulnerability crept through her bones as another squall attacked the car, rocking it from side to side. Instinctively she pressed the central locking device to insulate herself from the hostile elements outside and switched on the ignition. The noise from the engine muffled the general cacophony and, as the car picked up speed, Jane concentrated on getting home as quickly as possible.

Ten minutes later the headlights picked up the sign for Boundary Road and, with relief, Jane turned left and drove towards the steep hill leading down into Ashingham village.

The main street appeared to be deserted and the absence of any light from the cottages clearly indicated that everyone had retired to bed for the night. As she glided past Ivy Cottage to use the turning circle at the end of the road, Jane noticed a stationary vehicle parked by the footbridge. The heavy rain and murky blackness made it impossible to identify the car with its blazing headlights projecting a dazzling semi-circular glare of white light which cut through her windscreen and temporarily blinded her. She wondered what on earth anyone could be doing parked up by the bridge at such a late hour. Perhaps the driver had lost his way in the bad weather? Her curiosity aroused, Jane pulled up alongside the shadowy vehicle and opened her window to enquire if anything was wrong, and if so, whether she could help.

In a flash, before she was able to say anything, a hand grabbed her by the throat, catching her completely off guard. Jane's first instinct was to scream, but her assailant's grip tightened like a vice, squeezing and squeezing until the level of asphyxiation produced dancing lights in front of her eyes. In the ensuing struggle, Jane latched on to her attacker's wrist and grappled feverishly to wrench it away from her neck, but the more she strained, the more the powerful digits embedded themselves into her throat, cutting off her vital oxygen supply. She lay pinned hard against the seat, totally immobilised and unable to see the face of her aggressor, but from the strength of the grip and the abundance of hair on both the arm and hand she knew that her adversary was undoubtedly male. Excruciating ripples of pain flooded through her ribcage as she gasped for air and her temples pounded as the blood supply to her brain became severely constricted. A few moments later the stranglehold shifted slightly and a head appeared through the open window.

It wasn't difficult to recognise the ugly face of Arthur Briggs, even in the murky light. Their eyes met and locked together in a mutual hatred so acidic and inflammable, the intensity of the moment unnerved Arthur sufficiently to blink hard to clear his vision. He struggled to open Jane's door with his free hand but found it securely locked, as were the other three. The farmer inwardly cursed. He needed to gain access in order to finish her off quietly and not disturb the whole village.

'Release the door catch,' he hissed.

Jane stretched across towards the lever only to find it out of reach. Arthur's foul breath wafted into her face and she wrinkled up her nose in disgust at the smell of beer and tobacco. She gesticulated her helplessness to obey the order. He exhaled loudly, clearly irritated and grudgingly withdrew the hand pinning her down.

Jane was shrewd enough to realise that this was the time to act, if indeed she had any intention of escaping. She feigned an erratic fit of choking to give herself a breathing space. Arthur backed away as she jerked forwards with each raucous cough. While he waited, she slid her right hand across her lap, down the side of the seat and across to the door. Within seconds Jane had the window winder firmly in her grasp. Still coughing over the steering wheel, she began to close the window, sliding it upwards, gently and silently.

'Unlock the bloody door, damn you,' he snarled, reaching for the lever himself.

With her left hand, Jane grabbed Arthur by the hair and rammed his head against the steering column, jamming it neatly between the wheel and the dashboard, whilst at the same time she continued to wind up the window. Suddenly Arthur felt the top of the glass digging into his armpit and twigged what was happening. Just in the nick of time he wrenched his head free from her grasp and out of the small gap still open. Unfortunately, however, he failed to extricate the whole of his arm in time, his wrist caught between the glass and the metal frame as she finally closed the gap, her hand firmly anchored on the winder.

In all this time her car engine continued to tick over at a steady rate, neither of them having thought to switch it off.

Realising she had the upper hand she took full advantage of the situation by engaging the clutch, whipping the car into reverse and rolling away from the other vehicle. Arthur let out an agonising scream as he felt his arm pulled taut. In the next instant they both heard the snap as his wristbone cracked under stress followed by a tearing sound as the joint separated from its muscles and tendons. The farmer's cries reverberated around the valley only to be obliterated by the pounding torrential rain. No-one came to Arthur's aid because no-one, apart from Jane, could hear him. The villagers, asleep in their beds, safely tucked behind the thick stone walls of their cottages, slumbered on, completely oblivious, both to the storm and Arthur's predicament.

Jane gazed up at the grotesque protruding hand. Drained of blood, it dangled pathetically in space like a piece of blubbery tripe. The mere sight of it revolted her. Even in its lifeless state it was much too close for comfort as far as she was concerned. The fact it was in her car, invading her privacy, she found threatening and intolerable. But to remove the hand meant touching it. She shivered as an army of goose pimples crept over her flesh. A rapid glance around the interior of the car revealed nothing suitable she could use to remove the offending object.

'Damn,' Jane muttered to herself, although in reality she knew only too well she had no alternative but to physically eject it.

Easing the pressure slightly on the winder, she reached up and latched on to the solid forefinger with its pointed clawlike nail. It felt as cold as marble to the touch. The unpleasant sensation made her wince in disgust, and without further hesitation she rammed it through the narrow opening and reversed at speed along the deserted village street until she reached Ivy Cottage. With one eye firmly fixed on the other car, Jane fumbled in her handbag for her house keys, totally prepared to make a dash for safety, but Arthur made no attempt to pursue his victim. In the full beam of her car headlights, she watched him stagger from his vehicle and totter uncertainly across the footbridge towards Heronsford Farm.

For the first time since her arrival in Ashingham, Jane looked upon Ivy Cottage as a welcome refuge, a bolthole in which to recover and find her feet again. She ignored the cold murky gloom inside the living room, just grateful to be safely back in her own home. The untended fire had dwindled away to a pile of glowing ashes. Jane placed another log in the grate and sauntered into the kitchen in search of a glass. She needed a drink and a chance to unwind for a while before going upstairs to bed.

A sudden rustling sound from behind made her spin round nervously. Dee stood, framed in the doorway, brandishing above her head the heavy brass-knobbed poker, usually to be found by the living room hearth. Ashen faced and dishevelled, the girl clutched the deadly weapon with such grim determination that Jane froze automatically, fearful that any sudden move on her part might trigger off a spontaneous reaction from her friend. Instead, she waited for Dee to adjust her defensive train of thought to the realisation that the person she was about to attack was not an intruder. At last waves of recognition flooded into the girl's mind and the taut expression on her face softened.

'For Christ's sake, Dee,' said Jane as her friend lowered her arm. 'You scared me to death, creeping up like that. What on earth has happened? You look dreadful.'

'Oh Jane, thank God it's you. I thought it might be Paul coming back.'

Dee swayed unsteadily, her knees buckling and Jane grabbed her just in time to prevent her collapsing on to the stone floor. As she helped her to regain her balance the harsh lighting in the kitchen shone directly onto Dee's face, highlighting the livid bruising around her temples and the bloody abrasions covering her nose and mouth.

Jane gently guided her friend into the living room and sat her down in one of the large armchairs.

'Here, drink this,' she said, pushing the drink she had poured for herself into Dee's hand, whilst easing the poker away from her and returning it to its rightful place. 'You'll feel better in a little while.'

Jane returned to the kitchen to fetch another glass, stopping on the way to pick up an overturned chair. She wondered why she hadn't noticed it before. A sudden impulse made her turn round to cast an eye over the room. Dee followed her gaze.

'It's worse than this upstairs,' she said seriously.

Jane walked back to the fireside and sank into a vacant chair opposite Dee. 'Tell me what happened?'

Dee toyed with the glass in her hand, thoughtfully studying its contents, then she raised her head slowly and looked straight into her friend's eyes.

'Paul tried to murder Emma and myself.'

For several seconds Dee's statement failed to register. The words appeared to float over Jane's head, her brain refusing them access.

'What?' she gasped.

'Paul came home much earlier than usual this evening, saw the car was missing and demanded to know where you had gone. When I told him, he accused me of lying and ran amok.'

'Emma,' shrieked Jane, the realisation of Dee's announcement finally sinking in. She rose abruptly from her chair in panic, intent on dashing upstairs.

Dee stretched out an arm to intercept her.

'Don't worry. Emma is quite safe, unharmed and fast asleep in her cot.'

'Where is Paul?' Jane demanded.

'He's gone, but I don't know where to.'

In a flash, Jane was on her feet, moving briskly around the cottage as she checked that all the windows were securely fastened.

'You don't think he'll come back and try again, do you?' asked Dee nervously following Jane's movements.

'He won't get back into this house as long as I am alive to defend it,' she replied vehemently, the memory of her own earlier encounter with Arthur Briggs flashing through her mind as she slipped the iron bolts firmly into place on both the front and back doors. In view of the attack upon Dee and Emma and the sustained shock her friend was suffering, Jane decided not to mention her own problems. But the fact that attempts had been made this evening to murder all three of them made her blood run cold. The idea of coincidence she firmly dismissed as rubbish. The attacks had been planned, and although to date unsuccessful, she was in no doubt that they would be repeated.

At last satisfied that the cottage was impregnable, Jane returned to her chair and listened poker-faced while Dee related the chilling details of Paul's unmitigated attack.

'And yet, despite everything that happened, he didn't manage to hurt Emma in any way?' she interrupted at one point.

'No. The first thing I remember when I regained consciousness was hearing Emma screaming. Naturally I dashed into the baby's room to protect her and collided with Paul as he walked through the door. He'd obviously had some kind of accident, judging by the amount of blood streaming from his face and the fact he could scarcely walk.'

'Perhaps he tripped over something?'

'At first, I assumed that as well. So after he had gone I checked Emma's room thoroughly, but I couldn't find anything lying around that would have caused him to fall. Anyway, I cleaned up as best I could and changed Emma's clothes and bedlinen which were saturated, but although the baby was covered in blood, none of it appeared to be hers. There wasn't a single mark on her. It's baffling, isn't it?'

Jane nodded, her lips pursed thoughtfully.

'How do you feel now? Shall I call the doctor?'

'No. I'm OK. Just a trifle bruised and shaken up.'

'I'm not surprised. You're lucky to be alive.'

Jane stood up and started to tidy up the room, restoring the overturned furniture, table lamps and ornaments to their proper places.

'Did you get the information we wanted?' asked Dee, changing the subject.

'To be honest, I'm not sure. But I did learn quite a lot about the history of Ashingham this evening.'

'That's great. So what's the problem?' Jane sighed wearily.

'I've got that nagging feeling that something is missing, a link to connect the history of the valley to the psychology of its community.'

'How do you mean?'

Jane poured them both another drink and sat down.

'Historically speaking, Ashingham played an impressive role through the centuries, especially in view of its diminutive size compared to most other estates in England. The archives stretch back as far as the Norman Conquest, but, interestingly enough, the genealogy relating to the present community only dates back to the end of the Civil War.'

'Why is that? Was everyone killed?'

'Yes, in a manner of speaking.'

Briefly Jane explained the lead up to the siege of Ashingham Castle, and the tragic sequence of events during the hostilities which finally culminated in the total collapse of the Royalist stronghold and the slow and agonisingly painful death of the conscripted soldiers walled-up in the underground tunnel.

'So the valley lost all its menfolk at a stroke?'

'Yes,' Jane affirmed. 'Within the span of a single day, Ashingham was transformed into a village of widows and unmarried daughters.'

'But surely there must have been some male children in the village, small boys too young to participate? I can't believe they were all killed.'

'The children did survive, that is those ranging from babes in arms to about ten years of age, but the records clearly state that none survived to reach maturity. It's almost as if the lives of those little boys were doomed to destruction.'

'It's incredible. Things like that just don't happen in real life.'

'As far as Ashingham is concerned, it did happen. Moreover, I'm absolutely convinced that the psychological characteristics of the present male population stem entirely from that monumental tragedy three centuries ago.'

Dee pondered on Jane's theory for several seconds, somewhat puzzled.

'I don't understand how the catastrophe can possibly have any bearing on the make-up of today's inhabitants, especially in the absence of any kinship. And, from what you've already told me, it isn't possible for the present incumbents to claim direct descendancy from those unfortunate men. Is it?'

'No. That's correct. But curiously enough, despite losing their next of kin, the women came to accept, and indeed frequently crossed paths with the Roundhead soldiers, garrisoned up at the castle. When peace was restored and the armies disbanded, many of the soldiers, having taken quite a fancy to the valley, married the available women and settled down quite happily in the village, turning their hands to farming and raising new families.

'It all sounds rather odd to me,' said Dee. 'How could any woman marry a man directly responsible for the death of her previous husband?'

Jane pursed her lips and looked directly at her friend. 'Everything about Ashingham strikes me as odd. But it is important to remember that what seems strange and illogical to you and I, appears quite normal and commonplace to these people.'

Suddenly a low moaning noise wafted across the room from the direction of the cellar. Caught off guard, the sound made both women jump.

'Oh no. Not again. I've had a basinful of that already tonight,' said Dee. 'I don't think I can take much more.'

'If it will make you feel any better we could move the bureau in front of the door. It weighs a ton and I can guarantee that once it's in place nothing could possibly get past it, or for that matter, budge it an inch.'

Minutes later, and after a considerable amount of heaving and shoving, the desk stood in its new position, resolutely guarding the entrance to the cellar, and, although whatever it was that lurked at the top of the stone steps hammered relentlessly at the tongue and grooved door panelling, the two women felt safe in the knowledge that any attempt to break in was hopeless.

They adjourned upstairs, tired and weary.

'I've cleared up most of the mess in the bedrooms, but there are still minute fragments of glass embedded in the carpet by your bed,' said Dee apologetically.

'Not to worry,' said Jane, nonchalantly. 'Let's sort it out in the morning.'

'OK. By the way, what are we going to do tomorrow?'

'I'm driving you to Prestbury to catch a train home,' said Jane decisively.

'Oh no. You can't possibly do that,' Dee protested. 'We haven't finished our work here. And, anyway, I thought we had agreed to leave together.'

'I've changed my mind. There's no point in endangering more lives than is necessary, and, to be honest, I'd feel happier if you went home.'

'But...'

''Look, Dee,' said Jane, interrupting. 'I need a couple of days to pack up here, arrange for the cottage to be sold, and so on. As soon as I've tied up all the loose ends, Emma and I will move down to London, probably to stay with my parents.

I'm not intending to finish our little project if that's what is bothering you.'

'Fair enough. It's late, I'm tired and I don't want to argue with you. We'll talk about it again in the morning.'

'You can talk as much as you like on the way to the station, but you're definitely going home tomorrow, even if I have to put you on the train myself.'

Dee smiled and disappeared into Emma's room, quietly closing the door behind her.

With a sigh, Jane wandered into her own room and switched on the light, knowing what she'd see. She sat down heavily on the bed and stared dejectedly at the pretty kidney-shaped dressing table. Dee had placed all the broken ornaments on the plate glass top, obviously not wanting to take the responsibility for disposing of Jane's personal possessions. The rest of the room showed signs of the attack even though Dee had done her best to clear up the mess.

Instinctively she knew her decision to send Dee back to London was right. In view of what had happened, there was no alternative. It seemed that the entire village had finally pronounced judgement upon Emma and herself, a judgement that probably extended to anyone closely associated with either of them. She could only hope the cottage, with every window and door securely fastened, would provide adequate protection, at least until the morning.

Jane undressed slowly, pulled back the bed covers and slipped between the cool, crisp cotton sheets. Lying on her back, her head resting on the soft feather pillow, she gazed up at the ceiling, mentally compiling the list of tasks to be undertaken in the next day or two. She reckoned it could take up to at least forty-eight hours to pack and wind everything up.

As soon as Dee was safely on the train she would call in at one of the large Estate Agents in Prestbury and make the necessary arrangements for the disposal of Ivy Cottage. Unfortunately, the furniture would have to remain in situ for the time being, until she decided where her future plans lay. But the problem of the furniture would be something that could easily be dealt with by telephone. That only left the packing to contend with, and at least by having the car waiting outside to be loaded up in readiness for the journey, life had been made a little easier for her. If Paul had taken the car, the trek to London using taxis and trains with all the luggage and a small baby would have been horrendous, to say the least.

She wondered where her husband was at this moment in time. For some unknown reason she felt it was highly unlikely that he had taken refuge elsewhere in the village. Her mind went blank and she let the thought go - it really didn't matter any more, the family link bonding them together as man and wife had finally snapped, leaving her free to pursue her own destiny.

The overriding problem facing all three of them right now was the isolated situation in which they found themselves and the unquestionable danger surrounding the cottage on all sides. Jane prayed fervently that providence would look favourably upon them all and grant them the protection they needed to survive the next few days. The grim memory of Arthur's fingers around her throat welled up in her mind, reminding her how close they had all come to death this evening. Miraculously the attempts had failed, but Jane was in no doubt that further steps would be taken to eliminate them unless they escaped quickly.

With these thoughts weighing heavily on her mind, Jane turned on to her side, pressed her cheek into the pillow and pulled the covers tightly into her chin. She lay, mulling over the busy schedule in front of her until exhaustion finally overtook her and she drifted off into an uneasy sleep.

CHAPTER 15

Jane woke up abruptly to a harsh trilling in her left ear. She poked one arm free of the blankets and stretched across to the mahogany bedside table to switch off the alarm, vaguely remembering she had deliberately set the clock in order to ensure an early start to a busy day. She flopped her head back on to the soft feather pillows as she stretched each limb in turn, slowly but firmly to revitalise her sluggish blood circulation and tone up the sleepy well-relaxed muscle tissue. Wishing that she could turn over and sleep on for a few hours more, having spent most of the night restlessly tossing and turning, Jane sat up, albeit reluctantly, and pulled back the sheets before swinging her legs gracefully to the floor.

Her head felt like a lead weight, as it always did after a sleepless night, and, swallowing hard in an attempt to clear away the cobwebs, she experienced a burning sensation which seared up in her throat, extending from her glands to her ears, involuntarily making her wince. Gingerly running one hand across her throat she realised her whole neck was sensitive to the touch and that the soreness stemmed from last night's struggle with Arthur rather than from a viral infection of some kind.

A delightful dawn chorus of birdsong gently filtered into the room, reminding her of the importance of the day's schedule, and, casting her ailments to one side she resolutely donned dressing-gown and slippers, padded over to the window and drew back the curtains with a grand flourish. The dazzling sunlight burst into the room, its brilliance blinding her momentarily. She blinked several times until her eyes became accustomed to the harsh brightness, and then leaning across the deep sill she released the catch on the casement window and looked out over the countryside.

In the shining stillness of this hot early September morning the valley had an enthralling and spellbinding beauty that made Jane hold her breath and pause to admire its serene tranquillity. The sun shone down from a clear azure sky, gently caressing the tips of the undulating hills before cascading into the depths of the valley below. A shimmering haze rose up from the fields to greet the golden shafts of light creating an illusion of floating silkiness, an ethereal quality so breathtaking that Jane felt a sudden rush of warmth and tenderness surging through her veins, as she feasted her eyes upon the exquisite natural beauty of the scenery. Even the grim, forbidding castle, set high up on the clifftop seemed more hospitable on this glorious late summer morning, its crenellated battlements glinting in the strong sunlight.

Jane turned her head away from the valley and the castle to gaze reflectively at the picturesque stone cottages lining the village street. It was hard to believe that so much malevolence and inbred superstition could emanate from the inhabitants of these truly idyllic dwellings. She felt her brow furrow and her jaw tighten as she recalled some of the experiences she had witnessed or been personally involved in during the few months she had lived in the valley. She knew full well that the violence, the misery and the sadness affecting not only her own family but also the few close friends she had made in the community stemmed directly from the purchase and occupation of Ivy Cottage. She choked back a sob as she calculated the immeasurable cost of this disastrous decision, doomed to failure from the very beginning. Jane sighed with weariness and frustration.

The idea of settling into a country village and raising a family had always appealed to her. So when the opportunity to fulfil this lifelong ambition had presented itself in reality, both she and Paul had recklessly jumped at the chance without any conception of the wide-reaching social and cultural differences between city and country folk. Still, all that was in the past now, she told herself. Only the future mattered now, and to stay in Ashingham would be risking too much. In truth she would be endangering not only her own life but that of her daughter. Although part of Jane's make-up still hankered after a rural environment, the thought of someone harming the baby sent a series of shivers along the length of her spine, jolting her mind sufficiently to dismiss any notions of staying on.

She pulled herself together, resolute in her determination to embark upon her carefully formulated plans. To delay any longer would be dangerous and foolhardy to say the least, especially with so much at stake. Suddenly the silence was shattered as the sheepdogs from Half Acre Farm bounded out of the yard, barking and chasing each other as they raced up and down the road. Jane leaned across and closed the window, all thoughts pertaining to romantic ideology abruptly dismissed. Time was of the essence if she intended to leave Ashingham tomorrow as planned.

Opening the bedroom door, she stepped silently on to the landing. Neither Dee nor Emma appeared to be wake yet and Jane tiptoed down the stairs so as not to disturb either of them. While she waited for the kettle to boil, she padded into the living room to open the curtains and inspect the previous evening's damage in the cold light of day. To her relief, both the window and front door remained securely fastened, and from what she could see, no attempt had been made to force an entry during the night.

Her eyes strayed to the floor, as a shaft of brilliant light rebounded off a twinkling piece of yellow metal lying at her feet. She knelt down to retrieve the tiny gold Saint Christopher medallion that Paul had always worn around his neck. On close scrutiny Jane noticed that the link joining the talisman to its chain had broken. Instinctively she closed her palm tightly around the medal, acknowledging that her husband's fate now lay in the lap of the gods, his time having finally run out. At this moment she saw a trail of brownish stains meandering across the carpet from the front door to the stairs. Jane stood up and made her way to the kitchen to fetch a wet cloth to remove them. At the foot of the staircase the stains had smudged into each other to create a dark matted patch, and a quick glance upwards revealed yet more splattered marks on the wall leading up to the landing.

Gentle sponging erased the spots on the plaster quite easily, but Jane was surprised to see pink tinges on the cloth instead of the brown she had been expecting. In a flash she realised that Paul had injured himself during his struggle with Dee, and fairly seriously, judging by the amount of blood everywhere. At last, the final spots wiped away, she poured herself a well-earned cup of tea and wandered out into the garden.

The monotonous droning of the milking machinery reverberated across the valley, imposing the harsh reality of twentieth century technology on an otherwise idyllic and flawless landscape. One by one the cows from Half Acre Farm shambled out of the shed, only to plod a few steps before bending their heads to graze on the scanty tufts of grass in the well-used paddock. Jane smiled to herself, thinking how much she would miss her habitual early morning stroll among the carefully tended shrubs in her small garden. More and more cattle sauntered across the field in the vain search for fresh grass. Jane moved towards the rear fence where a large black and white Friesian had rested its head on one of the concrete posts and was studying her intently with its soft limpid eyes. She gently stroked the animal's head and offered it a handful of long grass.

Suddenly a piercing whistle cut across the silence and the sheepdogs dashed into the paddock to round up the herd ready for the slow journey back to one of the outlying fields. Jane stood and watched the animals move away, then turned on her heel and briskly entered the cottage to avoid being seen by anyone from the farm.

The hands on the delicately patterned ceramic plate clock on the kitchen wall pointed to seven-thirty and, as yet, there was no sign of any movement from the bedroom upstairs. Jane reckoned that she might just have enough time before preparing breakfast to compile an inventory of items to be boxed up later in the day ready for the journey to London. She made a start by emptying all the cupboards and drawers in the living room, placing everything to be packed in several neat piles on the sideboard, well out of Emma's reach. Satisfied that nothing more could be achieved in this room, she then moved into the kitchen to sort out what food, crockery and utensils she would need for the next day or so.

The minutes ticked by as Jane became absorbed in her work, for the present all other worries pushed to the back of her mind. Everything surplus to requirement she packed into a large black plastic sack which she carried outside and placed next to the dustbin ready for the next refuse collection. Returning to the kitchen she cleaned the empty cupboards and stacked all the remaining kitchenware and food in the larder.

A sudden creak followed by the sound of footsteps overhead made her glance swiftly at the clock. Without realising it she had let over an hour slip by. She closed the larder door and hurriedly set the table. While she waited for the kettle to boil she quickly leafed through the train timetable to find a suitable fast train to London, settling for the 11.15 as being the most convenient for all of them. About five minutes later Dee appeared in the doorway, carrying Emma.

'Perfect timing,' announced Jane, lifting the baby out of Dee's arms and lowering her into the highchair next to the table. 'Cereal and toast?'

'No, just coffee please,' Dee replied. 'I've got a splitting headache this morning.'

'I'm not surprised,' said Jane, looking at her friend's bruised and battered face. 'Would a couple of painkillers help?'

Dee nodded gratefully as Jane got up from the table and went in search of the small bottle of tablets she always carried in her handbag.

'I've been thinking,' said Dee, as Jane resumed her place and began to feed Emma. 'I really think we should all travel to London together. The thought of you and Emma here alone frightens me to death.'

'Don't worry. It'll only be for one night. I'm intending to pack and load up the car tonight so that we can leave first thing tomorrow morning.'

'Well, in that case I'll stay and give you a hand so that we can all drive down together. With any luck we might even be able to leave tonight.'

Jane studied her friend's anxious face and smiled.

'Look. I really do appreciate your offer, but my mind's made up. I feel responsible for what happened to you last night and I insist you go home this morning.'

Dee sighed heavily, defeated. There was little point in arguing with Jane, judging by the determined expression on her face.

'I've already looked at the timetable,' she continued. 'There's a fast train to London at 11.15, so we'd better get a move on if we want to get to Prestbury in time.'

'OK. You win,' Dee conceded. 'But I'll ring you tonight, just to make sure nothing has happened to either of you.'

'I'd like that,' said Jane. 'But I'm sure everything will be all right.' With that, she stood up and began to clear away the dirty plates.

'Why don't you go and pack while I clear up down here?'

'OK,' Dee replied, gingerly rising from her chair. 'I must confess, I feel as if I've been pulled through a bush backwards. Every muscle aches like hell.'

'If I were you, I'd take things pretty easy for a few days when you get home,' advised Jane. 'You look absolutely washed out.'

Dee headed towards the door, stopped and then swung round abruptly. 'Jane, what will you do if Paul comes back?'

The mention of her husband's name startled Jane and a shiver ran down the entire length of her spine. She quickly pulled herself together. Her carefully laid plans most certainly didn't include Paul, and she was resolute in her determination to carry them through single-handed, come what may.

'I think it most unlikely that he will come back,' she replied slowly. 'In fact, I'm positive he wouldn't dare after what's happened.'

'I hope you're right,' said Dee.

An hour later Jane loaded Dee's cases into the boot of the car and they set off for Prestbury. Although the village street remained as deserted as always, both women noticed how the brilliant shafts of sunlight protruded through the neighbouring cottage windows, clearly exposing several concealed onlookers. The two women exchanged a knowing look, after which Jane accelerated out of the village.

There was little traffic on the main road. Dee sat back in her seat and gazed out of the window at the passing countryside. It reminded her of the undulating terrain of Dorset where she had spent many happy childhood holidays. The car drew further and further away from Ashingham and Dee felt herself becoming more and more relaxed, almost as if a tremendous burden was being lifted from her shoulders. She began to view the prospect of returning to London with mounting· enthusiasm, tinged only with the regret that Jane and Emma would not be travelling with her. She turned to ask Jane to reconsider her decision to stay on, but seeing the determined expression on her friend's face, she bit back the words she was about to say and remained silent. In the distance the numerous church spires of Prestbury stretched upwards to meet the clear azure skyline, indelible landmarks, which for centuries had guided travellers on their journeys to this thriving market town situated on the banks of the River Ouse. Minutes later the car crossed the bridge marking the town boundary and headed towards the station. Jane managed to grab the last available parking space in the main forecourt. She switched off the engine, glanced at her watch and congratulated herself on how well her plans for the day were progressing.

They entered the concourse just as the tannoy was announcing the arrival of the London-Euston express on platform four.

'Great timing,' boasted Jane, triumphantly.

'You always prided yourself on being a perfectionist,' laughed Dee. 'But, on a more serious note,' she added. 'I'm worried about you staying on until tomorrow. You're taking a risk. For example, what if anything happened to either of you? That damned valley is so isolated you've no guarantee of help arriving quickly, if at all.'

Jane opened the carriage door, heaved the cases into the compartment and turned to face her friend.

'Now stop panicking, Dee, for heaven's sake. Nothing is going to happen in the next twenty-four hours.'

The guard walked down the platform, slamming the occasional open door.

'Get on the train. Have a safe journey and I'll see you tomorrow.'

Dee climbed aboard, shut the door and lowered the window to lean out. Almost immediately the train began to move slowly out of the station.

'I'll phone you tonight,' shouted Dee.

Jane smiled and nodded as she stood holding Emma and waving goodbye. At last the train finally disappeared from view and Jane walked briskly through the ticket barrier, across the concourse and out into the brilliant sunshine.

Turning left into the main thoroughfare, she skilfully manoeuvred the pushchair along the crowded pavement towards Messrs. Whalley & Tonge, the Estate Agents, with whom she left a set of keys and the authority to dispose of Ivy Cottage in her absence. Pleased with the morning's work, Jane drove back to Ashingham at a leisurely pace, stopping on the way at a small supermarket to buy fresh bread for lunch.

The countryside, basking in the hot midday sun, looked spectacular after the heavy rainfall of the previous day, the fields of ripe corn forming a glorious golden blanket that stretched as far as the eye could see. In front of her, the heat haze on the tarmacadam road surface shimmered like a floating veil of the finest gossamer, but the glare it projected through the windscreen was so dazzling Jane was forced to pull down the sun visor to protect her eyes.

A few minutes later she saw the turrets of Ashingham Castle rising majestically above the bank of trees and the familiar signpost that marked the left turn into Boundary Road. Her heartbeat accelerated, spontaneously triggering a surge of adrenalin to course through her veins. All idle thoughts instantly disappeared and her mind focussed its attention on the rest of the day's work schedule. With grim determination she drove down the hill, under the leafy canopy of trees and into the main street. The car pulled up to an abrupt halt outside the cottage. Jane leaned forward to extract the keys from the ignition and stared at the stone dwelling that had been her home for the last six months. For no apparent reason her instincts warned her something was wrong and an icy shiver ran the length of her spine. Clutching Emma tightly to her breast she climbed out of the car and cautiously approached the cottage with a terrible sense of foreboding.

A rapid glance around gave no indication of anything being amiss. A rush of unbridled anger flared up inside her and she severely castigated herself for allowing a sense of fear to override her determination to complete her outstanding tasks. Gritting her teeth in an effort to pull herself together, Jane opened the gate with a flourish, only to stop dead in her tracks. The blood drained from her face as she gazed at the gruesome spectacle in front of her.

Unable to move, she stood listening to the thudding of her heart while trying to think rationally. Whoever would do this and why? she asked herself repeatedly. The path leading up to the front door was strewn with entrails and gobbets of bloody flesh, the grisly remains of what had once been a chicken. The rest of the mutilated carcass had been crudely nailed to the front door itself. Jane's initial numbness gradually subsided and vivid memories of Oedipus flooded through her mind as she recalled the horrific moment of finding her cat crucified upon the inside of that same door.

Outwardly calm and erect, but inwardly aware that she was about to vomit, Jane picked her way through the gory mess and entered the cottage. The moment the door closed, effectively hiding her from the numerous prying eyes that watched her every move, she fled into the kitchen, dumped Emma unceremoniously into the highchair and was violently sick, again and again, until her sides ached from retching. Jane was still bent over the sink when an urgent tapping on the window pane directly above her head made her blood run cold. She held herself rigid, not knowing what to do, her brain reeling in panic.

'Jane. It's me,' said a muffled voice through the glass.

Jane looked up to see the anxious face of her neighbour Susan cowering outside in the garden. In a flash she unbolted the back door and hauled Susan inside.

Overcome by a mixture of personal grief and immense relief at seeing a friendly face, Jane fell into her neighbour's arms and completely broke down. Susan wrapped her arms firmly around her friend and waited patiently for all Jane's pent-up misery to escape as the floodgates opened.

'I'm sorry,' Jane sobbed, reaching into her pocket for a handkerchief.

'Don't worry, just let it all come out. It'll make you feel much better.'

Jane wiped away the tears and struggled to regain her composure.

'You shouldn't have come,' she said shakily. 'It's far too dangerous for you and Emma.'

'That's for me to judge,' said Susan brusquely.

'My immediate concern is for you and Emma, especially now that you are alone.'

'You've heard about last night then?'

'Yes. Graham was full of it this morning before he left for work.'

'I don't suppose you have any idea where Paul is?'

Susan shook her head. 'A long way from Ashingham I suspect. If he's got any sense that is.'

'What exactly did Graham say?'

'Apparently, Paul walked into the Castle Arms looking rather the worse for wear. Graham said he looked as if he'd gone fifteen rounds with a heavy-weight boxer and lost. From what I can gather Paul was quite badly injured.'

'I can well believe that, judging by the amount of blood I've cleaned up this morning,' said Jane flatly. She sat down with a sigh and waited for her friend to continue.

'There isn't much more to tell. Arthur Briggs was called to the scene and after a brief discussion and a vote Paul was expelled from the village.'

Susan bent down and clasped Jane's hands firmly in her own. 'He won't come back, Jane. The men will kill him if he ever tries to return.'

Jane began to sob.

'You still love him, don't you?'

'Yes, but I don't want to see him again, not after everything he has done to hurt us.'

'That's what I came to talk to you about,' said Susan. 'I saw you leave the village this morning with your friend Dee. Has she gone back to London?'

'Yes, I took her to the station in Prestbury.'

'I think you should do the same, if not for yourself, for Emma's sake. Surely you must realise it's not safe for you to remain here any longer?'

Jane nodded. 'Have you seen what they have done to the front of my house?'

'Yes. I watched John Mallen and Arthur Briggs nail up that chicken just before you came home. The men are determined to terrorize you into leaving, and the mess outside is only the beginning, you can be sure of that. Why on earth didn't you return to London with Dee?'

'I fully intend to leave Ashingham, just as soon as I've packed. With any luck I should be ready to go by the morning.'

'Thank God for that,' said Susan, standing up. 'Oh. I nearly forgot. I've got a message for you.'

Jane looked up enquiringly.

'While you were out this morning, a tall blonde woman called to see you. A Mrs Green I think she said.'

'Oh, yes,' replied Jane, perking up. 'She's the wife of the County Archivist. I wonder what it can be about.'

'She didn't say, but she asked me to tell you that she would call back this afternoon.'

'Thanks,' said Jane.

Susan smiled, then glanced quickly at her watch. 'I'd better be going.'

'Thank you for coming. I appreciate it,' said Jane.

Susan opened the back door a crack, checked the coast was clear, and bent almost double, dashed towards the hole in the privet hedge and the safety of her own garden.

After a hastily prepared lunch, Jane settled Emma into her cot for a sleep and set about the thankless task of clearing up the obnoxious and barbaric debris scattered across the flagstones and desecrating the front door. Swarms of ugly blowflies had settled on the pieces of rotting flesh and were contentedly gorging themselves in the hot afternoon sun. She made a start by fetching several bucketfuls of hot water and disinfectant to wash down the path and disperse the flies. The door, however, proved to be more difficult. Whoever had mounted the carcass on to the wood had rammed the nails in as far as they would go.

With a loud sigh Jane went in search of Paul's toolbox and returned several minutes later armed with a stout pair of pliers. One by one she prised each nail from the wood, cursing at the time she was wasting when there was still so much to do. To finish off she scrubbed down the door to remove as much of the blood as possible, although by now most of it had seeped into the grain, leaving a permanent reddish stain. As she worked, Jane sensed unseen hostile eyes boring into her back. At one point she whirled around and caught a glimpse of Ann Smith, the publican's wife, spying on her from one of the windows on the first floor above the pub. Her mind conjured up a picture of Dee, by now safely ensconced in her cosy suburban flat. Jane wondered whether her own decision to stay on an extra day had been foolish. She recalled the words Susan had used earlier 'The men are determined to terrorize you into leaving'. Time was running out, she knew that. It was imperative that she worked quickly.

Jane bent down to pick up the brush and pail, vaguely aware of a car approaching. She heard the vehicle slide to a halt outside 'The Hermitage' and prepared to beat a hasty retreat indoors, in case of trouble. A moment later the car door slammed and a woman's voice called her name. Jane turned at the sound of the well-spoken voice and spotted Sally Green walking towards her. Jane hurried down the path to meet her. The two women clasped hands warmly.

'I called earlier, but you were out,' Sally said, smiling.

'Yes, I know,' Jane replied. 'My neighbour gave me your message.'

Despite the oppressive afternoon heat Sally looked exceedingly cool and elegant in a pale blue linen suit, perfectly set-off by a simple white silk blouse. Her complexion, tanned to a soft golden bronze, was quite flawless, and the luxurious blonde hair shone in the strong sunlight. The overall effect was one of natural sophistication and, glancing down at her own cotton print dress, one which made Jane feel positively shabby in comparison. She ushered Sally along the path and into the cottage, anxious to get away from the uninvited audience watching them from behind closed doors.

'Can I offer you some tea or coffee?' she asked, as Sally sank into one of the armchairs.

'Tea would be lovely,' her visitor replied.

While Jane disappeared into the kitchen, Sally glanced around the low-beamed room. She inhaled the olde worlde atmosphere of the setting, admiring in particular the wrought-iron grate set inside the delightful old inglenook.

'What a charming cottage this is,' she called to Jane. 'Have you any idea when it was built?'

'The date stone above the porch says 1660,' Jane replied, returning with a tray of tea.

Sally's eyes cane to rest on the packing cases behind the door. 'I hope I haven't called at an inconvenient time,' she said.

Jane followed her gaze and laughed. Not at all, I'm delighted to see you.'

'But you are packing up to leave, if I'm not mistaken?'

'Yes,' Jane replied evenly. 'Things haven't worked out quite as I expected...'

Sally raised her hand to cut her short. 'There's no need to explain. To be honest, I'm not surprised you're going.'

'Oh. Why' s that?' said Jane, her curiosity aroused.

'Well, as you know I'm very interested in local history, and although Peter and I have only lived in the area a short time, we've both carried out a considerable amount of research already, not only from delving into the archives, but also by talking to quite a number of local people. The strange thing is that every time we mention Ashingham everyone clams up.'

'Rather like a no-go area?' suggested Jane.

'Exactly. I couldn't have expressed it better myself,' said Sally with amusement. 'But seriously, it seems that Ashingham is generally regarded as an evil place. So far I've only found one person who has shown any willingness to talk frankly and openly to me about this place.'

'I don't suppose it would be possible for me to meet whoever it is?' Jane asked speculatively.

'That's the reason I've popped over to see you today. From what you said last night it was clear that you hadn't found what you were looking for.'

'And you think this person may be able to help me?'

'I'm sure of it,' said Sally. 'She's become a very good friend of mine. Her name is Claire Adams. Have you heard of her?'

'No. Should I have?'

'No. Not really. She is a spiritualist, and, as it happens, one of the most interesting people I've ever met.'

'A spiritualist. How fascinating,' said Jane.

Sally laughed. 'I telephoned her this morning and told her about your project.'

'And?' Jane prompted.

'Claire said she would be delighted to help in any way she could. I suggested we all meet at my house tomorrow morning.'

'Marvellous,' said Jane enthusiastically.

'Yes, but what about your packing? When were you intending to move?'

'When I'm ready, there's no immediate rush,' said Jane offhandedly, deeming the question of little importance in the light of a further chance to unveil the dark mystery surrounding the valley. 'I don't want to turn down the opportunity of meeting Claire. She may well provide the vital clue I'm searching for.'

'Well, if you're quite sure. Shall we say ten-thirty?'

'That's fine by me.'

Sally rose to leave. Jane escorted her outside to her car, acutely aware that further along the row at 'The Barn', Dorothy Haresnape, although appearing to be innocently engaged in sweeping her front path, had in fact been posted outside as a look-out to monitor Sally and Jane's movements.

Sally switched on the ignition and rolled down her window. 'I'll see you tomorrow.'

'I'm looking forward to it,' said Jane. 'Give my regards to Peter.'

The car accelerated out of the village. Jane turned on her heel and stared hard at Arthur's sister-in-law, her mind filled with contempt and loathing for the spineless middle-aged female, despised and rejected by all the other women in the village. One day you'll get your just desserts, Dorothy, Jane muttered to herself, under her breath. Then, dismissing the woman abruptly from her thoughts, Jane headed back indoors to continue the packing.

CHAPTER 16

L ater that evening, having completed at last the arduous task of sorting out the items she wanted to take, and having filled the majority of cardboard boxes brought down from the loft, Jane briefly looked in on Emma, before settling down to relax in front of the fire. The heat of the day had dissipated rapidly with the sun's departure. In its place a cool breeze had sprung up and Jane observed there was definitely more than just a hint of an autumnal nip in the air. She sank back into the deep wing chair and rested her feet on the hearth to escape from the irritating draught around her ankles. The firelight danced playfully on the whitewashed walls and a warm glow was reflected in the rich mahogany furniture, creating an aura of cosiness in addition to the already charming ambience of the room.

For several minutes Jane lay back and succumbed to the tranquillity of the surroundings, feeling unusually relaxed and at peace with herself. She gazed languidly into the flames allowing the tension of the last twenty-four hours to gradually evaporate. A gentle smile began to flicker around the corners of her mouth as she convinced herself that everything was going to be alright. Slowly her eyes drifted away from the hypnotic incandescent glow of the fire to take in the remainder of the room, whereupon unexpected pangs of sadness welled up inside her as she realised how much she would miss her tiny cottage, despite all the painful memories associated with it.

Jane fought back a stray tear, swallowed hard and turned her mind to the forthcoming meeting with Claire. Perhaps tomorrow's get together would miraculously shed some light on the grey areas surrounding the village and its history, which would at least allow her to come to terms with the current situation, as well as making it easier to leave Ivy Cottage.

The clock on the mantelpiece struck the hour. Jane leaned across and switched on the television to watch the nine o'clock news. Her attention focussed on the female newsreader's immaculate white silk blouse and she remembered the one she had left on the kitchen table waiting to be repaired. With a groan at having to move from her comfortable position, she plodded into the kitchen to fetch it, pausing on the way back to pick up the small needlework box she had left on top of the sideboard. Delving into the wicker casket she pulled out needles, scissors and various reels of thread only to find she had completely run out of white cotton. Jane cursed under her breath. She had particularly wanted to wear this blouse tomorrow. At that minute the telephone rang.

'Hello Jane,' chirped Dee merrily. 'All packed and ready to leave?'

'More or less. Did you have a good journey?' replied Jane.

'Yes, not bad. The train got in halfway through the afternoon, so at least I missed the evening rush hour. I expect you've forgotten what it's like.'

Jane laughed. 'You sound in good spirits?'

'I am,' Dee replied. 'Saying goodbye to Ashingham was like having a lead collar removed from around my neck. The funny thing is, I didn't realise how oppressive the valley was until I actually left it behind me. I'm sure you'll experience the same feeling yourself tomorrow.'

Jane didn't reply. Instead her attention had been diverted towards the cellar door.

'Jane, are you still there?' Dee shouted down the line, perturbed by the ominous silence. 'Is everything alright? Jane, what's happening?'

Suddenly from somewhere deep in the bowels of the cellar or even further beyond in the passage that led into the labyrinth of tunnels honeycombing the entire valley, Jane heard a deepthroated roar. Although the sound was muffled and obviously some distance away, the stone floor beneath her feet responded to the reverberations that echoed through the underground maze by quavering violently. The shifting movement sent rippling vibrations through her feet as the whole room shuddered. The needlework box on the coffee table crashed to the floor, sending pins and cotton reels cascading across the carpet.

In her subconscious, Jane could hear Dee shouting at her, but for the moment her friend's pleas fell on dead ears. Without saying anything, Jane gently placed the receiver on the table and walked gingerly across the room to the large bureau barricading the entrance to the cellar. She gripped the highly polished writing surface and raised herself onto tiptoe, straining hard to listen. For a few seconds there was total silence.

A series of shivers raced up and down her spine as the suspense mounted, and in the eerie stillness Jane could hear her heart pounding uncontrollably. The time ticked by and then, once again, the floor began to vibrate as another guttural roar gathered momentum and raged unchecked beneath the cottage. At this point Jane knew, beyond any reasonable doubt, that the perpetrator of this hideous gutblasting vociferation had entered the cellar itself and was, in all probability, stationed directly below where she was standing. She clung to the desk, at a loss to know what to do for the best.

At the sound of a sudden clatter from somewhere behind her, Jane whirled round to see the telephone lying amid the debris on the carpet. Like greased lightning she shot across the room to rescue it, remembering that Dee was on the other end. A dull monotone whined plaintively at her as she grabbed the handset.

The bellowing from the cellar had stopped, leaving in its wake a chilly deathliness that hung in the air like an invisible mantle of doom hungrily devouring every last ounce of warmth left in the cottage. Within a matter of seconds the temperature had fallen so abruptly, Jane could see her own breath vaporising in front of her face. From down below the dry rasping sound of something heavy being dragged across the cellar floor drifted up into the living room. Jane's attention flashed towards the bureau again and she waited with bated breath for the first hint of movement on the stone steps. It never came. After what seemed an eternity, but was in all probability only a few seconds, Jane listened as the muffled shuffling and heavy panting gradually receded into the distance.

Immediately an effusion of peace and contentment permeated the atmosphere as the temperature rose and all traces of the earlier psychic phenomenon vanished. Jane, however, still clutching the telephone, remained rooted to the spot, as yet unconvinced that the creature had gone. Out of the corner of one eye she perceived several darting flashes of orange light from the fire as it burst forth into life sending violent streaks of flame hurtling up the chimney. The sudden warmth thawed the numbness in her hands and feet and her nose began to stream uncontrollably. It took several more minutes for Jane to accept that everything had returned to normal. She replaced the telephone receiver and quickly redialled Dee's number only to find the line busy. Anxious to set her friend's mind at rest she made a mental note to try again later. The clock on the mantelpiece struck the hour. It was getting late and the blouse on the coffee table was still waiting to be repaired. Her eyes swung back to the door as she inwardly debated whether or not to pop next door and ask Susan Entwhistle for some cotton. Time was short. The men would be leaving the Castle Arms shortly.

Jane rose with unusual swiftness, donned her cardigan and hurried next door. She stopped at Susan' front gate, one hand poised to release the catch. The 'Hermitage' stood in total darkness. Not a single glimmer of light protruded from any of its leaded casement windows. Jane paused, uncertain what to do. Susan had obviously gone to bed early. The sound of raucous laughter from the pub drifted across the deserted street. She glanced over at the brightly lit windows of the tap room and suddenly felt extremely vulnerable as she realised she was standing in a reflected pool of light. In a flash, she made a dive for the shadowy protection of the hedge, praying that no-one had spotted her.

Somewhere further along the row of cottages a door slammed, providing an open invitation for the numerous dogs in the village to outbark each other. Jane pressed herself further into the obscurity of the privet hedge, waiting for a chance to break cover and make a dash for home.

To her amazement nobody ventured out of the pub to see what all the commotion was about, but within seconds of the general cacophony reaching crescendo pitch, a male voice bellowed a stream of obscenities at the animals from somewhere within the farmyard immediately to her right. At a stroke the barking throughout the village stopped, leaving in its wake an easy calm. Jane let out a long sigh and edged slowly along the path to her own gate. Only Crabtree Cottage displayed any sign of life apart from the pub. As yet Eve Simpkins hadn't bothered to draw the downstairs curtains allowing light from the interior to flood across the neat little front garden.

On a sudden impulse Jane tiptoed towards the welcoming glow of light. Eve would have some white cotton, she felt sure. The front gate stood slightly ajar and Jane slipped through it easily and unnoticed. She stepped quickly into the deep shadowy recess of the porch and turned to look back at the street. As always it remained deserted and inhospitable, devoid of any form of human life. Facing the heavy oak door again, she was on the point of grasping the iron knocker, when she heard a muffled cry from within. Her hand poised in the air, Jane hesitated momentarily as she debated whether or not to disturb Eve this late in the evening. Then, she caught the sound of another cry, more desperate than the first, followed by a loud crash and the shattering of glass. Jane's initial instincts told her to run back to the comparative safety of her own cottage, but her inquisitiveness overrode any sense of better judgement, goading her on to investigate, if only to satisfy her own mind that nothing untoward had happened.

Using the garden foliage as protective cover, Jane crawled stealthily across the front garden as far as the living room window and tucked herself furtively behind a tall evergreen shrub. From this well-concealed position she had the advantage of a clear view of the Castle Arms as well as an unimpeded line of vision into the interior of the cottage. Several wet splashes pattered on to the crown of Jane's head. She looked up and felt raindrops gently graze both cheeks. Now she had two reasons to hurry. Not only would the men be leaving the pub before much longer, but also it wouldn't take long for her to become drenched.

With her back pressed flat against the cottage wall, Jane slowly stood upright and scanned the street. The coast remained clear in all directions. She made a sharp half-turn and peered into the room through the lower left-hand pane of glass. The scene that confronted her sent a series of shock waves flooding through her nervous system. At a first glance it appeared that she was witnessing a family dispute that had got slightly out of hand. Even from where she was precariously crouched outside the window, Jane could see the beginnings of a black eye forming on Eve's face. The petite, normally happy-go-lucky woman was holding on to the mantelpiece for support while at the same time attempting to ward off a rain of violent body punches from her husband. Apart from the livid bruising around her eye, the remainder of Eve' s face resembled a piece of white chalk. The assault had obviously taken its toll and Jane watched helplessly as the strain of holding on became too much and the woman's bloodless fingertips began to lose their grip. Bill Simpkins, his hand raised in readiness to mete out another vicious blow laughed mockingly as his wife's body crumpled and fell to the floor. Like a man possessed, he kicked at her delicate frame with the steel tips of his heavy working boots, ripping into bloody shreds of skin and clothing alike.

Outside the window Jane clamped one hand to her mouth to stifle a cry of horror, frustrated in the knowledge that physically there was nothing she could do to stop the attack, or help Eve in any way. She racked her brains for a solution, knowing full well that wife beating in Ashingham was commonplace, so help for Eve from within the village was out of the question. There was no-one to turn to, no options open. Jane could only think herself fortunate in that within twenty-four hours this ungodly village would be past history as far as she and Emma were concerned. The thought of Emma alone in Ivy Cottage worried Jane. She felt the need to return home.

At that moment a magnetic heart-rending cry from Eve Simpkins drew Jane's attention back to the grim proceedings inside Crabtree Cottage. The tiny defenceless woman, spreadeagled on the hearth-rug and battered, almost beyond recognition, had summoned up a last vestige of energy to make a desperate plea for help. It was only too plain to see why. Her husband had removed one of the swords that formed part of an extensive collection of weaponry that hung above the fireplace and was brandishing it contemptuously in front of her face. Unable to move, his wife lay helplessly on her back, staring up at her husband with an expression of disbelief at what she knew was about to happen. Bill lifted the sword high above his head. Jane felt her blood run cold as her eyes mechanically followed the downward swing of the blade and its deadly impact as it homed in on its victim. With one boot anchored on Eve's stomach, Bill tugged the sword free from its resting place, firmly embedded in his wife's chest cavity. Within a matter of seconds everything in the immediate vicinity turned crimson as blood rushed freely from the gaping wound like a geyser of fiery liquid. The body lay inert. The one blow had been enough.

Thunderstruck, Jane watched the impassive expression on Bill's face turn to one of hatred as he hurled the sword across the room and reached up to select another weapon from his collection. This time he chose what looked like a small short-bladed dagger. His eyes lit up sadistically as he slowly withdrew the blade from its leather sheath and tested the sharpness of the cutting edge against his thumb. Temporarily mesmerized by the whole bloody spectacle, Jane could only stare vacantly at the polished steel blade that sparkled in the glowing firelight. Bill lovingly caressed the dagger with his fingertips, the corners of his mouth curling upwards in a half smile of pride at being the owner of such an exquisite piece of handcrafted workmanship. Then, like a flash, he whirled round, threw himself on his knees and stabbed repeatedly at Eve's body. Like a maniac he hacked and hacked, tearing and gouging the corpse until it became impossible to tell that it had once been a human being. Jane looked away, her constitution unable to withstand any longer the carnage in front of her. The contents of her stomach surged violently up her oesophagus and she vomited behind an hydrangea bush. Angrily she brushed away the tears of frustration and self-pity that coursed down her cheeks. Crying wasn't going to solve anything. It certainly wouldn't bring Eve back to life. Bill

Simpkins had murdered his wife in cold blood and Jane knew she had no alternative now but to call the police.

With one eye firmly fixed on the Castle Arms, Jane scrambled towards the gate, still standing slightly ajar. The coast was clear back to Ivy Cottage, and after hesitating just long enough to take a quick glance back at Crabtree Cottage to check that Bill Simpkins hadn't spotted her, Jane made a bolt for home.

The hiss of rubber tyres slithering to a halt on the wet road surface outside alleviated the oppressive silence encapsulating the village. Jane, who had been on tenterhooks for the last half hour or so, shot out of her chair and crossed over to the window. Even before she drew back the curtains, she knew the police had arrived from the intermittent blue and white flashing light that blazed through the floral fabric covering the cottage windows. Thank God, she muttered to herself, wondering why on earth it had taken them so long to come. The front gate clanged shut and the strident thud of heavy footsteps approached the front door. Jane ushered the two uniformed police officers inside. Both men removed their hats and stooped to miss the lintel on the way in.

'I think it would be a good idea if you both sat down,' said Jane.

The sergeant lowered himself into the armchair nearest the fire, while the constable plumped for an upright one near the door.

'I'm Sergeant Roberts and this is Constable Deacon,' said the sergeant by way of introduction. Jane glanced over at the young constable and immediately recognised the policeman who had sat by her bedside, waiting to take a statement following the discovery of the surveyor's body.

'Constable Deacon and I have already met,' she said, smiling at the younger man. He smiled back, at the same time extracting a notebook and pencil from his breast pocket to take notes.

'Mrs Richardson, please tell me exactly what has happened,' said the sergeant, looking directly at her.

Jane described as concisely as possible what she had witnessed at Crabtree Cottage less than an hour previously, not forgetting to mention the extensive arsenal that Bill Simpkins referred to as his collection that covered the fireplace wall. The sergeant's expression turned to stone at the mention of firearms, swords and knives.

'Get out to the car and radio the Inspector,' he said, turning to Deacon. 'Tell him we'll need about another half-dozen men to deal with this and inform him that the suspect is armed.'

Constable Deacon disappeared in a flash.

While they waited for Deacon to return, the sergeant quizzed Jane about the internal layout of Crabtree Cottage and in particular all the access points to the front and rear. In less than a minute the constable returned looking somewhat harassed.

'Sorry, Sarge. I can't get the damned radio to work. I think the hills are blocking out the radio waves.'

Sergeant Roberts sighed impatiently and looked around the room for a telephone.

'It's over by the front door,' said Jane, reading his thoughts.

'Thanks,' he said. 'While I'm calling HQ, check out the rear of Crabtree Cottage, Constable. And, for God's sake, keep out of sight.'

Jane led the way in to the kitchen and unlocked the back door. Deacon slipped outside and vanished under the cover of darkness. She walked back into the living room just as the sergeant replaced the receiver. He turned to her smiling.

'Don't worry, Mrs Richardson. Everything's under control now. If you need me for anything I'll be waiting outside in the car. I want to keep an eye on the front entrance to No. 5 until the Inspector arrives.'

'I'll leave the door on the latch for you,' said Jane as he stepped outside into the porch. She watched him depart before returning indoors. Glancing at the clock she saw it was nearly midnight. It looked as if it could be a long night for all of them. Bending down, she selected a couple of logs from the scuttle and threw them onto the fire. An eerie stillness had descended over Ashingham again. It was almost as if the village was waiting for something dramatic to occur. It reminded Jane of the lull before a thunderstorm.

The logs began to crackle as tongues of orange flame curled themselves possessively around the rough outer bark. Jane stood for a moment, watching the fire take hold, reflecting for the first time on the full implication of her decision to call the police. Simply by dialling 999 she had left herself and Emma wide open to the inevitable hostile repercussions from the village.

It went without saying that everyone in Ashingham would know she was the one that had called the police, and, judging by their past actions, Bert and Arthur's revenge would be swift and brutal. From now on she was living on borrowed time. For Emma's sake, Jane decided to mention her predicament to the inspector. Perhaps he would be able to give them the protection they needed for their last remaining hours in the village. In truth, it was their only hope for survival.

The idea reassured her sufficiently to relax enough to push her fears to the back of her mind. She bent down and threw another log on to the fire for good measure before making her way upstairs to look in on the baby. As always Emma lay in her cot fast asleep. Jane smiled to herself, closed the door and returned to the living room at the very moment Sergeant Roberts walked in with his inspector, a tall and exceedingly handsome man, with black wavy hair and the most remarkable deep-blue eyes.

'Mrs Richardson. I'm Inspector Mason,' he said, extending his hand. 'I'm sorry to disturb you so late at night. Let's hope we can sort this lot out as quickly as possible.' All the time he was speaking the inspector's eyes darted about the room. 'Would you mind if I posted a couple of my officers in your back garden?'

'Not at all,' Jane replied. 'Is there anything I can do to be of help? I could make some tea if you like?'

'That would be most kind.'

Almost immediately the two men disappeared back outside and Jane found herself wandering into the kitchen to put the kettle on. She reached up into a cupboards to get the teapot and suddenly realised she had only left herself one cup and saucer. With a sigh Jane moved across the room and began to unpack the box of china standing behind the kitchen door.

The back door opened and she turned to see Constable Deacon slip unobtrusively into the room. He stood hovering by the door, rubbing his hands together to get the blood circulation flowing.

'My God, it's brass monkey weather out there tonight,' he announced ruefully.

His uniform was soaking wet and a small puddle had begun to form on the floor around as droplets of water steadily dribbled off his hat and cape.

'Go into the other room and dry yourself in front of the fire,' said Jane. 'I'll bring you in some tea, just as soon as I find enough cups for everyone.'

A few minutes later she appeared in the doorway, carrying a large tray which she set down on the coffee table.

Constable Deacon stood with his back to the fire and observed the young woman closely, a professional habit acquired during his training in the force. Instinctively he sensed that all was not well. An aura of tension and unease emanated from her despite all her efforts to sound relaxed and cheerful.

'Is the baby all tucked up and soundly asleep?' he enquired.

'Yes, she is, thank heavens,' said Jane, automatically glancing at the staircase.

Deacon sat down in the armchair nearest to the fire and gratefully accepted his tea. He sipped the steaming brew slowly to allow himself time to scan the room thoroughly just as the inspector had done earlier. His experienced eye missing nothing. Neither the bareness of the surroundings nor the packing cases in the corner by the front door escaped his sharp scrutiny. All the signs indicated that the Richardsons were about to move. But John Deacon sensed that the upheaval of moving house was not a contributory factor to the woman's anxiety.

Jane poured herself a cup of tea and placed the pot in the hearth to keep warm. The glowing logs in the grate crackled and hissed as the flames playfully darted around them, highlighting the warm red brickwork of the inglenook. The overall effect was one of luxurious comfort, and yet Constable Deacon felt unusually cold. He edged nearer to the fire and flexed his frozen toes several times to help thaw them out. He sighed inwardly as he glanced up a the time. There was no saying how long it would take the inspector to deal with the investigation. And, if Mrs Richardson's statement proved accurate as well as taking into account the fact that Simpkins was reportedly armed to the teeth, any chances of wrapping the whole thing up quickly looked pretty slim.

His thoughts returned to the woman opposite him. 'Is your husband out at the moment?' he enquired, as she refilled his cup.

'No, Jane replied bitterly. 'He's walked out. Deserted us. And, before you ask, I've no idea where he is and I don't think he'll come back.'

'Oh. I'm sorry,' he said, rather taken aback by her sudden ferocity. He had obviously touched on a delicate subject. 'You must be finding it rather difficult down here along with a baby?'

'Don't be sorry. We're better off without him.' Jane took a couple of sips of tea to calm herself. 'Please forgive me,' she said, apologetically. 'I didn't mean to bite your head off. It's just that my existence here is nothing short of living hell.' By the end of the sentence her voice had tailed off into an almost inaudible whisper, after which she sat in complete silence with her head bowed.

John Deacon edged forward slightly in his chair. 'Look,' he said gently. 'You can talk to me as a friend in complete confidence. I've been told I'm a good listener, and, who knows, I might even be able to help in some way.'

Jane raised her head and gazed searchingly at the young man sitting opposite her. Her brain was bursting to dispel all the pent up worry and she desperately needed someone to confide in, someone she could trust completely. The seconds ticked by. Neither of them spoke. To her surprise she found herself gradually unwinding as she looked into the depths of his warm brown eyes and became steadily engulfed in the overwhelming effusion of warmth that radiated towards her.

'Come on,' he coaxed. 'Forget I'm a policeman. Nothing you tell me will go further than these four walls.'

Jane still remained silent but this time she smiled, acknowledging the man's sincerity and genuine concern.

'Look,' he continued softly. 'I've lived all my life in Salesbury, a tiny village just two miles down the road from here, so I'm well acquainted with Ashingham's shadowy reputation. I'm quite prepared to believe anything you tell me about this place without being shocked.'

'Thank you,' said Jane. 'That makes me feel a lot better. I was afraid you might think I was mad.'

'No. Far from it,' he replied. 'In fact it may interest you to know that over the years many strange things have occurred in Ashingham, and yet the police have never successfully concluded any official investigation undertaken down here.'

'That doesn't surprise me,' said Jane evenly. 'The very location of the village, so cunningly hidden away in the depths of this valley, must make life very difficult for you. I'm sure that the majority of the passing traffic on the main road is completely unaware that a village exists down here at all.'

John Deacon nodded, pleased that she had found enough confidence at last to begin talking.

'How did you come to be living in Ashingham?' He enquired. 'Your accent tells me you come from the South, if I'm not mistaken?'

'From London actually,' Jane replied. 'We, my husband Paul and I that is, moved up here about six months ago to be near his new job in Prestbury.'

'But why Ashingham of all places?' he asked.

Jane laughed. 'We decided to buy a country cottage. I was pregnant and it seemed a good idea at the time to bring up the baby in a rural community rather than live in Prestbury itself.'

'So obviously you had no idea that you had chosen to settle in the most godforsaken village in the area?'

'None whatsoever, although I must admit I found the villagers most unfriendly when we first came to look at Ivy Cottage.'

'And yet you went ahead and bought it despite that?'

'Yes. We thought the situation would change as soon as they got to know us.'

'And did it?'

'Well to be honest yes and no. Paul adjusted to village life fairly quickly. He spent most evenings in the pub across the road with the men. I was the one that found it difficult. Making friends with the women wasn't easy. Quite apart from the fact I was a newcomer, my pregnancy made them wary of me.'

'That's odd,' interrupted Deacon. 'I'd have thought the impending arrival of a new baby would have delighted them.'

'It would have, had I been able to guarantee them a boy.'

'Sorry, I don't follow,' he said, scratching his head. 'What difference did it make?'

'To them, the difference between survival and catastrophe.'

'Now I'm totally lost,' he said, with a sigh.

'Well basically the root of the problem lies embedded in Ashingham's past history. At the time of the Civil War a woman born and bred in the village conspired with the enemy and, as a result of her treachery, the entire male population was wiped out. Since that time not one female child has been born in Ashingham, and even today women are regarded as beneath contempt.' Jane paused to take another sip of tea.

'Go on,' he urged.

'I'm afraid it didn't take me very long to cause trouble in their eyes. In the space of just one day I reported the surveyor's death to the police and only a few hours later gave birth to Emma.'

'I see,' said Deacon gravely. 'But at least you had your husband to support you.'

'No. That's the trouble. During the weeks immediately prior to Emma's arrival his personality had changed. It was almost as if he was being submitted to some form of indoctrination. As each day passed he became more like them.'

'So what happened?'

'Paul insisted we put Emma up for adoption. I refused of course and the bitter rows that followed killed what little was left of our marriage. To make matters worse, after the news of Emma's birth I became ostracised by everyone in the village. My neighbour, Susan Entwistle, the one close friend I had made in the village, was actually beaten up and raped because of our friendship.'

John Deacon raised his hand to stop Jane. 'It's not safe here for you and the baby. You realise that, don't you? Especially now that you have reported a second murder.'

Jane nodded. 'We're in danger from more than you think,' she said. 'If the villagers don't kill us, the creature that prowls through the tunnels under the village will get us. It's already broken through the cellar door once and I don't think I can protect either Emma or myself from its clutches much longer.'

'So Ashingham's legendary passages and the monster do exist then?'

'Yes. The tunnels honeycomb the entire valley.'

'Look. What do you want to do?' he said gravely. 'Have you made any plans?'

'Yes. It's all been taken care of. Emma and I are moving out tomorrow afternoon.'

'Where are you going?'

'I've decided to return to my parents in London for the time being.'

'Thank God for that,' he said with relief. 'When the inspector comes in I'll explain the situation and see if we can arrange some protection for you both until your departure.'

'Thank you,' said Jane. 'I would be most grateful if you could do that. The way things are at the moment, I don't think we will survive until tomorrow afternoon.'

'Don't worry. I'll sort it out for you. But first I'll check the cellar door if you show me where it is?'

Jane pointed to the bureau in the corner. 'It's behind there.' She glanced up at the clock and was staggered to see it was past four already. 'Do you think the inspector will be much longer?' she asked. 'He's been gone over three hours.'

'I don't know,' Deacon replied. 'Sometimes these things take all night.'

'In that case I'll make some more tea,' she said, pottering into the kitchen.

A few minutes later Jane heard the front door open and the sound of the inspector's voice. She deliberately took her time making the tea in order to give Deacon a chance to discuss her problem with his superior. Jane had already decided that if the police were unable to guarantee her safety, she had no alternative but to cancel her appointment with Claire Adams and leave for London first thing in the morning. From where she stood in the kitchen she could only hear the odd word between the two men so she waited for a lull in the conversation before picking up the tray and returning to the living room.

Both men stood up and made space for her to sit down near the fire. John Deacon smiled at Jane reassuringly.

'Mrs Richardson. I'd just like to confirm one or two details you gave us over the telephone, if I may?'

Jane nodded.

'You categorically stated that you witnessed the assault upon Mrs Simpkins?'

'Yes, Inspector, that's correct.'

'Can you tell me exactly where the assault took place?'

'In the centre of the living room, on the rug in front of the fire.'

'Now, you're absolutely sure about that, Mrs Richardson?'

'Yes. I had a clear view of everything that happened.'

'Did you see any blood?'

'Yes. The attack was so violent there was blood spattered everywhere. The walls were covered in it.'

'Thank you,' he said. 'That's all I want to know for now. We'll take a formal statement from you later.'

'Is everything alright, Inspector?' asked Jane. 'You look a little perplexed?'

'No, Mrs Richardson,' he replied gravely. 'Everything is far from alright. We haven't found a body, there's no sign of any blood and the hearthrug appears to be missing. We're taking Simpkins to the station for further questioning, but until the forensic team arrives, there's little more we can do. My officers are conducting a search of the whole village at this very moment, but I'm pretty sure we'll draw a blank.'

'Inspector Manson, you don't think I'm lying, do you, that I've called you out here on a wild goose chase?'

'No. Not at all. Stranger things than this have happened in Ashingham before. And, dead or alive, Mrs Simpkins is missing.'

The front door opened and one of the inspector's men stepped inside. 'No luck, Inspector. We've combed the entire area. It's as clean as a whistle.'

The inspector sighed. 'Thank you, Constable. Tell the others to get ready to leave. I'll join you in a minute.'

Inspector Manson turned back to Jane. 'Constable Deacon has told me about the difficult situation you're in down here and the likelihood of retaliatory action being taken against you and the baby. He also mentioned that you are leaving for London later on today?'

'Yes. This afternoon,' Jane replied. 'It's too dangerous for Emma and I to stay here any longer.'

'I agree entirely. I've asked Constable Deacon to stay behind, take a formal statement from you and remain here until we send a replacement to relieve him. That way you'll have the protection you need until your departure.'

'Thank you,' said Jane.

'Don't forget to let us have your address and telephone number in London. As our only witness to the crime, we'll need you to give evidence if we succeed in bringing this case to court.'

'Of course, Inspector. I'll give you all the help I can,' Jane replied.

He turned to Deacon. 'If you have any problems, ring HQ immediately. I'm leaving Sergeant Roberts on duty at Crabtree Cottage until the forensic boys arrive, which should be about eight o'clock. As soon as the day shift reports in, I'll send out a couple of replacements. Any questions?'

'No, sir.'

'Right. I'll be off then. Have a safe journey, Mrs Richardson and hopefully, we'll be in touch very soon.'

'Goodbye, Inspector,' said Jane opening the front door. 'And thank you.'

Seconds later the cavalcade of police vehicles swept out of Ashingham. As the last of the tail lights disappeared over the crest of the hill silence descended once more on what appeared to be a sleeping rural village. Yet beneath the surface a heaving cauldron of discontent was steadily reaching boiling point as the villagers watched both Ivy Cottage and Crabtree Cottage, waiting for the right moment to move in for the kill.

CHAPTER 17

A few minutes after ten o'clock Jane set off on the short drive across country to Hanslope. She felt surprisingly fresh considering she had only managed to snatch about four hours' sleep following the gruelling vigil of the previous night. John Deacon, on the other hand, looked tired and drawn as he stood at the cottage window waiting for her to drive away. As yet no telephone call had come through from Prestbury about relief for either of the two men and the forensic team currently working at Crabtree Cottage had come directly from County Headquarters and therefore had no information apart from their own specific instructions.

It had stopped raining at last, and once or twice on the journey Jane caught a glimpse of a pale watery sun behind the fast-moving cloud mass that streamed inland from the sea. She also saw the first golden hues of autumn had begun to appear on the trees and hedgerows, giving a soft burnished effect to the surrounding woodlands. A large flock of forktailed swallows passed overhead heading due south in search of warmer climes. Jane smiled as she found herself unexpectedly reminded of her own impending departure in the same direction. She glanced over her shoulder at the baby, soundly asleep in the carrycot on the back seat, then accelerated a little, conscious of the busy day in front of her.

Two miles or so further on she drove past Hanslope's medieval church and village hall and entered the main street. Immediately Jane saw that the atmosphere within the village contrasted markedly to that of Ashingham. The buzz of activity was everywhere. Over to her right children were running about in the school playground, laughing and chattering to each other during their mid-morning break, while opposite, at the village Inn, two burly draymen were unloading kegs of beer and openly flirting with the publican's wife. Women wheeling prams and pushchairs stopped every now and then to pass the time of day with people they knew in between calling at the various shops.

At the far end of the village she pulled up in front of Peter Green's house. Sally waved from the window and hurried outside to help Jane unload the carrycot.

'I'm so pleased you could come,' she said. 'Claire's arrived already and I know she's looking forward to meeting you.'

Once again Jane was ushered into the elegant and spacious drawing room, where the welcoming effect of a log fire immediately caught her attention. Sally carefully lowered Emma's carrycot on to the window seat and took Jane's coat.

'I'm just going to check that Claire is alright. She's in the kitchen making coffee. Make yourself comfortable. I won't be long.'

Jane drifted across to the fire and studied the impressive oil painting hanging above the carved oak mantelpiece. It depicted a wintry landscape caught in the grip of a violent storm. On the horizon the boughs of a sturdy poplar were bent almost double in an attempt to escape the rolling banks of cumulus cloud that swept across the dark purple sky. The bold brushwork and sombre colours added an eerie luminous effect to the already desolate scene. Jane shivered uncomfortably as she imagined herself encapsulated within the setting, a prisoner trapped in a timeless vacuum, miles from anywhere and at the mercy of the elements. She could feel the driving wind and rain lasing into her face as she physically toiled along the uneven winding track which meandered away into the distance.

At the sound of a sudden noise behind her she spun around, all thoughts of the landscape forgotten and stepped forwards to grasp Claire's outstretched hand. For one fleeting second, the tall, dark-haired woman glanced at the painting, then smiled directly at Jane.

'I'm pleased to see you. I've been looking forward to meeting you,' she said.

As their hands locked together in greeting, Jane experienced a tingling sensation in her fingertips, which reminded her of the tremendous electrical force she had felt on touching a prehistoric standing stone in the magnificent double circle at Avebury some years before. The shock made her jump as it had done on that previous occasion. Jane severed the contact by withdrawing her hand, but even as she settled into the nearest armchair, the powerful transference of energy swirled through her body like an injection into the bloodstream.

Sally, who had followed Claire into the room, deposited a large tea-tray on the low occasional table in front of the fire. 'It's lovely to see you both,' she said, handing out the coffee.

Picking up her own cup and saucer Sally sat back and turned to Claire.

'As I explained in our chat on the phone yesterday, Jane is doing some research into the history of Ashingham. But, although Peter, Jane and I spent the other evening together collating all the available documentation on the subject, I had the distinct impression that we didn't find whatever it was Jane was looking for. Unfortunately it wasn't until much later on that I suddenly remembered that you and I had once talked about Ashingham and it occurred to me that you might be able to shed some additional light on the matter.'

Claire smiled. 'I'll be only too happy to help in any way I can, although, of course, I cannot guarantee to possess the information you're looking for.'

'It's very kind of you to spare the time to see me this morning,' said Jane. 'In fact I really can't thank both of you enough for taking such an interest.'

' I think both Sally and I regard the subject as a challenge,' replied Claire, leaning forward to place her empty cup on the tray.'

'Yes,' agreed Sally. 'I'd like the satisfaction of being able to tie up all the loose ends.'

'Well in that case we'd better make a start,' said Claire. 'Sally tells me you're leaving for London later on, Jane, so you must be a little pressed for time?'

Jane nodded. 'Yes I am, but at the moment this meeting is the most important item on my agenda.'

'Have you any idea where you'd like to begin, Claire?' asked Sally.

'Yes. Since we spoke yesterday I've given the matter a great deal of thought. From what you've told me already it appears that the three of you have covered the historical facts relating to Ashingham since the eleventh century. So I've decided to approach the subject from a spiritual point of view in the hope that Ashingham's departed spirits might be willing to communicate with us and provide the missing links. I will need your full co-operation to achieve this, however,' she said to Jane. 'And I certainly wouldn't want to force you into anything against your better judgement.'

Jane tilted her head a little and gazed steadily into Claire's velvety brown eyes. 'You can count on my full support,' she replied adamantly. 'I have just spent the unhappiest six months of my life in what appears on the surface to be one of the most idyllic and picturesque villages you could ever wish to find. With any luck, in just a few hours from now, Emma and I will be travelling to London to start afresh. But before we go, I think I deserve some kind of explanation, if only in order to come to terms with everything that has happened to us in that brief period of time.'

'I'm glad you feel that strongly. Your strength of character will both guide and protect you as we probe into the deep recesses of the spiritual world. It's certainly not an experience I'd recommend to the faint hearted,' Claire added gravely. 'But, to begin, I need one of your most personal possessions. Something you wear or carry constantly. Your wedding ring, perhaps?'

Jane slipped the wide gold band from her finger and handed it to Claire, who clasped it tightly in the palm of her hand.

'Fine. Now the next step is for me to establish the requisite affinity to make contact.'

'Is there anything we should be doing in the meantime?' asked Sally.

'Yes,' replied Claire. 'I was wondering whether Jane could pinpoint any specific areas that are troubling her?'

Jane nodded. 'Actually there are several, but one particular phenomenon that I find quite baffling is the fact that since the Civil War only male children have been born in the valley.'

'But surely that no longer applies?' interrupted Sally quickly. 'Emma was born in Ashingham only a few months ago?'

'Yes, that's true. But I was already several months pregnant when we moved into the valley. So statistically she doesn't count.'

'Has Emma's presence in the village given rise to any difficulties?' Claire enquired, casting a swift glance in the direction of the sleeping child.

'Most definitely. In fact I have reason to believe that the men in the village mentally pressurized my husband Paul to get rid of the baby to the point where he completely cracked up under the strain and vanished into thin air.'

'I see,' said Claire thoughtfully. 'That is very interesting. What you are saying is that Ashingham has totally rejected Emma and you sense that the reasoning behind it lies embedded in history.'

'Not quite,' Jane replied. 'Only the men have ostracized her, the women are a little wary, that's all. But yes, I do detect the answer is buried in the past. To be frank, I'm absolutely convinced that the psychological characteristics of the current male population stem entirely from the tragic events that occurred during the siege and overthrow of Ashingham Castle at the end of that period.'

'Very well. I think I'm ready to make a start now, so we might as well begin at that point in time,' said Claire.

With Jane's wedding band securely cupped between both hands, the spiritualist closed her eyes. A cloak of silence descended over the room. Only the crackling of the logs and the ticking of the brass carriage clock on the mantelpiece broke the stillness in the atmosphere. Suddenly the furrows of concentration on Claire's forehead slackened and she visibly relaxed. Her eyes opened.

'I have managed to make contact with someone willing to talk to us,' she said softly. 'A young girl called Margaret, who lived in Ashingham during the time in question. She tells me that, although she lived in the village with her family, she was employed as a kitchen maid up at the castle.'

Sally's face lit up with pleasure. 'What a marvellous stroke of luck,' she exclaimed, edging forward in her chair.

Jane smiled, but said nothing, only too aware of the tremendous breakthrough Claire had achieved.

'Margaret has a story to tell, but has indicated to me her unwillingness to answer any questions, and we must respect that,' said Claire solemnly.

Jane and Sally both nodded simultaneously.

'Good. She has agreed to communicate directly with me and I in turn will then relay to you both the intrinsic details of her story.'

Claire closed her eyes once more. After a short interval of silence, the spiritualist opened her mouth and began to speak. 'Margaret's tale commences at the beginning of the seventeenth century, in 1602 to be exact. One bitterly cold April morning the castle servants gathered on the battlements and in the ward to witness the arrival, under heavy guard, of a number of witches. Manacled to each other hand and foot, the filthy old crones shambled through the barbican into the inner bailey where they met with a violent hail of abuse from the waiting crowd. The Sergeant-At-Arms took charge of the dishevelled group, quickly herding the women out of sight and away to the dungeons to await trial on charges of witchcraft.

'The female prisoners languished for many months in their subterranean black hole until a judge could be dispatched from London to try the case. During their imprisonment, they were closely guarded by a detachment of men from the village. The witches endeavoured to bribe their gaolers, one of whom was Margaret's father, and although two of the men were sorely tempted to help the women escape in return for riches beyond their wildest dreams, the majority stood firm, refusing to be swayed.

'Late in the December of that same year the women were finally hauled before the court and charged with indictments ranging from the illicit practice of the black arts to necromancy, namely witchcraft. Margaret watched the whole proceedings from behind a pillar in the minstrel's gallery above the courtroom.

'In the absence of any defence counsel to represent the prisoners, no godfearing advocate prepared to risk his reputation on a lost cause, the judge pronounced verdicts of guilty on all counts against the accused and duly passed the death penalty, condemning the witches to be burnt at the stake within the confines of the castle. The courtroom erupted in euphoria and the news spread like wildfire to the masses waiting outside in the courtyard.

'The witches were led away and incarcerated once more in the dungeons while work got underway to prepare the execution site. Celebrations and feasting commenced immediately both inside and outside the castle walls as everyone rejoiced at the court's decision.

After five days, the witches were brought up from the cells for the last time and ceremonially paraded in front of the jeering crowd before being bound to stout oak poles, each one shaped to form a sign of the cross. The castle militia stood shoulder to shoulder in a circle around the site while the village chaplain offered up the souls of the condemned women to the mercy of God. Seconds later the brushwood surrounding the stakes burst into flame and the assembled mass fell silent as sheets of roaring flame engulfed their victims.

'Suddenly, at the height of the inferno, a piercing cry rang out, sending gasps through the crowd. The flames on the centremost pyre parted to reveal the hideous face of the coven leader, Anne Grimsdyke. Despite the heat and dense black smoke, the toothless old hag opened her mouth and bellowed obscenities at the gawping onlookers who visibly shrank back in terror. Then drawing what turned out to be her final breath, Anne directed her steely gaze towards her gaolers and places a curse upon them, swearing that at a given time in the future Ashingham would be betrayed by one of its own women and they would die in the service of their feudal lord. Accordingly in 1648, during the Civil War, the curse became reality.'

Claire paused for a moment and then turned to Jane. 'Margaret has just described to me Sir Francis Ashingham's defence strategy during the siege. However, I think I am right in assuming you have covered this ground already, and are familiar with the existence of the tunnel and the tragedy that followed?'

'Yes,' replied Jane. 'But I didn't know that a village woman was responsible for betraying castle secrets to the enemy.'

'Well spirits don't lie, so you can rest assured that it's true,' said Claire gravely. 'The woman in question married General Fairfax, the Officer Commanding shortly afterwards in a hastily prepared ceremony in the tiny castle chapel, thereby guaranteeing her protection from certain death at the hands of the local community. Margaret goes on to say that after the war had ended, the Roundhead garrison defending the castle disbanded and a number of soldiers, having made friends in the valley, married the widows of the men who had perished in the tunnel. Village life appeared to settle back into its old familiar pattern, but unknown to the outside world some remarkable changes had taken place.

'Firstly, the souls of the dead soldiers had implanted themselves into the bodies of their widow's new husbands where they were to lie semi-dormant waiting for freedom and revenge. Secondly, from this time onwards Ashingham only produced male offspring; the valley was never to forget its betrayal by one of its own women. Thirdly, as time progressed the absence of females meant that the men, on reaching maturity, had to look outside the valley for suitable women to continue producing the male line. The new brides remained totally unaware that, without fail, eight weeks following conception further dead souls forcibly entered the tiny foetuses developing inside their wombs.'

Claire opened her eyes and sat back in her chair.

'I think Margaret has answered your question, don't you?'

Jane nodded. 'It's incredible!'

'There's just a little more,' said Claire.

'Margaret tells me the pattern continued unchanged through the centuries that followed. When the mill was erected during the Industrial Revolution, even the bodies of additional craftsmen drafted in from outlying districts were infiltrated – no-one escaped, only the women themselves remained immune. She also says it is important to stress, however, that these spirits played a comparatively low key role in all this time, the only noticeable difference between the male community and outsiders being the introvert and guarded behaviour of the Ashingham men. Only when the secret tunnel was unblocked recently by a team of surveyors examining the mill foundations did the restless and vengeful spirits finally gain the freedom they required to become fully active once more.'

The spiritualist exhaled loudly, rubbed her eyes and gazed into space. She looked tired and drawn. 'Margaret can't tell us any more,' she said rising slowly and making her way towards the fire. 'Her story is finished and she is unwilling to predict the future. I've thanked her for telling us what she knows and she has gone in peace.' Claire knelt down to warm her hands. 'I feel very cold, Sally. Do you think we might have some more coffee?' she asked.

Sally jumped up immediately and grabbed the tray. 'Of course. I won't be a minute.'

'Yes, After Sally had left the room, the two women sat silently, each pondering on their own thoughts. Suddenly Jane said, 'Claire, Paul changed radically during the time we spent together in Ashingham. By the time he disappeared I hardly knew him at all. Do you think he was affected in the same way as all the other men?'

'Yes, I'm sure of it,' replied Claire.

During all this time, Emma had lain peacefully asleep, but now Jane heard the faint snuffling sounds that signified she had woken up. Claire, who had glanced over at the sleeping child several times during the previous hour or so, approached the carrycot and smiled down at its gurgling occupant. Emma stretched out her tiny arms towards the spiritualist in an attempt to touch her. Laughing, Claire lowered her hands into the cot and stroked the delicate little fingers. The initial contact was enough to confirm the strong vibrations Claire had experienced all morning from that corner of the room.

At this point Sally breezed in with another tray of coffee and sandwiches and the three women settled down to their lunch while Jane gave Emma her midday bottle.

'I know this sounds rather odd, Jane,' said Claire. 'But when you have finished feeding Emma, I wonder if you would undress her for me?'

'Yes, it does sound strange, but seeing the request comes from you, Claire, you must have good reason for asking,' Jane replied.

'I'm intrigued,' said Sally. 'Are you going to tell us why?'

'No,' said Claire. 'Because I might not find what I'm looking for, in which case I'd rather not say anything.'

'Well we'll soon see,' said Jane, replacing the bottle in her large handbag. 'Emma needs to be changed anyway.'

She spread a clean nappy across her knees and swiftly removed the baby's clothing. 'Do you want to hold her?' Jane enquired.

'No, I can see perfectly well from here,' said Claire, staring at the tiny third nipple on Emma's chest. 'Thank you, Jane. You'd better get her dressed before she catches cold.'

'Well?' said Sally. 'Did you find anything?'

'Yes,' the spiritualist said solemnly.

She turned to Jane. 'Have you ever wondered about the small dark blemish on the baby's chest?'

'No, not really,' she replied. 'Actually Paul was the first to notice it when he saw Emma in hospital. The ward sister called it a third nipple and told us it could easily be removed.'

'Yes that's true, although its removal wouldn't make a ha'porth of difference.'

'What exactly are you saying, Claire?' asked Sally.

'The so-called third nipple is in fact a witches' mark. Furthermore, there is no doubt in my mind that Emma, although only a baby, is indeed a witch. All morning, even though she has been sleeping quietly, her brain has been actively transmitting messages both to Margaret and myself.'

Jane froze.

'My God. I don't believe it,' said Sally, reaching out to comfort Jane. 'It's not possible. She's only a few months old.'

All the colour had drained from Jane's face. She sat, rigidly clutching Emma protectively to her chest as if afraid that someone was about to snatch her baby away.

'Jane. Listen to me. It's nothing to be frightened about. In fact it's wonderful news. Few people are lucky enough to be granted such a precious gift. I have the power to communicate with the other world and you're not afraid of me, are you?'

'No,' answered Jane shakily. 'It's just a bit of a shock, that's all.'

'Yes, I realise that,' said Claire. 'But you must consider the advantages of possessing such a skill, the tremendous benefits Emma will derive from such power and knowledge throughout her life. Already her mind is advanced way beyond her years.'

'Are the villagers aware that Emma is a witch?' interrupted Sally.

'I shouldn't think so,' replied Jane. 'I've only just found out myself.'

'You're wrong there, Jane,' said Claire with a sigh. 'Mark my words, the men in the village know. They will have known, in fact, from the first day Emma arrived.'

'So that's why they made life so difficult for us. All the pieces of the puzzle are beginning to fit together at long last.'

'Yes. It's easier to understand now just how much consternation Emma caused within the community. If she had been a boy, life would have continued as normal and your family accepted into the village. But the fact that you produced a girl, which in itself is intolerable to them, and furthermore a child possessing the mystical powers of a witch, posed a threat to their very existence.'

'Paul never acknowledged Emma as his daughter,' said Jane thoughtfully. 'And I can see why, under the circumstances.'

'Yes. Your husband found himself in an impossible situation. On the one hand the villagers insisted he remove the child and yet as one of them he was powerless to touch her. The pressure on him must have been unbearable. I'm not surprised he disappeared.'

'My God!' exclaimed Sally. 'It's horrendous, a complete nightmare. No wonder everyone clams up whenever I mention the name Ashingham. It needs wiping off the face of the earth.'

Claire nodded. 'Jane, there is something vitally important you must know,' she said, looking her straight in the eyes.

'The only reason you are still alive is because you are under Emma's protection. If you become separated from her your life will be placed in grave danger. While you remain in Ashingham the men will collectively do everything in their power to destroy Emma and kill you. I strongly advise you to go home, collect your belongings and get the hell out of that accursed place for ever.'

'That's a decision I have already made,' said Jane, standing up. 'And now, thanks to you, I also know the reasons why I have to leave Ashingham.'

'There's just one more thing that might be of interest to you before you go,' said Claire also rising. 'Emma has just told me about Eve Simpkins.'

A shiver ran down Jane's spine and she felt her legs buckling as she waited for the spiritualist to continue.

'While you were waiting for the Police to arrive last night, the villagers carried Eve's body to Half Acre Farm, where it was fed through an industrial mincing machine. At this very moment her remains are being spread as slurry on the fields.'

At that moment Jane cracked.

'Sally, please fetch my coat, I have to go.'

Dumping Emma in her carrycot Jane turned to Claire. 'Thank you for all your help. Please excuse me rushing away, but I've got the feeling that time is not on my side.'

'I understand. I wish you luck,' she said, shaking hands.

Sally returned in a flash with Jane's coat.

'Thank you for everything, Sally. I'll write to you as soon as I get to London.'

With that, Jane picked up the baby, rushed out to her car and drove away.

CHAPTER 18

The small Ford saloon careered along the country lanes at breakneck speed. Jane sat stony-faced, clutching the wheel like a vice, her eyes staring dead ahead. Occasionally she glanced at her watch, only too aware how late it was. The picturesque scenery hurtled past the car windows unnoticed this time by the woman whose sole objective lay in reaching her destination in the fastest time possible.

Jane struggled hard to concentrate on the tasks to be completed at the cottage, but the gruesome details of Eve's disposal constantly tormented her already troubled mind, causing her accelerator foot to judder and the vehicle to lunge erratically along the road. She flexed her leg and brought the car under control just in time to negotiate the next series of double bends before the T-junction at the main road. Ten minutes later the turrets of Ashingham castle appeared above the golden treetops skirting the formidable rocky escarpment and Jane drove into the village for the last time.

The sun, an enormous orange ball of fire low in the western sky, cast gentle reflections of itself in the cottage window panes, creating a mellow ambience to the picture-postcard setting. The car slid to a halt outside Ivy Cottage. Reaching behind her, Jane hauled Emma's cot from the back seat and placed it carefully beside her. Next she scanned the empty street for any sign of life. The silence was eerie. Jane began to sense that something was wrong. Ashingham was deserted at the best of times, but today the stillness seemed to cloak the village like a mantle of doom. She stared at Ivy Cottage expecting to see the friendly face of a policeman awaiting her return but the place looked empty and lifeless.

Then suddenly she saw Oedipus, sitting on the front wall by the gate, gazing mournfully at the car. At the sight of him, tears welled up in Jane's eyes and rolled unchecked down both cheeks. The late afternoon sun shone on to the cat's black sable coat accentuating its rich silky texture. Instinctively Jane felt the urge to rush out of the car and throw her arms around his neck, but the haunting coldness that emanated from his beautiful luminous eyes served as a grim reminder that what in fact she looked upon was only a spiritual materialisation.

Oedipus was dead, killed by the very people persecuting Emma and herself. Jane recalled the last time she had seen him, the day Oedipus had led her down to the river bank to witness the mangled body of the young surveyor. Bearing that in mind, she acknowledged that his presence on the front wall at this time could only be conceived as a warning to her of impending danger. She glanced down at the carrycot and noticed Emma had woken up, was wide awake staring up at her as if she also sensed a feeling of uncertainty.

Clutching her house key in one hand and the cot in the other, Jane scrambled out of the car and approached the cottage, her pounding heart beating in her ears. As she drew near to the cat, Oedipus lifted his head towards his former mistress, miaowed plaintively as if asking to be stroked, then leapt from the wall and disappeared into the undergrowth. Jane fought back another wave of tears, struggled on up the path and inserted the key in the lock.

The door swung open and Jane stepped inside. As she did so, she felt a chilly wind run through the room, and the heavy oak door slammed shut behind her.

'Is anybody there?' she called nervously, hoping to hear the familiar voice of John Deacon, but knowing in her heart that the cottage was deserted. Nobody answered, the only sound coming from the clock on the mantelpiece that steadily ticked away the seconds. The room was chilly, the grate heaped up with cold grey ash from the previous evening's fire, long since dead.

Suddenly Jane began to feel frightened and uncomfortable, sensing something unnatural, something cold and strange within the cottage. A sour rotting smell curled around her nostrils growing stronger by the minute, tightening her stomach muscles. She stared across the murky low-beamed room, struggling to see in the failing light, but apart from the shadowy outlines of various items of furniture, the source of the smell continued to elude her.

Dumping the carrycot across the arms of the nearest chair, Jane reached for the wall switch and turned on the light. Immediately her attention focussed on the large mahogany bureau blocking the cellar entrance. It had been moved away from its position flat against the wall and now stood obliquely facing towards the fireplace. Jane froze, her feet rooted to the spot as her mind grappled with the impossible task of deciding what to do for the best. Seconds later, after a backwards glance at Emma, she took the only course open to her and approached the corner.

In two strides Jane reached the bureau and peered behind it. The cellar door lay on the floor, its hinges, wrenched and twisted, still attached. An overpowering stench of putrefying flesh billowed up the cellar steps and into her face. Jane grabbed the writing desk to maintain her balance as a wave of nausea swept through her body.

Noticing Paul's toolbox by the kitchen table she hastily considered the possibility of quickly nailing the door back into place, but abandoned the idea on seeing the badly splintered frame hanging loosely from its supports. Instead she kicked the door out of the way with her foot and heaved the bureau back against the wall to block up the hole.

Jane's shattered nerves told her she needed a stiff drink if she had any intention of completing the outstanding work to be done. Automatically she opened up the drum cabinet only to realise she had already packed away all the alcohol. Emma began to whimper and Jane glanced at her watch to see it was past five-thirty and the baby's feed time.

'OK,' she said in exasperation. 'I'll put the kettle on for your bottle before I have a drink,' hurrying into the kitchen. While she waited for the water to boil Jane rummaged agitatedly through the boxes on the kitchen floor, found a bottle of Talisker single malt and poured herself a healthy measure. The whisky burned down her throat and into her stomach but remedially steadied her nerves and suppressed the waves of hysteria that constantly crept up on her.

She sat down at the table for a few minutes to collect her thoughts, leaving Emma's bottle on the draining board to cool. Where on earth was John Deacon's replacement? Inspector Manson had guaranteed to provide the necessary protection until her departure for London, and she had trusted him implicitly. Had the inspector let her down or was he unaware that nobody had turned up? Jane hoped for his reputation's sake it was the latter because if anything happened to either Emma or herself, he would have to account for the consequences of his decision. It occurred to her that, in fairness to him, a replacement probably had arrived earlier in the day, while she had been with Sally and Claire, and finding no-one in at the cottage assumed she had already left and returned to headquarters. But that still didn't explain what had happened to Deacon, unless he had been ordered to leave with Sergeant Roberts when the forensic team had finished at Crabtree Cottage.

Jane twisted the whisky tumbler backwards and forwards in the palms of her hands and toyed with the idea of telephoning the Police to let them know she was still at the cottage, and without protection. What was the point?

But on reflection she decided against it. It would take them at least thirty minutes to reach Ashingham and she had every intention of being on the M6 within the hour.

Jane lifted Emma out of her cot and sat down to feed her. The baby, gazing up into her mother's eyes, drank quickly, as if anxious not to waste time, and Jane at last understood the full significance of the inseparable bond, formed between them from the first moment they had looked at each other as Claire's words flooded back into her mind. The only reason you are still alive is because you are under Emma's protection.

At that moment the telephone rang. Still cradling Emma in her arms, Jane walked into the living room to answer it.

'Jane, it's Susan from next door,' said the caller on the other end.

'Hello Susan. Are you all right?'

'Yes. I'm fine. It's you I'm worried about. What are you still doing here? When we spoke yesterday, you assured me you would be packed up and ready to leave by this morning.' 'I know. But events overtook me.'

'You're not kidding!' said Susan. 'What on earth possessed you to call the police last night? Don't you think you've enough problems on your plate already?'

'Susan. Do you know what happened to Eve's body?' asked Jane.

'No, and I don't much care at the moment,' she replied.

'Well, whether you care or not, I'm going to tell you, and you're going to listen.'

Jane heard Susan exhale in exasperation at the other end.

'Eve's body was mashed into a pulp and sprayed on to the fields.'

'Look, Jane,' said Susan quietly but firmly. 'If what you say is true, then what happened to Eve is barbaric and I can only express my shame at being associated with such depravity. But surely you must acknowledge that the men will stop at nothing to eliminate you and Emma as well. That's why I'm phoning you. My husband saw you return this afternoon and now Arthur Briggs has called a meeting. Everyone is over at Heronsford Farm discussing the situation.'

'Thanks for the warning, Susan. Don't worry. I'll be gone within the hour.'

'Oh Jane. I just pray you and the baby will get out in time.'

Jane replaced the receiver. 'OK, little one,' she said, placing Emma into her cot. 'Let's get this show on the road.'

She made a start downstairs, packing the last few essentials into boxes which she secured with string and deposited by the front door. Next she opened her handbag, took out her keys and moved across to the window to check the coast was clear. Satisfied the street was deserted, Jane opened the door, and laden with boxes, sallied forth to the car.

As she opened the boot, her eyes strayed across the road towards the 'Castle Arms'. To her dismay Jane noticed Oedipus sitting on the front step silently watching her. She pretended not to see him, wishing he'd go away. Three trips later she firmly bolted the front door behind her, and picking up the baby, headed upstairs to the bedrooms.

She stood on a chair and lifted down the two large suitcases from the top shelf of the fitted wardrobe in Emma's room, carried them through to her own bedroom and dumped them on the bed. Emma, still wide awake, looked on as her mother speedily emptied the cupboards and drawers in both rooms, walking to and fro with piles of clothing and bedlinen which she neatly laid in the cases.

'I think that's the lot,' said Jane, snapping the lids closed. 'Come on, Emma, don't look so serious. Give me a big smile. In a few minutes' time we'll be out of here and on our way.'

At that moment there was a loud knock on the front door. Mother and daughter both jumped. 'Dear God, no. Not now,' Jane whispered to herself, suddenly feeling very chilled and very frightened. She decided to ignore it, and instead heaved the heavy cases on to the floor ready to take downstairs.

Seconds later the knock was followed by a fist pummelling on the wood. 'Stay right where you are,' she said to Emma, forgetting the baby was incapable of leaving her cot. 'I'd better go and see who it is.'

Jane stepped on to the shadowy unlit landing and peered across the bannisters towards the living room window in an attempt to catch a glimpse of her caller, but outside darkness had fallen and she could only see her own ghostly reflection in the glass. The hammering continued. By now Jane had reached the foot of the stairs and was approaching the heavy oak door. Her mouth felt dry and stale, and her gastric juices rumbled noisily in a stomach that felt hollow and empty.

'Who's there?' she called out. Her voice harshly reverberated around the cold empty rooms, making her feel helpless and vulnerable as she waited for an answer.

'Arthur Briggs,' came the reply. 'Open the door, Mrs Richardson. I want to talk to you.'

Jane stood firm, holding on to the back of a chair for support. 'Go away,' she shouted. 'We have nothing to talk about.' 'Don't play games with me, young lady. Open up, or I'll batter the bloody thing down.'

'I wouldn't do that, Mr Briggs. You'll regret it if you do.'

'Where's the baby?' he asked, a hint of caution creeping into his voice.

'In my arms,' Jane lied, glancing anxiously towards the stairs.

Everything went quiet. An icy draught curled around Jane's ankles as she waited for Arthur Briggs to make his next move. Her heart beat and the clock on the mantelpiece ticked in unison, the atmosphere fraught with tension. After what seemed an eternity, but in all probability was only a matter of seconds, Jane heard the farmer's footsteps moving away from the door and down the path. The gate clanged shut and then there was silence.

Jane wiped away the beads of perspiration dotting her forehead and took several deep breaths to recover her composure. She stepped across the room to draw the curtains, not only to shut out the inky blackness outside, but also to obliterate the prying eyes watching her every move.

Suddenly the glass in the front window exploded, scattering lethal splinters the length and breadth of the room. In the same instant a hand shot like greased lightning through the jagged hole and grabbed her arm. Jane screamed, wrenched herself free and backed away towards the stairs. The hand withdrew, but only to be followed by more glass breaking as the remaining pieces were hacked out of the frame by what appeared to be a large wooden club. Jane looked on in horror at the devastation. Arthur Briggs' departing footsteps had been a clever ruse to catch her off-guard. A pair of hands gripped the sill as the first man levered himself through the window. They were coming in.

At this point Jane galvanised herself into action and fled upstairs. By the time she reached the landing three men had successfully climbed in to the living room. She rushed clumsily in to the bedroom, grazing an elbow on the protruding iron latch, plucked Emma from her cot and cradled her defensively in her arms. At the sound of pounding feet on the stairs, she spun round to face the intruders as they barged in to the room.

The men, brandishing knives and clubs, stopped dead in their tracks at the sight of mother and child unarmed, yet bravely confronting them. For a second or two nobody moved. The atmosphere smouldered with malevolence. Then Arthur Briggs, who had cunningly rejoined the men, lunged forwards towards Jane, aiming a double-edged blade straight at her heart.

Instantaneously Emma jerked herself upright into a sitting position effectively shielding her mother from attack. Her dark eyes blazed with hatred as she stared directly at the farmer, rendering him totally immobile, while her fully dilated pupils generated intense flashes of radiation through his eye sockets and on into his brain. The power transmitted from the tiny body was overwhelming and Jane found it increasingly difficult to hold on to the child. The spell held for at least a minute, and the second Emma relaxed her grip, the men, almost blinded and with tears streaming from their eyes, fled down the stairs. Arthur Briggs staggered backwards, clutching his damaged head. He collided with the door and went sprawling on to the landing.

With his fingertips the farmer groped feverishly for the bannisters and hauled himself up. 'You'll never get out of here alive, either of you,' he hissed through bared teeth, then disappeared down the stairs and out into the night.

Jane sank down on the bed, her head reeling with shock. She looked down at Emma, who lay back gazing intently at her mother. Their eyes locked in mutual understanding. Together they would come through this nightmare and survive to see another day.

The sound of voices outside filtered up to the bedroom. Jane sat stock still, her senses prickling like static electricity as she strained to hear what was happening. Bert Grimshaw appeared to have taken charge, bellowing orders in all directions, but about what she was unable to ascertain. Acknowledging that Emma and she were engaged in a fight to the death and round two was about to commence, Jane crossed over to the window and peered down into the street below to find out what all the commotion was about.

At first it was difficult to see anything at all through the funereal blackness, but gradually as her eyes became accustomed to the dark, she was able to perceive the villagers scuttling to and fro laden with armfuls of timber and brushwood. All too soon it became clear what all the frantic hubbub was in aid of. Jane opened the window and leaned out to confirm her worst suspicions. The men had piled the kindling around the base of the cottage walls and Bert Grimshaw was busily dowsing the wood with petrol. 'OK, Terry, we're ready,' he shouted, vaulting across the wall to the pavement.

The publican appeared from the back of the crowd, carrying several stout poles, the ends of each one tightly bound up with thick cotton wadding on to which Bert emptied the last remaining drops of liquid. John Mallen stepped forward brandishing a lighted taper, set fire to the torches which in turn were systematically hurled at Ivy Cottage. Some hit the brushwood which kindled immediately, shooting sparks high into the air, others crashed through the broken window catching the curtains before landing on the carpet.

Ivy Cottage was on fire. Within seconds the living room burst into flames, the close boarded ceiling and low beams adding additional fuel to the blaze. The acrid smell of smoke from the dry timbers drifted up to the bedroom and Jane, dashing on to the landing realised it was only a matter of minutes before the staircase caught fire. It was becoming increasingly difficult to see for the thick black smoke and Jane began to cough violently as she fought for breath.

The intense heat pushed her backwards to the bedroom, and turning to glance at Emma, she noticed a blue cloud haze drifting past her in to the room. At this point Jane knew that the only way to get out alive was to protect themselves from both the smoke and the heat. She grabbed Emma and sprinted along the landing to the bathroom.

By now the fire had reached the staircase and tongues of flame were beginning to lick at the bannisters. Jane groped blindly for the bathroom pull cord and turned on the light, only to stand in the doorway staring into the room, unable to speak or move at the sight she encountered. John Deacon lay stretched out in a full bath of water, his bulging eyes staring vacantly at the ceiling. As Jane stepped nearer she saw the bath chain tightly wrapped around his neck had been successfully used as a garotte to throttle the last living breaths out of him, although she suspected that the main cause of his death was from drowning, judging by the constable's bloated appearance and the fact that his body was floating on the top of the water.

A loud crash down below reminded Jane of the purpose of her visit to the bathroom. For John Deacon time had run out. For herself and Emma the same would be true within a few minutes if she didn't act fast. Jane plucked one of the towels from the heated rail by the wash hand basin, dowsed it in the bathwater and wrapped it around the baby, taking care to cover her head. Then she repeated the process, this time using the larger bath sheets to protect her own body. Satisfied there was nothing more she could do, Jane carried Emma back along the landing.

They were greeted by the deafening roar of the blaze, billowing poisonous smoke and scorching heat. Beams crashed down willy nilly as the fire steadily ate its way along the ceiling in search of the bedroom floorboards. Jane heard the tinkling of glass as the kitchen windows disintegrated in the holocaust. The stairs had turned into a wall of flame. They were trapped.

Jane looked down at her daughter and smiled. 'Have faith in me, Emma,' she said calmly. 'We're going through.'

Emma gazed up at her mother and returned the smile.

With an inexplicable air of confidence Jane descended into the roaring inferno, clasping the baby firmly to her breast. Instantly the sheet of fire parted as if by magic, leaving a safe passage for both of them to pass through unheeded, the wall of flame acting now as a protective barrier from the evil all around.

Down the staircase, through the living room, out of the front door and along the path Jane walked, Emma snug in her arms, her ebony eyes never leaving her mother's face. The flame barrier illuminated and protected their escape route as far as the edge of the pavement where it ballooned outwards to form a circle around the car.

On impulse Jane glanced across to the 'Castle Arms'. Oedipus still sat on the steps keeping watch, the firelight dancing reflectively in his glistening luminous eyes. She held out her hand towards him in a parting gesture, knowing she would never see him again. Opening the rear door of the car she placed Emma gently on the seat and turned to look back at the cottage for the last time.

Suddenly a shout went up. A woman armed with a carving knife broke through the crowd and headed straight for Arthur

Briggs. Susan Entwistle thrust the blade deep in the man's chest and, as he staggered backwards into the cottage porch, a surging mass of flame engulfed the farmer, dragging him in to the blazing interior. For one fleeting moment he appeared at the window, let out a blood-curdling scream, then disappeared.

Flames were leaping through the roof in anger, shooting skyward. Slates rained down on the assembled crowd who scattered in all directions. Only the shell of Ivy Cottage remained intact. It was time to go.

Hesitating no longer, Jane got into the car, turned on the ignition and, as the protective flames drew apart, accelerated away into the night.

EPILOGUE

Jane had seen the hate in the baby's eyes, and she knew instinctively that this affair was by no means over. Emma would return to this evil place at a time in the future, and then ...

ACKNOWLEDGEMENTS

I would like to thank my daughter Ailsa and my son Andy for their support & enthusiasm from the outset. I would like to thank my husband Peter for his commitment to this project and arranging for the book to be published and also using his own editorial skills in this field from his previous work as a Sales Manager in publishing. I want to thank the author PETER TREMAYNE for his support and for writing the blurb on the back cover of the book. My thanks to Regina Osborne for her encouragement. I would also like to thank Ruth, Jay, Judith & other members of the team at ukbookpublishing.com for producing my book

Sonja Williams ☺